The
Ache

N J KERNS

authorHOUSE®

AuthorHouse™ UK
1663 Liberty Drive
Bloomington, IN 47403 USA
www.authorhouse.co.uk
Phone: UK TFN: 0800 0148641 (Toll Free inside the UK)
UK Local: (02) 0369 56322 (+44 20 3695 6322 from outside the UK)

Published by AuthorHouse 10/25/2021

ISBN: 978-1-6655-8954-3 (sc)
ISBN: 978-1-6655-8953-6 (e)

Print information available on the last page.

This book is printed on acid-free paper.

For my wonderful family, my soulmate friends and my gorgeous little children. For each individual person who makes my life truly magical.

CHAPTER 1

Present

She opened her eyes suddenly, raked in a panicked breath and held it. The blackness prickled in front of her as she adjusted to the darkness. Her burning lids and aching sockets told her it was far from morning. An ear-piercing scream had woken her. She quickly tilted her head to lift her ear off the pillow, tuning in and muting out all her other senses. Her mouth was dry, and her throat tightened, her breath shallow and short, eyes dancing from left to right scanning her brain for sense.

"Help me please! I'm scared, please stop!" Cries echoed through the still, quiet house.

She was standing before she knew it, woozy and wobbly, adjusting to being vertical, waving her hands out in front to feel for the wall or door. The disturbing cries continued to fill the moonlight airwaves, terrifying pleas of mercy ricocheting off the walls. Out on the landing, her eyes adjusted; a cool glow from the streetlamp outside streaking through the window, lighting her way. She stepped outside her bedroom door onto the cold landing laminate, hearing whimpering and pleading emanating from the room across from hers. She opened the door to see her 5-year-old daughter laying in her single bed, duvet predominately on the floor. Her fists and her sweaty face were clenched. Nancy rushed over to her panic-stricken daughter, wrapped her back in her duvet, held her tear-stained face and gently touched her cheeks, planting soft kisses of comfort over her wet skin. She swept her short, messy, autumnal crop back into its usual side parting, gently shushing her, sprinkling comforting words over her until she visibly relaxed, muscles loosening, shoulders dropping, jaw unclenching. Lottie muttered a few words of nonsense then gently purred back into a deep sleep and Nancy sighed. She stared into the dark, feeling like her eyeballs had been rolled in the dust of what was left at the bottom of a bag of salt and vinegar crisps. She planted one final kiss on her daughter's cool forehead, told her she was safe and loved and shuffled back across the landing towards her room and flopped into bed with a dramatic groan. She slung her left hand out of the bed and let it creep around on the hardwood floor like an inquisitive spider until she felt the shape of her phone. She gently pulled it towards her until the charging cable tightened and pinged out of the phone port and snaked onto the floor. The screen illuminated her face and she squinted. 3.45am and 3 messages. She squeezed her eyes shut and pressed her eyelids with her fingertips. She calculated her sleep total; just over 6 hours. Could she get up and function today on that, or should she force herself to roll over and fret until the sun came up? No, she decided that she wasn't prepared to risk several hours of swimming in her own uncertainty, so widened her eyes in the contract that she'd committed herself to wakefulness. She counted down from five like she always did and quietly sat up on the zero, swung her legs out of bed, grabbed the gym kit she'd carefully laid out the night before and quietly snuck downstairs. There, she went to the toilet, and stared at her phone, deleted a bunch of spam emails and inhaled a handful of motivational quotes she'd saved for herself on Pintrest the night before, in a bid to make her feel lucky to be alive. Afterwards, she heaved her black lycra leggings over her bottom, wrestled with her sports bra until her breasts were contained, crept out of the bathroom and threw on a hoody which was hanging over the banister. She fumbled around for her trainers and, not bothering to untie her laces, lazily pushed and crushed the heel of the shoe with her foot until it finally let her in, something she regularly told her daughters off for doing. She took the key off her set, popped it in the zipper pocket in her leggings and quietly slipped out the door.

It was dark; the chill in the September morning air announcing that summer was almost over. The streetlamps created spotlights on the wet ground. She took her first step straight into a puddle, which soaked her trainer and sock and she wondered what the hell she was doing. But the feeling of not giving in to what could have been hours of staring deep into her soul filled her with relief, and she was glad she was up and out to distract herself. She was doing something productive before the rest of Britain's alarms went off, which made her feel she was doing one thing right. She shook her soggy foot and set off, falling into a decent rhythm, neither a depressed plod nor an annoyingly enthusiastic stride. She wanted to allow her thoughts to come and go like a wave upon the shore. Sometimes they gently slid into the shore and retreated peacefully. But more recently, like today, they rolled up high and crashed onto the rocks, barely time for a breath before the next one followed and hammered the surface of her psyche. They were loud, erratic, and she didn't know how to find the quiet she so desperately craved.

She followed the lights to ensure she was well seen, as her overactive imagination about creeps and drug addicts lurking on every corner to attack her always sat at the forefront of her mind on her runs. She deliberately didn't take headphones at this time of day, as, although the music maintained her motivation and lifted her mood, the image of someone silently leaping on her back and dragging into a bush never to be seen again, overrode any pleasure she would get from her carefully created running playlist.

Her feet hit the ground over and over, as rhythmic as a steady heartbeat. Her body was on autopilot, her breathing even, arms bent and swishing beside her. She began thinking perhaps if her body knew what to do, then maybe her mind would follow. Her thoughts felt like a bluebottle trapped in a jar. She couldn't take the lid off, yet she couldn't calm it down inside the jar. It was just panicking, trying to escape. But to let it out would lead to more problems, it would climb all over everything, infecting things, bothering people, so she kept the lid firmly on, and watched it suffer. It would eventually suffocate, but it was better than setting it free.

She came to a zebra crossing, and momentarily paused to check for cars before running across. She tried to stay on the white stripes, just a childish challenge she had given herself since she was small. She smiled to herself that she was still doing that in her 30's and vowed to never stop. As she reached the pavement, she saw someone walking away from her in front, black coat, hands in pockets, hood up. She wondered what kind of mental person was out at this time of day, probably the kind of person that stabbed people in the throat for no reason. But then she remembered she was out as well, so thought maybe that theory wasn't completely accurate. Nancy really did want to overtake them; she hated people being behind her, but she was catching up fast so didn't really have much of a choice. She looked over her right shoulder to check for cars and stepped off the pavement to run around them in the road, to give them a wide birth.

"Morning" Nancy breathed quietly, trying to be polite and not make them jump.

She took a quick side glance to her left as she passed, but the person was looking down, hood so far up she couldn't see their face. She ran steadily along the pavement, looking over her shoulder a few times. The person seemed to be walking faster, gaining on her. Nancy's heart rate and pace picked up until she was sure she alone.

She was panting as she came back through the door and walked straight to the kitchen sink for a glass of water. The house was still quiet so she slumped down on the sofa in the lounge and stared at her phone, clicked on Facebook and scrolled, the light from the screen shining on her blotchy red face. Funnily enough, swiping through other families' happy snapshots that were worthy enough to share with the world, did nothing to appease her. She knew it was all a lie, but somehow, she still believed it. Reams of images of people looking happier, healthier, luckier, wealthier made her stomach twist. There were shots posted of family holidays, capturing smiles and laughter, even though the children were most likely being little shits before and after the perfect image was captured. Nancy knew it to be true, because her girls had behaved the same way before and after she'd forced them to smile for a snap. She saw selfies that had been taken over and over, then filtered, edited and shaded so the person looked nothing like themselves and more like a Japanese cartoon. A spurned woman mysteriously ranted on her wall, cracking the curiosity of a few who commented below, either checking she was alright, sending their love or publicly asking her to message them privately, to show that they cared more than the others. Some simply liked it with a blue thumbs up.

Nancy sighed, and placed the phone face down on the leather couch and felt agitated. Should she shower? No, too early. Yoga? Meditate? She could. She was working from home today, so there was no real rush to do anything other than get the girls to school. She should meditate; that always helped. But instead she picked up her phone again, infecting her brain with more images of perceived perfection and slipped into an even darker mood.

She was falling down into a scroll hole, bombarded with filtered images and videos until she felt anxious, inferior and like she wanted to spend money to feel better. She'd wasted over an hour consuming advertising without really realising it and felt fidgety, unattractive and irritable. She was just about to buy an expensive collagen supplement until she was interrupted by the sound of a little barefoot child padding down the wooden stairs. It was Lottie, she could tell, by the lightness and carefulness of her step. Nancy put her phone face down and waited for her entrance, like the anticipation of a young groom in a church waiting for his bride. In she came, her elfin, chestnut curled crop, wild and untamed, her eyes sleepy and her arms outstretched to her mother.

"Come here, you" said Nancy grabbing Lottie and pressing her close to her chest. Lottie's soft arms wrapped tightly round Nancy's neck, before pulling away to press her forehead against her mother's, her stale but sweet morning breath filling Nancy's nose. They stared into each other's perfectly matched light chocolate brown eyes and Nancy's heart skipped a beat. Lottie told her mother she loved her, gave her several kisses and asked her what day it was.

"It's Wednesday poppet, a school day".

"What have I got for lunch Mumma?" Lottie asked. Lunch was her favourite part of school.

"Same as yesterday darling. Sandwich, veggies, yoghurt and crisps".

"Yay" she said, smiling softly.

Satisfied, Lottie securely plopped herself onto the sofa next to her mother and turned the television on. When Nancy tried to pull away in order to get into the kitchen to start breakfast, Lottie's grip tightened and she begged her mother to stay.

"Just five minutes mama" she pleaded, staring into her eyes to secure the promise. Nancy felt irritated by Lottie's persistence, followed by a slap in the face with shame, wondering why getting on with chores was more important than capturing a moment of peace with her baby. They would one day be gone, she should treasure them. *Because it was just more time she would have to sit alone with her own thoughts.*

In walked her 8-year-old daughter Tilly, dressed only in her pants, with the same sleepy expression as her younger sister. Her hair was longer, but the exact same colour as Lottie's. She kissed Nancy and Lottie on the mouth, grabbed a blanket out of the hamper next to the sofa and wrapped it round the three of them. Nancy tried to get up, but the two of them demanded she stay. Nancy agreed, but after just one minute of sitting still, her mind and heart were racing and she could wait no more, so she prised Lottie off her arm to make a coffee and tidy the kitchen, leaving her whining daughter behind. She felt guilty. She always felt guilty when it came to Lottie. She had wronged her, and she feared the day she would find out.

As Nancy dried up, she stared numbly out of the kitchen window at the near empty park which her house overlooked, one dog walker dotted in the distance. His feet had been swallowed by the white mist that swam across the top of grass, his dog springing out of low fog and disappearing once again like a dolphin breaching the ocean only to dive back down again. The clouds had cleared, and the sky had turned a murky blue as the sun started to rise, streams of light bolting through the gaps between her neighbours' houses. There was hope, and she could feel the weather trying to persuade her that her mood could improve, much like it had. She tried to believe it on her inbreath, but on her exhale, all she could feel was rain beating down inside her, muddy puddles pooling in her soul.

CHAPTER 2

Then

Age 3

"Hello!!!' The door swung open and a warm light shone from indoors out onto the front porch, illuminating their excited faces.

"Come in, come in! It's freezing out there!" Grandma said, as she quickly ushered her family inside. With the front door firmly closed behind them, they proceeded to remove the hats, scarves and thick coats, which were essential on the early December night. Grandma took and hung their items on the coat hooks opposite the front door and they were ushered from the hallway of the bungalow into the lounge where Granville, her Grandma's husband, sat in his comfortable worn brown floral armchair.

"Nancy!!! Come here you!" he growled, shuffling to the edge of his seat cushion opening his arms open wide for her to toddle into. She wrapped her silky arms around his neck and he swept her up onto his lap and bopped her on the nose with his finger, the smell of stale smoke lingering from his 40 a day habit. Her brother swished in behind her in his aqua and purple shellsuit, and slumped down on the 3 seater with his Gameboy and resumed his game of Tetris, pausing only to offer a nod of greeting his babysitters. Nancy's mother was excitedly chatting to her mother-in-law about what time she and Nancy's father would arrive at the B&B in the Cotswolds, and the walks and pub lunches they had planned for their romantic weekend away. Nancy's father came in with the last gift bag and popped it under the tree, shimmering red Christmas paper and curled gold ribbon poking out the top.

"I put their overnight bags in their bedrooms and their welly boots by the door, and the address and phone number of the place were going to are by the phone" Dad said, shaking his step-father's hand with an 'alright?'

Grandma fussed around offering drinks and nibbles to everyone. The children squealed, requesting squash and opening their eyes innocently wide to see what else was going to be offered, avoiding eye contact with their mother who would have certainly been pursing her lips in judgement at a treat before tea. They ran into the kitchen following their grandmother and crowded her at the treat cupboard. She shooed them away so they climbed up onto the kitchen stools and waited politely and hopefully with sweet smiles on their faces, fluttering their eyelashes like angels. Their parents laughed, admiring their children's ability to obey when sugar was involved. Sensing the children were happily settling in, Nancy's mother and father started to make noises about getting on the road, kissed their children on the top of their heads, refusing to break eye contact at Grandma who was still rummaging in the treat cupboard. They exchanged a sideways glance with one another which said "let's go" and silently waved to Grandma in the kitchen and through the lounge door to Granville on their way out.

Grandma placed the treat tin on the work surface. "Just one each because it's nearly bedtime and you'll never sleep." Both children dove into the tin, frantically searching and selecting a treat, putting it back when they found something better. After a few moments, both were satisfied with their selection and hopped off their stools to return to the lounge to eat their lollies. Grandma stayed in the kitchen to start preparing the dinner, pulling potatoes out from the cupboard to peel. She took her pinny off its hook, carefully hooped it over her head of short white curls, and wrapped it around her round tummy. She would make bangers and mash with peas and onion gravy, Granvilles's favourite.

Back in the lounge, the children stared at the tv, licking and sucking their lollypops. Gladiators was on; their new favourite programme. They both loved Jet and Wolf, although Nancy only liked them because her brother did. She idolised her brother and he knew it. He was completely in charge of playtime and always decreed what they would do and what the rules were on that particular day, to ensure the game ended with him victorious. He also led the way with popular culture, and she decided whether she loved or hated tv stars, based on his opinion. She followed him around like a shadow, and even when they argued and fought, she would return to her room full of rage to hide under her desk, tell her teddies all about it and then feel lonely without him. They'd soon make up, not with an apology, but by laughing at something their mother had said earlier and dove straight back into another game of his choice.

She looked to her right as the couch sunk with the weight of Granville joining them, lighting a fresh cigarette, which sat snuggly in the corner of his mouth and could be drawn on without even getting his hands involved. They all joined in with the Ref shouting in his broad Scottish accent 'Gladiators, Ready!? Contenders, Ready!? 3, 2, 1" The whistle blew and the crowd went wild. Bouncing up and down on the sofa, Nancy and Robert squealed and clapped for the contenders swinging high across a huge crash mat using the silver hoops attached to the arena ceiling. The sound of the whistle blowing signified that the Gladiators could now and they swung, catching up fast behind the contenders, trying to grab them with their dangling legs and yank them onto the crash mat below. Two hands slipped under Nancy's armpits and she was hoiked onto Granville's lap where he wrapped his arms around her. The smell of fresh smoke enveloped her, so she craned her neck to her left, taking a large gulp of fresher air. She was desperate not to make Granville feel bad about smoking, even though she absolutely hated it. Her Dad once told them he smoked before they were born, but gave up when their mother was pregnant. She was very glad he didn't smoke any more. It absolutely stank and she'd heard it made you die early. Even when Granville wasn't smoking, he smelt of it. His white hair smelt stale and his pitted, reddened skin held onto the stench too. She looked down as a sprinkling of ash from Granville's cigarette landed on her lap and he reached down to brush it off, leaving a grey streak on her black leggings. He lifted his thumb to his mouth and deposited a hefty slick of saliva onto it, before returning to her leg to erase the evidence from her clothes. "There we go, good as new" he growled, satisfied with his efforts. She stared at the dark grey streak that now clung to her leg and smelt more smokey than the actual cigarette. She turned her attention back to Gladiators and tried to enjoy the next game. He was holding her tight on his lap and she really wanted to get down. She waited for him to reach for his ash tray to stub and tried to wriggle out of his grip, but he just lifted her back onto his lap with a 'there you go'. She stared at the telly, and glanced towards her brother who was engrossed, awaiting the infamous Jet. Just then, Grandma came in, red in the face and donning her favourite pinny.

"Right you two! Dinner is almost ready but it's getting late. Why don't you go and pop your pajamas on now, and then that's one job out of the way. Go and wash your hands too and make sure you do them properly now".

Nancy excitedly hopped off Granville's lap, grateful for the permission to be free. She raced her brother to the bathroom but lost, so he took centre stage at the sink. She tried to squeeze in next to him before he elbowed her to one side and she was stuck with the cold tap and couldn't reach the soap. He finished cleaning his hands, dried them on the towel, stuck his tongue out at her in the mirror and went into the bedroom he was sleeping in to get changed. She rubbed the disc of soap resting in a small pool of water on the basin, and washed her hands under both taps, and turned them off as tight as she could. They still dripped, but she was sure a grown up would finish the job later. She dried her hands on the towel and what was left was wiped down her red tartan jumper. She walked out of the bathroom and started along the bungalow hallway towards her bedroom to get her jammies on. But as she walked along the carpet, her heart sank as she sensed that there was someone following her.

CHAPTER 3

Present

"Bye darlings!" she called out to them as they ran into school. Lottie's oversized satchel banged against her bottom and the neat hairstyle Nancy had tried to create for her this morning was now fluffy and wild as she bolted into her classroom. Tilly caught up with her friends, and they walked into to their entrance, chatting and gasping, excitedly exchanging stories with one another. They didn't turn back when she called, which both comforted and saddened her. She was overjoyed that they were so confident and secure, of course she was, but the fact that they didn't turn back, was a reminder that they needed her less and less every day. She made a mental note to squeeze them extra hard tonight, and that she would try and capture every school story in the car on the way home into her long term memory bank, rather than ignore them and lazily say 'wow' at all the right parts. When Nancy saw they were safely in school, she turned and quickly walked back to the car, head down. She hadn't showered yet and was a sweaty mess. She did not want to see her reflection in one of the other school Mum's disapproving looks, so she picked up the pace into a slow jog. She managed to get away with mouthing a quick 'hi!' to a pair of Mums who were deep in conversation, dove into to the car and drove home.

She felt numb. Hedgerows rushed by. Irritating jingles on radio adverts slipped into her subconscious brain to ensure she thought of them next time she wanted to clean her washing machine. People walked along the pavement, chatting and laughing. She sighed, and drove robotically until she pulled into the driveway and wondered how on earth she got there.

She wasn't working; she worked part-time from home and today wasn't one of them. The house was a mess and she had the girls coming round tonight, so grabbed a notepad off the side to make a list of the things she needed to do to focus her mind. She was still in her clammy gym gear, so she decided showering should be the first thing she ticked off. She ascended the stairs and walked into the bathroom, locking the door behind her. She turned the shower on, peeled off her sticky leggings like a wet label off a beer bottle and stood on the scales. She had squishy hips and a soft tummy, but was slim enough. She never really felt happy with what she saw under her feet when she stood on that thing and wondered why she did it to herself. There wasn't a number on there that would make her feel happy. She stepped into the shower, closed her eyes and let the steaming water cascade over her face and body like a waterfall. She stood still and hoped it would wash away the feeling of her insides being gnawed at like a dog chewing a juicy bone.

Nancy turned off the shower and stood dripping for a moment. She reached through the shower door to grab her towel off the hook and took it straight to her face, pressing it firmly into her skin. She blotted the rest of her body and wrapped it tightly around herself, under her armpits, binding her breasts. She flipped forward so that her wet hair was hanging down, dripping on the tiles. She grabbed the hair towel off the floor and wrapped it around her head, stood back up and neatly secured the turban at the nape of her neck. She saturated a cotton pad with cleanser and mopped the remnants of make- up off her face. She deposited a dab of moisturiser onto her index finger and dotted it on her cheeks, forehead and chin and looked up at herself in the mirror. This was the first time she'd looked at herself all morning. Her eyes took centre stage in the reflection and they saddened her the most. Dull, lost, tired and afraid. She smeared the moisturiser across her face to erase the observation. She opened the bathroom door and walked out onto the landing and straight into Alex. She was shuffling along the landing carpet with her eyes almost shut, hardly any of her wavy blonde hair left in its loose ponytail, the majority of it twirling around her face and neck.

"Mornin,." Alex dramatically yawned like a lioness, her arms stretching high in the air, interlocking her fingers. She stepped forward and captured Nancy like a butterfly being caught in a net, like she did every morning. They squeezed each other until their backs clicked, Alex childishly pinged Nancy's sports bra and they asked how each other had slept. Alex let her go and stepped past Nancy into the bathroom to have a wee. She started, still telling Nancy through the crack in the door how the man she'd eye-fucked on the tube the other day had made his way into her filthy dream last night. Nancy stood on the landing smiling to herself. Nancy loved her best friend. Everything about her, she loved. Even the things other people hated about her, Nancy adored. She was crass and loud, funny and crude. She'd had her behavior described as 'unbecoming' by the generation that had preceded them, which Alex wore like a badge of honour. It was the nicest way she'd ever been described in fact. Nancy knew the bones of Alex, and never told others that her persona was a front and that she really was soft as butter on the inside. She was gentle and patient and understanding, she would give you the shirt off her back. But only to those who really deserved it, who'd earned it, and fortunately, Nancy was one of those.

What Nancy loved most about her, was that her bold behavior was not a shield to protect herself. She simply didn't care anymore what people said behind her back or even to her face. She didn't want to hurt anyone, she just felt no inclination to disguise her feelings or to tell a story in anyway that wasn't hilarious and dramatic. She knew who she was and was completely at peace with it. Nancy craved to feel like that too.

Alex flushed, washed her hands and walked out of the bathroom wiping them down her pyjamas, kissed Nancy on the forehead and padded downstairs to make their coffees.

Alex had come to stay with Nancy when she found out that her husband, Grayson, who'd been spending an inordinate amount of time at the office, had, in fact, been sleeping with his co-worker, Emma. Alex had come to stay with Nancy and naturally raised the roof, blaring out *You're So Vain* whilst cleaning the kitchen. They'd spent many evening consuming copious amounts of Malbec, Alex angrily telling Nancy how she would like to rip his testicles off and shove them up his arse.

"Actually, one up his arse, and one up the arse of his cheap whore!" she'd growled.

When they'd hung out with Sophie and Sam, she was laugh a minute, not banging on all night like most spurned women, but just delivering a quick overview of the latest drama, calling him names mostly beginning with the letter C, and then she'd want to move on and change the subject. When everyone had left and they'd cleared up, they'd say goodnight and go up to bed, but Nancy would often hear Alex crying in her room. Nancy would get up and slide in next to her, and Alex would roll over and cry it out on her chest. When Alex finally fell asleep, Nancy would place her head back on her pillow, and stroke her hair, tears in her eyes that this man could have hurt her best friend so badly. Nancy would sleep in with her on those nights, incase Alex woke up hungover and lonely and needed her.

One night, when they were about to open their second bottle, there had been a knock at the door. It was Grayson. Nancy's immediate thought was he wanted her back, and it was clear it was Alex's too by the look of hope on her face. But no, he'd come to ask her to check her emails (she never did, it was mostly spam) because his solicitor had been trying to contact her, as, he not only wanted to file for divorce, but he wanted to buy her out of her house, so that he and Emma, the co-worker, could live there together. Nancy simultaneously held Alex back and slammed the door shut with her foot before Alex calling him a cheating cunt echoed out into the neighbourhood.

Months had passed, filled with angry crying, drunken texting and point scoring, until she finally walked away with a decree absolute and a deposit to buy a small house just down the road from Nancy. She'd covered her heartbreak well and to an outsider, you'd have thought she was happy he'd screwed her over. But that was Alex, she only let a few people see her. She was like a Crème Egg, hard on the outside and sweet and gooey on the inside. But she just didn't allow many people to crack the shell.

Alex often still slept over in her old room, like she had last night, even though it was only a 2 minute, pyjama-clad shuffle back to her place, but sometimes Alex just didn't want to be alone, and neither did Nancy. She'd invited Alex to stay as long as she wanted to, and she had. She'd been incredible company, Amazing help with Tilly, a great role model (she'd kept the fuck's and shit's for after the watershed) and Tilly adored her, as much as Alex adored them. Alex being there and so keen to help, gave Nancy the freedom to go for her early morning runs, work late when she needed to and catch up with other friends too, almost an impossible task as a single mother. It worked brilliantly for both women, and the children loved it. But Nancy was furious for Alex. She'd done everything for Grayson, dedicated her body, mind and soul to him and his needs. A feminist by nature, of course, like she and every other woman she knew strived to be, but they'd all slipped into this horrendous pattern, where taking care of their men had become the main focus of their lives. They'd sacrificed their own dreams, wants and desires and rarely put themselves first, and were apologetic if they did. Then, if they'd had children, they never thought of themselves first again. Yet they believed that, because they liked powerful quotes from powerful women on Facebook and slagged men off around a wine glass-cluttered table, that they were also strong, independent and free. Nancy realised now that despite their best efforts, this had all been utter bullshit.

Nancy dried and dressed herself in blue jeans and a loose-fitting cream v neck jumper, combed her wet hair into place so that it could dry naturally and she decided to go for a walk. She needed the fresh air and also needed to pick up some more bits for dinner that night. She grabbed her backpack, refilled her water bottle and put on her trainers, calling to Alex as she slipped out the door. She made a mental list of what she needed to get as she paced along the pavement. Smoked salmon, horseradish, crème fraiche, sourdough, that would be for when they were having drinks when everyone arrived. Then she'd get pork belly, sticky rice and greens for main. She'd need chocolate, cream and butter for the fondants Alex always insisted she make. She loved to cook and was reasonably good at it but hated the stress it could bring. She'd made the mistake more times than she could remember, where she'd been so inspired by a cookery show or recipe book that she dove head first into the idea of impressing her guests, head racing and mind whirling at the praise she would receive, before realistically calculating how much pressure she was putting herself under. She'd ruined countless weekends for herself, excitedly making lists and working out timings, decluttering and cleaning, revolving her entire week around one meal served on a Saturday night. She'd feel so tired by the time her guests arrived that she'd swan dive into a bottle of wine and be nodding at the table come 10 o'clock. It was always gone midnight by the time everyone left but she'd still load the dishwasher, and tidy round before flopping into bed, tipsy and exhausted, wondering whether if she'd done a simple spag bol, her friends would have had less of an enjoyable time. She would wake up 2am with a sandy mouth and sore head, proceeding to run a postmortem on the evening. She'd convince herself that they were just being polite when they said it was delicious, that the meat was overdone and dry, and she laughed too loud after her third glass and most likely took a joke too far, until the sunlight slid underneath the blind to confirm it was morning.

She was almost at the supermarket and shook away her daydream as she prepared to cross the road. She pressed the button to cross and waited for the silhouette of the little green man to give her permission to walk. To her left, she felt someone join her to wait. Nancy looked ahead but felt the eyes of this person on her cheek. She wondered if they wanted to know if she'd actually pressed the button or was just standing there, assuming that someone else had pressed it on the other side of the road. Nancy fidgeted, cleared her throat and glanced left and right at the traffic to signify she had indeed pressed the button and was doing everything she could to ensure they all crossed the road safely. She felt the eyes of the stranger continue to burn into her, so Nancy felt compelled to look round. A woman dressed in black sports clothes, younger than her, looked away the second they made eye contact and stared straight ahead. White blonde curls fell just below her shoulders, and she had a freckled button nose and pouty mouth. Nancy politely smiled and with a tiny nod, resumed her position of staring forward. The green man flashed and Nancy hoiked her backpack firmly onto her shoulders and strode out across the road in the direction of the supermarket. She walked faster than usual, and when she felt she'd made some ground, took a casual glance back and found herself alone.

CHAPTER 4

Then

Age 3

"We are only going for a few nights Poppet. We will be back before you know it" Mum assured her.

Nancy clung harder to her. A few nights felt like a month to her. "Please Mummy I want to come too" Nancy begged.

"I know my Darling, but it's Uncle Reg's 30th and no one else has children like Daddy and I do. They just want to do adult things. You would be bored my Darling".

Nancy shook her head, refusing to believe for a second she could ever be bored in her mother's company. Besides which, her parents and their friends were going to Center Parcs, her favourite place in the world. Woods, play parks, bowling, miniature trollies in the supermarket just for her size and to top it all off, a sub-tropical paradise with a huge wave pool, slides and her favourite, steaming, fast flowing rapids which ran outside in the fresh air. She couldn't swim very well yet, but her Daddy let her wrap her arms round his neck and ride down the river on his back. He would take the brunt of all their collisions against the walls and he would pull her out of the bubbling landing pool at the end. They would go round and round for hours and no matter how many times they went, she always felt quietly short-changed when it was time to get out.

Grandma placed her hands on Nancy's shoulders and saved her daughter-in-law from any further negotiations.

'You go, we'll be fine! We've got an action-packed weekend planned and we're going swimming too Nancy, so you don't have to be sad that you are missing out'. Missing out wasn't the real reason she didn't want to be left behind. Her Mum tried to smile at her, but her eyes looked too sad for it to be convincing. Grandma closed the door and walked back down the hallway to get the dinner on. Nancy stood staring at the closed door for a moment, then dashed to her bedroom window, pushing the door to behind her, to get one last painful, private glimpse of her parent's blue car driving down the road. The car's brake lights burned red as they reached the junction and a firework of hope exploded in Nancy's heart. *Maybe they have changed their minds!* she thought. But then the right indicator blinked and they made their maneuver onto the main road and drove off out of sight. She stared hopefully for a minute longer, gasping when another blue car drove along the main road. It coldly carried on past and she sighed, feeling lost and lonely. She walked away from the window and laid on the bed, grabbing the sandy teddy, Wilfred, who lived on the pillows at Grandmas and squeezed him close to her chest.

Her lip trembled and she felt a painful fluid run up her throat, under her ears and along her signaling that tears were sure to follow. She clenched her back teeth together and pressed her face into Wilfred's fur, telling herself she couldn't crumble now. She was going to have to be brave, at least to start with. Once a few sleeps had past, Mummy and Daddy would soon be coming home. She would get up, get ready for bed and find Grandma. She would let her drink out of her favourite cup and eat dinner out of her favourite bowl and then it would be bedtime. Then she would only have two more sleeps left, instead of three until Mummy would hold her again. 'That was a good plan' she thought. A few tears had fallen, which betrayed her, so she used the back of her hand to swipe them away, and took a big breath in and out. She hopped off the bed and unzipped her duffle bag to get her pyjamas out. She took off her jumper and was just about take off her bottoms when something caught her eye, which made her stomach twist like a flannel being wrung out. In the gap between the door and the doorframe, a pair of eyes were watching her.

CHAPTER 5

Present

"Nancy, this is fucking delicious" Sophie said between mouthfuls. "Every time I come here, I literally have to waddle out" said Sophie.

"Crawl out you mean" snorted Alex and the girls laughed, loudly cheering and clinking their wine glasses above the centre of the table.

Nancy scanned the glasses, and noticed most were running low, so she zizzed into the kitchen to fetch more Sauvingnon Blanc out of the fridge and brought it back to the table, topping up the white wine drinkers. She grabbed the Pinot Noir off the side table and topped up hers and Sam's glasses, reminding herself to discretely massage her tongue over her teeth to wipe away any dark residue left behind from the wine. The food was going down well and the playlist she'd created was prompting mid-course sing songs and she knew the evening would end in a drunken dance off. The four girls had been friends since school. First Nancy and Alex who'd made friends at the ripe old age of 6 in the playground. Nancy had been picking daisies to make a necklace for her mother, and Alex had come over to help. They'd ended up making an entire collection of floral jewellery; necklaces, headbands and even rings and proudly gifted them to their teachers and took what was left home to their mothers. Nancy's mother had wept when she was given the sweet necklace and held her very tight. Nancy had felt worried at her mother's reaction but her mother assured her they were happy tears. Nancy couldn't wait to see Alex the next day, and fortunately, neither could Alex. In silent agreement, they became inseparable and school was a joy, simply because they had each other. They made friends with Sophie and Sam in year 5, and though were closest in their own pairs, they became an exclusive foursome, a sisterhood that had spunned through the decades. Their paths had led them to different universities, jobs in other countries, marriages, babies, divorces. But now as grown women, they'd gravitated home and to each other. And although it seemed their individual stories had moulded them into the people they were today, their experiences in their friendship and the memories they shared, made them who they really were.

"I don't know" Sophie said. "It just seems like one minute you were young and in love and building this exciting life together and then… they unload the dishwasher "for you" and expect a fucking blowie!" she said as she slammed her hand down on the table.

They all jumped at the bang, then cackled and mock wretched.

"See girls, this is where Nancy got it right' said Alex, slightly slurring.

"Just her and the girls. Of course, there have been sad times but hey, you gotta make the best of it. Yes, you had a good relationship with Nate, the prick. Amazing holidays and drunken nights but when you both started your careers, he hated the responsibility and wanted to travel more. I know you were happy to go wherever he wanted to go but did he ever ask you where you wanted to go? No. And then when you found out you were pregnant, he still went travelling, the cock", she said as she gritted her teeth.

"I did say he could go though" Nancy interjected.

"Yeah, for a couple of months, not forever!"

Nancy picked up her glass and took a deep drink. Alex was going a bit far. She wasn't cross at Alex though, she knew it was the wine talking and that it was from a good place, she was just starting to feel hot and bothered.

"Heart of gold you Nance. You knew if you stopped him, he would have resented you, so you did the decent thing and stayed behind for all your appointments with the plan that he would be back in plenty of time before the baby's born and you would settle down together as a family. Funny old thing, he met someone else in Oz and never returned. Cry cry cry. Heartbreak bla bla bla and then boom. You come into your own and raise that baby like a machine. And look at Tilly, proper decent human being. Love that kid. And now you've got darling Lottie too. You've got it made love."

Nancy shuffled in her seat and looked uncomfortable. She was hurt that Alex had summarised her relationship with Nate like that, and felt stupid that she believed he would come home to her. She knew Alex meant it as a full compliment that she'd overcome it, but she still felt the blood rush to her face in embarrassment and hurt. Not to mention talking about Lottie. She wasn't meant to be talking about her. Alex spotted Nancy's expression and straightened up, realising her mouth was running away from her. Alex snapped out of her wine-soaked ramble and mouthed 'sorry' to Nancy and she winked back. Alex slid her chair back.

"Right, I am going to put Nancy's fondants in the oven and take all the credit. Give us your plates then" she said, holding out her hands for them to pass to her.

Nancy was grateful for the interruption and tried to pause her inward descent by taking the conversation back.

"Look, just do the jobs yourselves girls" she said, grinning. "A bloz for unloading the dishwasher is not an even trade".

CHAPTER 6

Then

Age 4

"Sausage, burger or both Mum?" Nancy's Dad asked her Grandma.

"Oh um… just a sausage please Darling, I'll never eat both"

"Onions?"

"'Oh no dear. I like them but they don't like me"

Nancy's father tonged a sausage onto her plate and pointed to the table, Nancy's mother had laid out with homemade potato salad, a tomato salad, crusty French stick and a plastic tub of coleslaw with a spoon standing in it. Grandma helped herself to a small spoon of each and carefully walked across the patio to take a seat on the white plastic garden furniture.

It was summer, a British summer. They had planned a barbeque, they'd bought the stubbies, the sausages and burgers and they were going to go ahead with it, whatever the weather. Even though the forecast changed that morning from sunny intervals to just cloud and no intervals, now with a chance of rain showers sprinkled on the top. Dad had spent all morning sweeping the patio, getting the garden furniture out of the shed and hosing it down, then cleaning the kitchen window where the mud had sprayed, to reveal Mum's furious face.

Mum worked inside, hoovering and dusting, furiously cleaning the kitchen and bathroom then preparing and cling-filming crudites and dips, and a variety of salads. And of course, Beryl's trifle, the only trifle to ever grace their table, recipe courtesy of their dear neighbour. It was sherry-laden with lots of cream and strawberries, and everyone seemed a lot chattier after they'd eaten it, which Nancy liked.

The clouds had continued to roll over and there was a chill in the air, but Mum and Dad had kept positive, beavering away to get ready for the party, exchanging squeaky chatter, convincing themselves and each other that the sun would most definitely come out later. Nancy had been given a few jobs, but she felt perhaps she was more of a hindrance than a help, judging by the way her parents grimaced when she joined in. Still, she carried the sauces out one by one, and laid them out on the wobbly plastic table outside, and put her garden toys away in the shed and she'd had her hair ruffled by both of her parents afterwards, which made her beam and flush red with pride.

Robert was on the computer still, and Dad had shouted at him to get off and make himself useful before hurrying back outside. Rob had huffed and sulked and pouted, which was a complete waste of time because their parents were too busy to care, shoving tongs, Dad's bbqing apron, that transformed him into a topless man wearing Speedos, and a kitchen roll into Robert's arms to carry out into the garden.

The crunch of gravel down the side of the fence, heralded the arrival of their guests.

"Shit they're here!" Mum shrieked from upstairs, saying that she wasn't quite, if at all, ready. Nancy poked her head out of the backdoor, and saw her Grandma dressed in trousers and a big grey coat, crunching down the path with a carrier bag in each hand. Nancy smiled, until she saw the larger silhouette of a man behind her, his wispy grey hair wafting in the ever-increasing wind. Nancy swallowed, waved and then ran into the back garden to stand by Dad.

An hour had past, she'd eaten too many crisps and had been sitting on Granville's lap for the most part. She'd been talking to Grandma mostly, about her new school, which she was told she was starting after the summer. Adults seemed very excited to talk to her about school, and she didn't really know what to say. What was it like there? When would it end? Would she go there for a few days or more than that? She wasn't really sure but Robert seemed fine with going, so she was sure she wouldn't mind it too much either. The jumper was red which she liked, and Robert said there was somewhere called the Zig Zag playground, with lots of hiding places. It sounded fun, but she was worried about being away from her Mummy. Hopefully if she was worried she could go and find Robert and he would find a way for Mum to come and get her. He was good like that, always looking after her. Well, as long as he knew she was in trouble.

"Dinner's ready!" Dad announced and bottoms shuffled to the edge of their cheap squeaking seats. Mum handed Nancy a paper plate and she walked over to her father who was engulfed in the grey smoke emanating from the barbeque. "What would you like poppet?"

Nancy tried to see what was on offer through the fog. Dad waved his large hand around to disseminate the smoke, which made them both cough and splutter as they inhaled it. They both laughed.

"A sausage please Daddy" asked Nancy.

With a wink, he gave her two, and kissed her on the head. She walked over to the salad table and tried to put some potato salad on her plate but as she lumped a spoon onto it, one of her sausages rolled off onto the floor and she yelped. She turned to put the spoon back in the salad bowl and when she turned back, Granville was bending down next to her and putting the sausage back on her plate. She looked down at it, with a few crumbs of gravel on it, and frowned. Her Mummy would be mad if she didn't eat all of her food, she hated waste but Nancy really didn't want to eat food that had been on the floor. Granville saw her expression and took the sausage off her plate and put it on his. "Our little secret eh?" he winked and squeezed her shoulder too tightly.

Nancy stared at the grout between the paving slabs.

CHAPTER 7

Then

Age 28

"Tequilla?"

"No!!" they all shouted as Alex spun round and stalked off to the bar to order the shots.

"This is going to hurt in the morning, I can tell" Sophie wailed, leaning her head on Nancy's shoulder.

Nancy empathetically patted her friends face. She knew how she felt. She was only a few cocktails in, she could stop, have a water, it wasn't too late. And she knew once the tequilla hit they were going from classy cocktails in a fancy bar to ending up in a sticky club they were much too old for. Normally Nancy would have just come for the cocktails and pre-planned her early exit to save herself from a day of hugging the sofa. But her mother had Tilly tonight at hers and was keeping her until teatime the next day. This gave Nancy unspoken permission to behave irresponsibly and wallow in self-pity the next day. She didn't have to, of course, she knew she would spend the entire day regretting it. In fact most likely the week. Hangovers in her twenties were merely shrugged off after a couple paracetamols washed down with a glass of fresh orange juice, before going out again later that night. Nowadays it was a week of dragging her feet and her anxious mind behind her, moonlight soul-searching, detoxing with mindful yoga and turmeric water which promised to cleanse the liver, and a bucketload of reassurance from Alex that she wasn't really the complete twat she knew she had been. Nonetheless, the times of getting together out of the house were becoming few and far between. The girls these days always opted for dinner in, walks and yoga classes to spend time together these days, which she loved, but on the occasion that it called for her to be wild and free, she had to answer with a "fuck yes".

Alex walked back towards them, closely followed by a young male waiter who carried a tray of cocktails, surrounded by tequila shots.

He rested the edge of the tray on their table, and decanted the drinks to the centre, all of them selecting which cocktail they'd ordered on sight, Soph and Sam swapping when they realised they'd picked up each other's.

Alex licked the back of her left hand and sprinkled salt which clung to the line of saliva. She gestured for her friends to follow, and shook the saltshaker onto the back of their hands. She picked up her lime wedge, held her shot glass into the centre of the table and said loudly "To being out out!"

She lapped at the back of her hand and threw her shot back, but Nancy hesitated. She watched her friends squint and choke on the alcohol, flapping their hands trying to waft the sensation away. Nancy knew she'd left too much time to think about whether this was a good idea, and was going off it. They girls looked up to see Nancy looking down into her glass and went for her, goading and scolding for being so wet. Nancy reluctantly ran her tongue along the crispy line of salt and lifted the rim of the shot glass to her lips. She swiftly tipped the glass up and the acrid liquid burned down her throat. She winced, and pressed the lime wedge into her teeth, citrus squirting around her gums. She shook her head and hung her tongue out of her mouth and clamped her eyes shut. When she opened her eyes, the girls were all laughing, and wrapping their arms around one another's shoulders. The heat of the alcohol warmed her heart, numbed her cheeks and made smiling effortless. She felt glossy, fortune flooding through her veins. She wanted to live for the moment and no longer cared about tomorrow. With that, the lights turned down and the music turned up, and the energy between them accelerated. Another round of shots appeared, which they eagerly threw back, and found it difficult to sit still in their seats. Nancy stood up and fought the urge to climb on her chair. She felt like she could touch the ceiling, the combination of music and alcohol flooding through her veins, making her feel invincible. She felt free of responsibility, and young. She usually felt old beyond her years, the length of life's to-do list wrapping around her throat and pulling her down to the ground, hopeless and too tired to do anything wild beyond 9pm. She loved Tilly, more than she could have ever imagined, more than she could bear most days, but on these rare nights out, she loved pretending she was carefree and once all sense of reason had gone out the window, she was on the open road to obliteration.

Alex wrapped her arms around Nancy, and they squeezed each other tight, shouting words of devotion, love and empowerment into one another's ears, when there was a tap on Nancy's shoulder. They pulled away from one another and looked to find 4 much younger, well-dressed men smiling, one holding a tray of shots.

"We couldn't help but notice what a brilliant evening you ladies are having and wondered if we could join you for a drink?"

Nancy looked at Alex, who was grinning and nodding, and Sophie and Sam were high fiving that they still had the ability to party and attract the opposite sex, even though neither of them were available. The man holding the shots slid the tray onto their table whilst the other men dragged free chairs from neighbouring parties and sat down to join them. Nancy plopped herself down on her seat, the least excited of them all to be invaded by a bunch of boys, who looked like their Mummies still bought their underpants.

"I'm Rupert" said the one nearest to her and held out his hand. He had an accent that reeked of family money and privilege. He was tall and lean, and she could smell his expensive aftershave immediately. He wore a smart, well fitting, pale blue shirt, with a navy suit, no tie. He was handsome, and he knew it.

"Nancy" she grimaced and shook his hand.

"So, are we having a good night?" he asked.

"We are" she replied.

She looked around at her friends, each paired off with one of the boys, predators sectioning off the herd so they could pounce. Alex was giggling and playfully hitting her man on the shoulder at whatever compliment he'd just whispered in her ear and Nancy felt her irritation grow.

"So, what do you do Nancy?" he asked. She sighed as discretely as possible.

"I work in travel and leisure" she replied as vaguely as possible, bored and reserved. She hated that question too. The last thing she wanted to do was be interviewed on what she did for a living. Who wants to think about work on a Saturday night, for fuck's sake.

There was a pause and she felt obligated to return his question.

"How about you?" she asked, taking a deep sip of her drink.

"Well..." he paused for dramatic affect and smiled, clearly gleeful that she'd returned his question.

"I am actually due to move to New York next year. My father has a lot of connections out there, so I have a few potential job opportunities on Wall Street. I'm going to fly out in the New Year to look for an apartment. All of us are going actually" he gestured to the men trying to worm their way into her friends knickers.

"Tie in something dull with a vacation" he finished.

Yuck, she thought.

A) you are not American, say holiday, you absolute knob. And B) How could you call apartment shopping in New York dull, you spoilt prick? 3) Will you just fuck off? It's a girl's night.

She smiled politely, nodded and sighed at the thought that her night as she knew it was almost certainly over and the end of her night would most likely be filled with stories of wealth from Rupert.

Noticing he was losing her, as if he'd ever had her, Rupert offered her a drink. She didn't like accepting drinks from men in bars. She believed men thought it was like a currency to be used in exchange for her vagina. But her friends were so ensconced with his friends, she felt she had no other choice, but to spend the rest of the evening

31

getting drunk with Rupert instead. She could have gone home of course, but she was beyond the stage where sense prevailed.

He lifted his hand and beckoned the waiter, and ordered cocktails and shots for the table. Nancy excused herself to use the ladies, and dragged Alex up by the armpit to join her.

"Okay, okay I'm up" Alex laughed.

She loyally slipped her arm round Nancy's waist and giggled in her ear whilst walking to the ladies, saying her man was forward and that's just how she liked it.

"Oh come on Nance, live a little! The other two can't shag their blokes, but we can!" Alex said as they entered their toilet cubicles.

"How old are they Al??" Nancy said under the door whilst they wee'd.

"Who gives a fuck? Everyone looks amazing tonight and it shows we can still pull a bunch of lads. We should be celebrating!"

"True" Nancy agreed as she wiped and flushed.

They met in the mirror at the sinks, washed their hands and opened their clutch bags to reapply their lippy.

"Listen, no one is saying you have to shag him" Alex reassured her.

"But yours is the fittest out of them all, and he chose you. So, what if they are jumped up little bastards. Let them pay for the drinks and let's have a brilliant night. Whatever happens after that is down to fate."

Nancy backcombed her roots, and then combed almost all of it out when she realised she looked like she'd just taken a ride in a convertible.

She blotted her lipstick, whilst Alex badgered her some more. Nancy took a large breath in and smirked at her friend, lowered her shoulders, readjusted her bra and looked in the mirror. She felt attractive, she looked attractive, although she wasn't sure how much of that was down to the tequila. She smiled to herself and with numbing confidence, decided to straighten her dress and rejoin the table with a better attitude. Alex threw her arm around Nancy and squeezed her shoulder. "That's more like it!" Alex cheered, and they walked back to their table hand in hand.

Nancy sat back down in her seat, crossed one leg over the other and smiled at Rupert. He passed her the Cosmopolitan she'd ordered and held his flute of champagne up to toast.

"Cheers" he smiled, and she clinked her glass against his, and returned his smile.

Nancy looked at him as she took a sip of her drink, the sharp red liquid slipping down her throat. He was gorgeous. Horribly arrogant, far too young, yes. But it was only flirting, and it did feel good to be selected for his attention above every other woman in this bar. She was always suspicious since Nathan. She didn't believe she would ever throw herself into any kind of relationship with a man ever again. She would forever exercise extreme caution, even when it came to lighthearted flirtations like this. She always felt, well knew, a man always wanted something from her, and would take it and run. She had accepted this, and protected her heart, by becoming a strong, single mother, with a pillar of decent women around her, never allowing a man to get the better of her. It had become such an obsession, she struggled to even have a conversation with a man without thinking he was going to try and steal her bank details and stamp on her heart.

He passed her a shot of tequila with a nod. She told herself this would be the last one. She felt drunk, but logical. She gently lifted the glass to her lips and tipped it back slowly, whilst maintaining eye contact with Rupert. She fought the urge to stomp and crumple her face at the taste, and with a lick of her lips, returned the glass to the table. Rupert laughed, and leaned in.

"You are quite a woman aren't you?"

Her heart thumped and she gently flicked her hair, loving that she'd managed to fool someone into thinking she was a lot more sophisticated, than she actually was.

He tried to reach in and hold her chin, to pull her in for a kiss, but she dodged his hand, and stood up to dance, just as the beat dropped.

She moved, circling her hips, avoiding eye contact, mouthing the words to the song. She could feel him watching her. She looked up slowly through her hair to see him sitting back in his seat and crossing his ankle across his knee. They made eye contact and he smiled slowly. She felt her breath catch in her chest and her heart beat to the music. She was aware of her sexuality, and was enjoying performing for him. She looked over at the girls. Alex was sitting on her boys lap, his hand on her bottom and her hands around his neck, kissing. He was sliding his other hand up and down her back, into her hair, pressing her face into his. The other two girls had joined together on the sofa, and were showing their boys something on their phone. Due to the defeated expression on the men's faces, Nancy guessed Soph was showing pictures of her children. Sam was laughing away, and was holding onto her engagement ring, twisting it from side to side. They had enjoyed the initial flirtation, but were clearly bringing out the big guns to stop the boys thinking they had a chance. It had worked, and one of the guys kept checking his watch and shuffling to the edge of the sofa to show they were thinking leaving. Nancy snapped out of her observation as Rupert, now standing, pulled her close to him. She slowed her dancing and smiled awkwardly.

"I can't keep my hands off you a second longer" he said as he pulled her in closer.

He pressed his lips softly against hers and she felt a spark ignite in her tummy. He pulled away gently and looked her straight in the eyes, smiled and kissed her again. This time he slipped his tongue into her mouth and massaged his with hers, the spark in her tummy travelling south. She wrapped her arms around his neck and pressed her body against his, the kiss making her want to moan into his mouth. She hadn't been kissed in so long. She tried to contain herself, and hold back, but the more he slipped his tongue in and out of her mouth, the tighter she held onto him. She felt light, weak, and needy. She felt herself getting wet, a steady throbbing in her knickers. He cupped her buttocks and parted them slightly, she was hot and aroused. She pushed herself lower further against him, shameless and primal. She knew she would regret it, but right now nothing was going to stop her from going home with him.

CHAPTER 8

Present

Nancy woke suddenly. It felt like an elephant was standing on her head and that something had crawled into her mouth and died. She took a deep breath and rolled out of bed, onto her knees, pulled herself up and shuffled to the bathroom. She plonked herself down on the toilet and tried to lubricate her mouth She peeled her tongue off the inside of her cheek, like she was opening a Velcro wallet to get some money out. She could barely open her eyes and certainly did not want to see her reflection. She fumbled around for some tablets, which she'd left by the toilet roll on her left. She thanked her sensible self for putting them out, popped two out of the packet and tried to swallow them down with the small amount of saliva she'd managed to muster. She washed her hands, and walked back to the bedroom to get her water bottle. The chalky, acidic tablets were lodged and were making her feel sick. She glugged the liquid back, and gasped. Placing the water on her bedside table, Nancy flopped back into bed, clutching her head and groaning. She replayed what she'd had to drink, and she couldn't remember, once all the food had been served the wine had just flowed. She felt a tightness in her tummy, something telling her they'd touched on an uncomfortable subject. She scanned her brain, seeing the girls smiling faces and thought the alcohol must be playing tricks on her. No, there was definitely something. She remembered Alex bolstering her, and remembered her referencing Lottie's father. The tightness in her tummy changed into a punch and she felt sick. She squeezed her eyes shut and prayed for the tablets to kick in.

CHAPTER 9

Then

Age 28

He opened the car door and walked round to her side and offered his hand. It was the first time a man had ever helped her out of a taxi. Well, like this. She'd been carried out several times. He paid the driver and the taxi pulled off and left them standing at the end of a driveway. She looked up to see a very large, detached house with several expensive cars parked outside. She spun around and noted that the house stood alone; not a neighbouring house to be seen. He slipped his arm around her waist and kissed her.

"My parents are away for the weekend so we have the house to ourselves" he whispered and kissed her again, but she pulled away.

"Your parents?" she smirked.

"Yes well, I've sold my place ahead of the move to NYC so I'm staying here until I go. They're never here though, so I pretty much have the place to myself."

Nancy hesitated.

"Listen, I know I'm young but don't let that put you off. I have a pool…"

"A pool?" she smiled.

"Yep. And a jacuzzi" he whispered as he leant in to slip his tongue in her mouth.

She ignored her responsible self, screaming at her and enjoyed the tightening in her tummy and the tingling in her underwear.

So what if he's young and lives with his parents. Just laugh at it Nancy, don't ruin the fun by acting like a bloody Mum. It was Alex in her head, ruffling her hair and shoving her into Rupert's arms. He ran his hands over her back and bottom, and his kiss deepened. She felt warm in his embrace. She had never had a one night stand before, she couldn't stand the idea of waking up alone and feeling used. She'd never looked at sex as something that could just be done and dusted. But she had missed it, the touch of a man. And maybe the odd one night stand was what had been missing from her life. She had made the decision to just be her and Tilly, strong and independent. No man was worthy to come in and take over everything she had provided for them. But maybe the occasional, no strings attached dalliance was what she needed, to lighten her load. And she knew Rupert was going away, so this was perfect. He was young, handsome and polite, he wouldn't want anything from her apart from her company tonight, and even if they met up again, it would purely be for sex. She would never introduce him to Tilly. But if it was just for tonight, then she would be able to tick a one night stand off her bucket list, not that it was ever on her list, and laugh about it with Alex in the morning. And if she fell in love with him and he left, which he would, then she could add it to the long list of things she would never do again.

"Shall we?" he asked, holding out his bent arm for her to hook onto.

CHAPTER 10

Present

Nancy sloped into the kitchen, relieved to see that she'd loaded the dishwasher and cleared most of the empty bottles from the night before. There were a few undrunk glasses of wine on the side next to the dishwasher so she swilled them down the sink, a puff of alcohol hitting her in the face making her groan in disgust. She opened the kids' treat cupboard and grabbed a carton of apple juice, ripping the plastic off the straw and frantically stabbing it into the box until it found the tiny silver foil hole. She placed the straw in the corner of her mouth and desperately sucked, until it she'd drained the contents. She launched it into the bin and missed, threw her head back and groaned like a teenager being asked to make their bed.

"Mum why are you drinking our juice?" asked Tilly

"Umm because I'm thirsty, why do you think?" Nancy snarled sarcastically.

Tilly looked hurt.

Nancy was horrified at her reaction and guiltily reached out for her, squeezing her close to her chest and kissing her rusty locks.

"Sorry poppet. I just fancied some juice that's all"

"That's okay" said Tilly and hopped into the lounge to watch television.

Peering through to the lounge, Nancy could see Tilly was happily watching some American kids' show with her little sister, so she quietly nudged the kitchen door shut. She returned to the cupboard, and scoffed her way through a mini bag of cookies, two fistfuls of Haribos and a sherbet dib dab.

Sighing, sugar pulsing in her head and sherbet crumbling off her lips, decided she should probably make herself a proper breakfast now. She opened the fridge and took out 6 cold eggs. She opened the bread bin, selected 4 slices of seeded bread and placed them the toaster. She cracked the eggs into a jug and whisked them to a sunshine yellow froth and popped a frying pan over a low heat. She added butter to the pan and poured the eggs in, nursing them slowly with a wooden spoon. The toast popped up and she laid out 3 plates, 2 slices for her and one each for the girls. She sliced an avocado and laid it out on hers and Tilly's toast, and sliced some peppers for Lottie who openly hated avocado. The eggs were loose, almost cooked, so she turned off the gas and let the eggs finish off in the heat of the cast iron skillet. One more stir and she spooned the eggs onto the toast, and finished with a sprinkle of sea salt and a grinding of black pepper. She added a pinch of dried chilli to hers and called the girls to the table. They ate, and Nancy could feel the virtuousness of the meal overriding the wine she'd guzzled and the sugar she'd just inhaled. She welcomed the taste of the salty eggs, the creamy avocado and the crunchy carbs, and was already thinking about what other goodies she going to eat today. The girls bombarded her with questions; 'Why was there a moon?' and 'how did it stay in the sky?' 'How do we breathe?' and' how old would they be when Nancy was 100 years old?' The worst one, 'where do eggs come from, and what came first'. She was simply too delicate to have the chicken and the egg debate. She answered what she could and suggested they google the rest later, her alcohol-soaked mind trying to find the answers to their anxiety inducing questions. She put her knife and fork down and excused herself from the table, taking her plate and loading it into the dishwasher and leant against the worktop. Her headache was subsiding but she felt shaky and could still taste stale alcohol. Anxiety engulfed her, with every beat of her heart, sending uncertainty through her veins. She couldn't identify what was making her feel so worried, but the familiar twist in her stomach reminded her that she was. She'd gotten so used to the feeling that, although it was unbearable, it was a comfort to recognise it. Pain was her companion. She hated feeling like this, but she'd forgotten what she felt like without it. She wanted to feel better, but she didn't know what better felt like or how to even start to get there. The pain meant she was staying still but she was safe. To move forward would mean significant change which she simply did not want to acknowledge and put into action. She knew, deep down, that if she wanted to feel better, she was going to have to open up compartments of herself and she did not know what they would look or feel like, and what consequences would come of unearthing them. Her past was dark and undealt with, and she didn't know where to start. And it had followed her into adulthood, like a pair of shoes she'd never grown out of. There were so many layers, so much confusion, betrayal, disgust, fear, anger. *Why had this happened to her? But why not? Why not her? Why was she so special to be excused from trauma? Why was she thinking about this now? Stop being so ridiculous*, she told herself.

She turned around and looked out the window. The garden was beginning to decay, deep in autumn's grasp. She thought back to the night with the girls and smiled. Why was she ruining the memories of a good night with a morning of soul-searching? *You're hungover Nancy, that's it. Nothing even happened to warrant these thoughts, she need not go on a quest of self-discovery because she enjoyed wine with her dearest friends.* But the fact that she had felt like this for a long time, long before she'd experienced hangovers, kept nudging her. Her mouth filled with salty saliva and she gulped it down. Her stomach turned over like a cement mixer and she ran to the downstairs toilet and threw up. She stared at her vomit in the basin and hated herself. She spat the foamy coating that remained on her teeth into the toilet and wiped her mouth with toilet tissue. She reached forward and flushed the toilet and sat back on the cold tiles. She felt better, and tried to rise above the self-loathing that was washing the shores of her inner being. She'd had a lovely evening, the house was mostly tidy, the girls would be perfectly happy with park and a cosy day, so she didn't need to push down any walls, and she felt no worse than she had most of her life. Today was no different and she didn't need to spend it pulling at a thread. She was simply hungover and tired, and in a few days, she would feel better and could manage her feelings, like she always had. She stood up and swilled her mouth out in the sink and washed her hands. She walked past the lounge door and told the girls she was getting in the shower, and then would join them on the sofa for a film. The girls cheered, and then squabbled about who would get to choose what they watched. Nancy told them it was going to be an all day snuggle club, so they would both get a chance to choose which appeased them. She walked quietly upstairs so as not to wake Alex. She would most likely sleep in for another few hours, and join them on the sofa where they would eat rubbish and throw popcorn at each other. A wave of relief and lightness crashed over her. How could she forget she wasn't alone, and that her best friend in the whole world was here, feeling equally rough but secure in the fact that it was just a hangover, and as grown women were allowed to be. As soon as Alex woke, she would tell her it was all alright and they would have a lovely girly day together. As Nancy started to ascend the staircase feeling much more positive, there was a knock at the door. She sighed, and crossed her arms over her braless chest under her pyjama top. As she walked past the hallway mirror, she brushed her lips and teeth with her index finger to remove the red wine stains, and dragged her pinkies under her eyes to remove mascara residue. The person knocked again, this time with more intent and Nancy felt irritated. She opened the door just a crack to cover as much of her body as possible. There on her front porch, stood a young woman. She looked a few years younger than Nancy, most likely in her early twenties. She looked nervous, shifting from one foot to the other.

"Yes?" Nancy questioned when the girl did not identify herself.

"Hello"

"Yes?" Nancy impatiently repeated, feeling the heat rush from inside out.

"Is your name Nancy?"

Nancy bristled at the mention of her name by a stranger.

"Can I ask who you are?"

"You don't remember me, do you Nancy?"

Nancy felt anxiety rush in through the gap in the door with the cool autumn wind.

She stared at her to provoke a memory. She had almost white blonde curly hair, her complexion signified it was natural and not from a bottle. Pale skin and a button nose, and large, glassy blue eyes with thin shadowy skin underneath. She wore black jeans, boots and a black duffle coat.

There was something about her that rung a bell, maybe her hair, but Nancy couldn't place it. She felt irritated that she was even engaging in this guessing game. All she wanted to do today was to shower, put on fresh pyjamas, and spend the day with Alex and the girls. Nancy shook her head.

"Listen, I'm sorry but I don't know who you are and I've got something on the stove, goodbye" and she shut the door in the woman's face.

Nancy stood at the door trying to catch her trembling breath and fought the urge to re-open the door and find out what she wanted and how she was supposed to know her. She moved away from the door and into the downstairs loo and sat down on the toilet lid, out of sight.

"Who was that Mummy?" Tilly called.

"Postman" Nancy replied, leaning forward for the door handle and closing the bathroom door.

Stupid cold callers, Nancy thought, shaking her head. *They even get your name now to get your attention,* she laughed to herself. She was being paranoid. That woman didn't know her, she knew her name as many companies did. The amount of time and money she spent shopping online, it's no wonder that these companies knew her name, address and email. They just knew she never read all the spam they sent her every day. Her inbox was now so full of shit it was too big of a job to reduce it, so she just left it and only decluttered it when she'd tired of scrolling through social media, which was hardly ever. Yes, that's what it was, she convinced herself and took a deep breath in and out to calm her racing heart. Without alcohol she would have been mildly curious and irritated by the cold caller. With stale wine still beating through her system she seriously considered turning her house into a fort and digging out a moat so no one could ever knock on her door again.

"I know you are still there"

Nancy's head jolted upwards to where the voice came from through the crack in the W.C window. She didn't breathe, and just shrunk down and stared with wide eyes at the gap where the voice was coming through.

"I know who you are, and you might not remember me right now, but you will"

Nancy's heart thumped in her throat and she pressed the heel of her hands into her aching eye sockets, trying to visualise her face to try and remember where the fuck she might have known this woman from.

"I know where you live now, so you can't ignore me. I'll come back another time".

"No you won't! If you come back I'll call the police okay?" Nancy shrieked out of nowhere.

Nancy sat there panting, sniffing salty tears away, ears pricked for a reply. But there wasn't one.

CHAPTER 11

Then

Age 28

Nancy saw white. White ceiling, white walls, white light streamed through the window. It was bright and her head hurt. She was in an asylum. They'd finally realised she was crazy and locked her up. She fanned her fingers over her face, casting strips of shadow across her eyes to create a more diluted and digestible picture for herself. As her eyes adjusted to the glow in the room, she made out she was in a large bed with white sheets. Her bare legs touched one another, and she slipped her hand under the duvet and patted her body to realise she was naked. Probably not an asylum then. At least she hoped not. She gasped and pulled the sheet up to her chest and shuffled backwards until she was sitting up, pillows propped up behind her. *Tilly, where's Tilly?!* she panicked. *Calm down*, Nancy told herself and took a deep breath like she always did when she was reeling. *She was at Mum's*, Nancy remembered and breathed out a sigh of relief. *She'd gone out with the girls. Did she go back to one of theirs? Those boys, they came over. What was her one called again? Rupert?* Yes, she thought. *Did she go home with him?* She must have. She'd never done that before in her whole life. She was mortified, horrified at her lack of responsibility. *He could have been a murderer! He still could still be a murderer! Where was he, hiding under the bed, waiting to kill her?* She looked at the bedroom windows for bars, assuming she was probably in some kind of white sex dungeon, never to be seen again, but the windows were open, a gentle breeze rippling the curtain and the sound of birds tweeting their morning chorus. Nancy realised she desperately needed the toilet, so she wrapped the large sheet around her body twice tightly and hopped to the en-suite, where she locked the door behind her. She dropped the sheet on the expensive looking tiles, and sat down on the toilet. She winced as she started to go to the toilet, urine stinging her, prompting flashbacks of her riding Rupert like a bucking bronco last night.

"Oh God!" Nancy slapped her hand over her face and clenched her teeth at the memory.

She dabbed her delicate genitals with tissue, flushed and stood up at the sink. She looked at her naked body whilst she washed her hands and dried them. She didn't look too bad for someone who'd had a baby. Running had been her savior, both mentally and physically. She'd walked Tilly wherever she could and always drank slim line tonic with her very large gins. Nancy decided that. although she was certain she would beat herself up for this irresponsible act for the rest of her life, for the next few minutes, she shouldn't. Was Rupert going to beat himself up over shagging that woman in the bar last night? No. She was sure he was going to do quite the opposite. He would have winked at his mates as he'd walked her out of the bar, with his hand on the small of her back, and he would be arranging to meet with them later today at the pub to confirm that he did in fact, fuck her. Nancy hated that term, and frowned at the thought of someone using it to describe what they did to her. All of a sudden she felt dirty and the moment she thought she could be proud of her sexual emancipation had disappeared in the blink of an eye. She bent down to pick up the sheet of the floor and smacked her head on the marble basin on the way back up.

"Fuck!" she shouted and clamped her hands over the back of her skull.

Nancy stood up and felt woozy, alcohol still pumping through her veins.

"Everything alright in there?" came a voice from the other side of the door.

Nancy hesitated. Could she remember what he even looked like?

"Err fine thanks, I just um, hit my head"

"Shit! Are you okay?" he asked.

"Fine, just give me a minute, thanks" Nancy said.

She wrapped the sheet firmly around her breasts and made sure it covered her all the way down to her feet, tucking the loose ends in under her armpits. She swilled her mouth out with water and took a squeeze of toothpaste from the bathroom cabinet and swiped it over her teeth with her finger. She swished and spat, and rinsed the bowl clean. She still had make-up on from last night. She'd treated herself to a new foundation which promised to last 24 hours, which at the time, she thought was a ridiculous amount of time for make up to be on one's face. Now she was hugely grateful to her past self for making a decision which made her look mildly fresh in this awkward scenario. Her blow dry was still in reasonable tact and with a quick root push from her fingers, was revived to a post-shag style. Nancy looked at herself and smirked. Despite feeling a bit like a cheap whore, the whole thing was quite amusing, and if she could get over herself, could probably laugh at this with the girls, tick the one night stand box off life's to do list, and get on with it. Nancy took a deep inward breath and told herself not to spoil the whole experience by overthinking, and opened the door. Rupert was sitting on the edge of the bed in navy, checked pyjama bottoms, with no top, a tray of coffee and orange juice next to him, with a toast rack, butter and jam in a little dish each. Seeing him topless in the cold light of day was embarrassing, and Nancy hardly knew where to look; yet her gaze kept finding it's way back to his toned, tanned torso.

"How's your head?" he asked.

"Sore, for two reasons now" she smirked, rubbing her hand over her forehead where the tequillas sat and the back where she'd cracked it on the sink.

"I thought you might be hungry" Rupert smiled.

"Oh I'm fine thanks" Nancy started to say, just as her stomach let out the most unattractive rumble that told Rupert she was lying out of her arse.

Nancy clasped her hands over her stomach and pressed hard to stop it gurgling like a drain.

Rupert rolled back on the bed laughing, the coffees spilling over the rim onto the tray.

"Oh my God, I'm so embarrassed, sorry"

"Don't be sorry" laughed Rupert. "Here, come and have some breakfast"

Nancy smiled sheepishly, and hopped back over to the bed in her sheet dress and perched on the end of the bed next to the tray.

She picked up a coffee cup, blotted the bottom of the cup on a serviette and held it up to her lips and blew. Rupert copied her and looked at her over the top of his cup.

"Fun night" he smiled.

"Yeh" Nancy laughed into her cup. She could see herself from above, acting out a cliché scene with a younger man, and couldn't believe she was actually the one playing the part of Mrs Robinson.

"What's so funny?" Rupert smirked.

"Oh I don't know. It's just, funny that's all."

"Why?"

Nancy looked at him and stopped smiling, and looked around the room to search for an non-insulting answer.

"It's just…you are younger than me and…"

"So?"

"You have done this lovely breakfast in bed scenario, you would see in a film"

"And?"

"Well, I'm a Mum"

"Yes?"

Nancy looked at him as though the answer was obvious.

"Why would any of that stuff matter to me?" he asked.

She shrugged and looked down into her coffee.

"Listen, sex and breakfast in bed is not exactly a marriage proposal" he smirked, maintaining eye contact.

She flushed with embarrassment, that she was making more of this than any man ever did. She picked up a triangle of toast, furiously buttering and blobbing jam on it, before shoving it into her mouth.

"But I do like you. And the fact that you are a Mum, and that I'm a few years younger than you, or the fact that you have jam in the corner of your mouth, does nothing to put me off" he smiled.

Nancy swiped at her mouth, dragging jam down her chin until she looked like a vampire who'd just finished its lunch.

Rupert laughed again and leant forward to kiss her, kissing the corner of her mouth.

"Mmm I love jam" he murmured.

She flushed red at being so clumsy with her food, and the cheesy declaration from Rupert. Well it was hardly a declaration. She really needed to get out more. But it had been a very long time since someone told her they liked her, despite all the things she thought took her off the dating market.

He pulled away when he felt her reluctance to kiss him back.

"What's wrong?" he asked.

"I don't know. I'm just in my head" she laughed and shook her head and looked down at her lap.

"Well, let me help you get out of it" he smirked.

He took the tray and placed it on the sideboard. She was excited but also annoyed that he'd moved the toast.

He stepped in front of her and slowly unwrapped her bedsheet dress. She could see he was hard through his bottoms, shamelessly pressing and straining against the material. He kept eye contact whilst he bent down onto his knees on the fluffy carpet. She looked down at him, feeling vulnerable and exposed. Her breath quickened as he placed his hands on her knees and parted her legs wide. She wanted to clamp them shut, tell him this was ridiculous, and she should be getting off. But when she felt his hot breath on her inner thighs as he moved in closer, she knew she wasn't going anywhere.

CHAPTER 12

Present

Four days had past since Nancy had been visited by the curly haired cold caller and she'd almost forgotten about it. Her panicky hangover had clung on for two, almost three days but on the dawn on the fourth day, the feeling of pending doom had subsided, along with the things the blonde had said. She told Alex about it when she'd finally woken, and she'd laughed and said it was probably a Jehovah's going for a more personal touch. It had comforted Nancy immediately, and she wondered how much of what she remembered was even true, and how much was just her drunk imagination. The story kept changing in her mind, so she wasn't exactly sure what was actually said anyway. Alex had given her a big hug, reminded her that they'd got through a bottle bank's worth of wine the night before, and on that kind of a hangover, she would probably have thought the milkman was trying to kill her. She'd taken herself out for a few early morning runs when she couldn't sleep, and was feeling physically and mentally stronger again. She had packed the girls off to school and since she didn't have her first meeting of the day until 11am, she decided to swing into the supermarket and do her big shop. She took her token off her keyring and pushed it into the trolley, the chain falling and clanging into the trolley in front. She yanked the handle and swung it round, fumbling for her list and realising she'd left it at home.

"Fuck's saaaaaake" she growled and gritted her teeth in frustration.

She walked down the aisles, aimlessly throwing fruit and veg into the trolley. She got to the chiller section and paused to recall which meals she'd planned for the week. She closed her eyes tightly to try and see her list on the breakfast bar. All she could remember was a chicken for Sunday and mince to make spaghetti meatballs, Lottie's favourite. She opened her eyes and picked up a ready to roast chicken in a bag and a kilo of mince; she would make a double batch of meatballs and freeze the rest for another day. She reached for sausages and some chicken breasts, and thought she could fashion anything with those ingredients. She vowed to herself she would look up some vegetarian options and try and reduce their meat intake the following week. She knew the girls would make a fuss and she would probably end up cooking two meals, but she was sure Alex would appreciate a change of scene from the same midweek meals she kept knocking out. Not that she ever complained, Nancy did all the cooking and Alex cleared up. It was an unspoken agreement seeing as the last time Alex cooked for the family, she'd burnt egg and chicken onto Nancy's new fancy pan. Nancy didn't even know what Alex was trying to cook. It was like a family funeral.

That night they'd thrown the meal and pan away and ordered a pizza, put their pyjamas on and snuggled on the sofa together to watch Disney films. It was a wonderful evening and Nancy felt very lucky that Alex lived so close to them, and hoped she always would. She imagined one day Alex would fall in love with a tall dark handsome stranger and remarry, but until that day, she would enjoy every moment with her best friend and her girls. When Nancy would sometimes share her fears, Alex pretended to slap her, saying after what Grayson did, she would never remarry and she had everything she needed right here. Then when the girls left home, she and Nancy would join a walking group and go on coach trips for widows and lesbians.

Nancy picked up milk and cream, then a bunch of lunchbox paraphernalia, some of which would make it to school and some which she would eat in the car on the way home. She moved away from the confectionary section before she was tempted to sweep anymore into her trolley, when she saw a man in front of her that made her stop dead in her tracks. He was at the end of the aisle but she was sure it was him. He had white hair combed over his scalp, gold-rimmed, yellowing glasses and a large, red, bulbous nose. Pitted. He wore a grey cardigan over a beige striped shirt, beige trousers and lace-up tan shoes. He was looking at the tins, and although he wasn't completely facing her, his stance was so familiar, even though he was older since the last time she saw him. She couldn't take a step further, gripping onto the trolley until her hands turned pink and her knuckles white. He turned from her and walked away and disappeared to the right, possibly down the next aisle. She drew a jagged breath in and blew it out through her mouth. He was here. She should run, dump the trolley and do an online shop. She felt like she was going to burst into tears right there next to the KitKats. Her lip trembled and her throat felt tight, hot lumps rising under her ears along her jawline. *Why was he here? Why is he shopping half an hour away from his home?* Almost every time she'd bumped into him when she was younger, she'd been with her parents, and they'd quickly ushered her away, protecting her and shunning him from her life as quickly as possible. Now she was on her own, and even though she was a grown woman, she found herself looking side to side, wishing her parents were with her to shoo him away like a bad dog. But they weren't. And she had a choice. She could run or she could continue her shopping like she intended. She should hang back, give him a chance to get ahead and she wouldn't have to see him again. *Yes, that's what she would do, she would hang back.* But before that thought had finished planting its seed, she lunged; striding forward, pushing her trolley fast, running straight past the tins and crisps, and careering around the end of the aisle and into the household aisle. She didn't know what she was doing, but she couldn't stop. She saw him standing there, looking at the toilet cleaning products. She paused for a moment, blood-red rage pumping through her body. Before she could even think, she ran forward again, driving her trolley right for him. She wanted to crash it into him, smash him into a million pieces, and then cover his sin with the products he was browsing, burn and bleach his dirty soul clean, whatever soul he even possessed. She was charging like an avenged warrior, crazed. All the pain, all the fury and disgust driving her forward to cause him rib-crushing pain. All of a sudden, she winced inside, her mind catching up with what she was about to inflict. It was like watching a You Tube video of someone skateboarding, about to fall on their face, which Nancy always paused before impact. Her teeth unclenched and she dug her heels in to the tiled supermarket floor and pulled back on the trolley handle until screeched to a halt, just inches before she reached him. He gasped and dropped his basket, took a wobbly step backwards onto a tin of new potatoes that had rolled out, which spun from under his foot, sending him flying backwards and crashing onto the top of his spine, his body curling up as though he would go into a backward roll. There was a collective gasp from nearby shoppers as they watched the old man crash onto the ground with his legs over his face before rolling back so he was laying flat on his back, still and motionless. Customers rushed to his side, someone lifted his head and propped it on their lap, another woman barked not to move him. Someone called an ambulance and teenagers started filming on their phones. An old lady touched Nancy's arm and asked her what had happened. She stuttered, looking down at his bloodied nose where he'd obviously kneed himself in the face. She realised, now she was up close, that it wasn't him. It was an old man that looked very much like him. Her stomach knotted so tight, she thought it might throw her breakfast back up. She watched people crowd around and try to help him whilst she just stood there, frozen and horrified.

"It was her, she ran at him and knocked him over with her trolley"

She snapped out of her daze, a grey-haired old lady telling the security guard what Nancy had done.

He walked over to her and she shook her head fiercely.

"No I didn't hit him, he fell over, I was just rushing past and must have scared him" Nancy fibbed.

He held onto her elbow and as she tried to wriggle away, his grip tightened.

"Alright, ow, do you mind, you are actually hurting me. I didn't do anything".

Paramedics pushed past them and waved the crowd back. The lead paramedic talked to the white-haired old man, trying to get a response. He groaned and tried to touch his nose, but the paramedic held his arm down and asked him not to move.

"I think we better take you to the manager's office Madam" the security guard said to her.

"Well, I don't see what good I can do to help, like I said I was just rushing past him and he fell over" Nancy explained again.

"Nonetheless" he said as he led her by the elbow down the aisle, whilst being filmed by several hooded teenagers.

"I do not give consent to be filmed!" Nancy scolded, holding her hands up to cover her face.

"Free country Bitch" one muttered and the others sniggered before the security guard opened the manager's office door, took Nancy in and closed the door behind them.

CHAPTER 13

Then

Age 4

"Got your gloves, hat, scarf?" Mum called.

"Yeh!" they all replied as they put their welly boots on.

"Gloves, hat, scarf, hipflask, check!" said Dad, grinning at Mum. She smirked as he grabbed her for a kiss, squeezed her bum and she squealed, hitting him with her gloves. Nancy and Robert pretended to throw up and their parents laughed.

"Wait until you get a girlfriend mate" Dad said as he ruffled Robert's hair.

"Yuk, no thank you!" he said indignantly.

"I'll remember that when you bring her round for the first time" Dad teased.

Nancy laughed, enjoying the opportunity to wind up her brother in the safety of her parents' company. It gave her little in the way of protection, as once her Dad nipped into the downstairs toilet, Robert punched her on her upper arm, the blood rushing to her numb limb.

"Owwww" she whined.

"Stop it you two" Mum warned from the kitchen and Robert smiled.

Nancy rubbed her upper arm, sulking.

"Right everybody out, or we'll miss the fireworks" Mum said as she ushered them out the front door.

It was a dark, cold night, the wind whipping up what dry leaves were left on the ground. She was glad she had wrapped up so tight and felt a frisson of excitement in her tummy to be out in the dark. Mum reached down and held her gloved hand and started marching them along the pavement at a speed too fast for Nancy's little legs. She ran alongside her mother, her brother and father following behind, her father already sipping out of the hipflask and smirking to himself like a schoolboy.

She looked up and there was a moving fug of smoke in the sky from where fireworks had already been set off from peoples' gardens. They, along with the rest of the town, were walking towards the football ground where they held their annual firework display. The smell of blown out birthday candles was in the air, along with hot chips and greasy fried onions. Nancy squealed with delight and squeezed her mother's hand tight. Mum looked down and beamed at Nancy, wearing a red bobble hat and matching red wellington boots.

"Your nose matches your boots Niknoodle" said Mum, bopping her on her cold nose.

Nancy loved it when Mum called her Niknoodle. She didn't really know how she got that from Nancy, but it made her feel special to have a silly name tailor made just for her.

As they approached the football ground, the crowd thickened as they tried to squeeze through the turnstiles one by one. Mum kept a firm grip on Nancy's hand, Dad put his arm round Robert, and slipped his hipflask into the inside of his coat pocket, hiding it in case the stewards confiscated it.

"There they are!" Mum announced and pulled Nancy along.

"Who Mummy?" Nancy asked, looking at the back of lots of strangers' legs.

"Grandma and Granville! Surprise!" Mum exclaimed.

Nancy's stomach flipped as she saw Grandma and Granville waving to them, wading through the crowds to get towards one another.

"Happy Fireworks!" Mum said, giving Grandma a kiss and hugging Granville.

Dad shook Granville's hand and planted a kiss on his mother's cheek. Grandma lifted Nancy up and squeezed her tight. Two chubby smokey fingers reached across and pinched her cold numb cheek.

"Hello you" he crackled, the overpowering stench of salty smoke lingering.

Nancy offered a smile and slid out of her Grandmas arms and hid behind Mum's leg.

"Nancy don't be rude, isn't it a great surprise?!'

Nancy nodded and looked away.

"Probably tired" Mum said and patted Nancy's red hat.

"Let's go in shall we?" Dad said, ushering his family forward towards the entrance.

Nancy held onto her mother's hand and dawdled to keep a distance.

"Nancy stop dragging your feet, we'll get separated" Mum scolded.

Nancy's felt cross at her for not understanding her reluctance to join them, but nonetheless, held her hand tightly and picked up the pace. She didn't want Mummy to be cross and send her to stand with Grandma and Granville. Once they took their place in the stands, Dad took everyone's orders and walked over to the burger stand to join the queue. Nancy saw him sneak a sip out of hipflask and return into his pocket, looking around with a cheeky grin on his face. Even though he looked old to her, Nancy loved that he behaved a bit like her friends at school, when they were doing something they shouldn't. Almost everyone was in their seats* now and the atmosphere was electric. The families that gathered were wrapped up tight, a sea of brightly coloured hats swaying in the stands. Children squealed and adults laughed, the excitement building in the stadium.

"Scuse me, scuse me, coming through"

Dad returned with 6 cones of chips, huddled together in a steaming bouquet. He distributed the chips to each person, with a warning that they were piping hot.

"Yes, I added lots of salt and vinegar, don't worry" Dad exasperated, when asked multiple times if he had.

Nancy looked down in her cone, which was smaller than everyone else's. She was disappointed that she had less, even though she was the littlest there. It didn't mean she wasn't the hungriest.

She took her little wooden fork and stabbed one of the chips and lifted it to her mouth. The smell of vinegar shot up her nostrils and made her cough. She smiled at Dad for putting plenty on, just as she liked it. As she lifted the chip up to her mouth, she could feel the heat of the hot fat radiating off of it, and she took a tentative bite, lifting her lips away from it, hoping that her teeth would take the brunt of the heat. She bit down and broke off the end, steam gushing out of the end of the chip.

"Itsh hotch" she said between her teeth and looked up at her family, all doing he exact same thing and making the exact same face. She let the chip fall into her mouth, and opened wide to let the heat out, fanning the steam as it puffed into the night air. The chip had already scolded her tongue, but it tasted so delicious she didn't care. Mum rarely gave them chips, but having them outside on Fireworks Night was the best way to have them. She didn't mind if she only had them once a year, as long as it was like this. She swallowed, heat travelling all the way down to her tummy and warming her from the inside out. She looked down in the cone to stab another when her fork-holding hand was nudged sharply from the elbow and the fork went flying. She tried to grab it with the hand that was holding the chips, letting go of the cone and tipping it all onto the floor.

"No!" Nancy cried.

"Oh Nancy, how did you do that?" Mum moaned.

"I don't know Mummy, sorry Mummy, it just flew out of my hand!"

She looked down at the concrete, her delicious chips scattered across the floor, her fork nowhere to be seen and the paper cone soaking into the damp concrete.

"Honestly" Mum said, shaking her head and kicking most of the chips to one side. Nancy tried to fight back the tears. Not only was her delicious tea ruined but Mum was cross with her.

"Sorry Mummy" Nancy looked up through her tear-filled eyes, her lip wobbling.

"Oh darling don't be upset! Sorry my love, I just was cross for a second but don't be silly, here, have my chips. I shouldn't be eating them anyway" she winked.

The tears flowed out of Nancy at her mothers kindness, and she wrapped her arms around her, climbing her way up until her mother put her hands under her arm pits and lifted her onto her hip. Mum wiped Nancy's tears away and kissed her cheek and told her not to worry a moment more. Nancy sniffed and braved a smile.

"You'll have to feed me though my darling. My hands are full!" she chuckled, one hand holding the cone and the other her. Nancy took a chip, blew on it and popped it in her Mummy's mouth, and then one in hers and savoured the taste. Nancy wrapped her arms around her mother's neck and squeezed tight.

"I love you Mumma"

"I love you more my darling"

Nancy didn't believe her. Mummy couldn't love her more than Nancy loved her. Nancy loved her more than anyone or anything in the world. She always had and she always would. She loved everything about her, even if she was a bit strict. Mum did everything for her and Robert and made them feel like the most important people in the world. Nancy never felt more happy than when she was in her mother's embrace. Nancy was sure that there would never be a love better than that.

They finished the chips and smiled. Mum passed the empty cone to Dad and he folded it and to put in his coat pocket. Nancy could feel herself slipping off her mother's hip, and Mum bounced her back up to where she'd been.

"Cor you're getting heavy my darling, you won't be up here for much longer" she chuckled.

"Here, she can go on my shoulders".

Nancy froze.

"Oh thanks Granville, are you sure, she's quite heavy" Mum strained.

"No problem at all" he reassured.

Before she could protest, his hands were under her arm pits, pulling her off Mum's hip and lifting her high onto his shoulders. Nancy looked down at her mother, who was readjusting her coat and getting a tissue out of her pocket to blow her nose.

Nancy looked down at the top of Granville's head, white hair starting to thin at the top revealing a liver-spotted scalp. She didn't know where to place her hands, so placed them on her own thighs. The fog lights went off and everybody cheered into the darkness.

"10, 9, 8, 7..."

The countdown to the fireworks had begun.

"6,5,4"

"You excited Nancy?" said Granville from below.

"3,2,1,0!"

The first firework went up, Nancy was relieved there was no screech or bang. Just a *phut phut phut* and the crowd *oooing* and *ahhing*. Nancy looked up at the sky and tried to ignore the fact that Granville was holding onto her legs too tight. She wanted to get down desperately, but she was worried her Mummy would get cross that she had to hold her again. She sat up there, looking up at the sky, wondering what fireworks were made of. She remembered a story about a man who tried to blow up a building in London and the country celebrated this day because of that. She didn't really understand what blowing up more things would do to help, but she did enjoy the pretty colours and the tradition. Nancy loved tradition. She loved the routine of something familiar, something to look forward to, something to celebrate. The excitement as families gathered to enjoy these days in the calendar in their own special way. It helped her to focus on exciting things like this when she felt sad and worried. She didn't really know why she felt sad and worried, but she did. All of the time. Even when she felt happy, her tummy told her she was wrong to be so. She felt like she didn't have a voice, and she didn't really understand why, because she had one to talk and sing and be loud with. But there was something inside her that was quiet, mute even. Like another little girl who lived inside her with a hand clamped over her mouth. And that little girl made her tummy hurt. But she'd gotten used to her so there didn't seem much point talking about it. She couldn't if she wanted to. Because if she did. bad things would happen to her Mummy, Daddy and brother. Grandma would die. Everyone would be cross with her. They wouldn't believe her anyway. Children made things up all the time after all. And Granville was an adult too. If he knew that, then she was sure all the adults knew. Adults always talked about things without children when they went to bed. If he said it was important to keep playing his game and to not tell anyone, to keep them safe, then she would.

"Bang!"

The firework made her jump and she wobbled backwards on Granville's shoulders. She grabbed onto his hair to steady herself and he cried out.

"Ow careful!" he growled.

Mum turned round and saw Granville ungripping Nancy's hands from his hair.

"Oh careful Nancy, you'll hurt Granville! Are you okay?" she asked him.

"Yes, yes fine thanks my love" rubbing his scalp.

"Say sorry Nancy" Mum directed.

"Sorry" Nancy said, her lip trembling.

"That's okay" said Granville.

They all looked back up at the sky to watch the rest of the fireworks whilst Granville stroked Nancy's leg.

CHAPTER 14

Present

"Listen, honestly I was shopping and then I remembered I hadn't turned the oven on, I mean off, and thought I better just rush down the aisles quick as a widget and get home, that really is the truth of it" she assured, putting on her best telephone voice.

The security guard and store manager were obviously loving the opportunity to play good cop, bad cop. The office, which was more like a poorly lit large cupboard, consisted of a desk, a spinning chair and a computer, and another chair that she was sitting on. The room stank of cheap stale coffee and vape. The security guard stood in front of her, his shirt buttons straining over his round rock-hard belly. She reckoned if she bolted now, neither one of these men could catch her. She reckoned she could actually out walk them.

"Problem is Miss, we've got security tapes that say differently."

Nancy's tongue dried and stuck to the roof of her mouth. She thought her tummy might fall out of her bottom. She crossed her legs one way and then the other and cleared her throat.

"Okay, yes I was running but that's because of the oven, I told you this."

The manager spun round on his chair to face the computer and wiggled the mouse. The screen was split into four, and in each square, there was a small picture of her from different angles in black and white. She swallowed and crossed her legs again.

"Let's see shall we" he said.

He pressed play and all four images played. She pushed her trolley down the aisles collecting fruit and vegetables. She paused at the meat and closed her eyes.

"I was visualizing my shopping list I'd left behind" she fake laughed nervously.

"Seems you're quite forgetful today, aren't you Miss" said the manager, raising an unkempt eyebrow.

She continued to shop, putting an embarrassing amount of biscuits in her trolley and stopped. They all looked in at the screen.

"See that's where I realised about the oven" Nancy narrated.

The manager clicked on another angle. One that included the old man.

"You are staring right at him" he accused.

"I was staring into space! This is ridiculous, honestly" she said impatiently and started to gather her things.

The old man walked round the corner and Nancy stayed still, frozen to the spot. Then she changed, teeth clenched, snarling, fury radiating from her. She swung round the end of the aisle and stopped and focused on him. She put the weight of her body behind the trolley, her lip curled, red with rage. She shifted uncomfortably in her chair. She tried to think of an explanation, but she had nothing. She didn't even recognise herself, she looked like an angry lioness. She pressed her foot into the ground and lurched forward, heading straight for the old man. She picked up speed, pelting towards him. She winced, watching and waiting for a collision, even though she knew there wouldn't be. She halted to a stop, just moments before smashing into him. She didn't want to see what happened next again, it was horrifying enough seeing it in real life.

"Okay okay let's just calm this down, it's obviously a trick of the camera, I just needed to get home" she said, her voice wavering.

The manager and security guard exchanged a look. The manager reached over his desk and picked up the phone.

CHAPTER 15

Then

Age 28

The leaves had almost all fallen now. A few weeks back, the trees had been reaching up to the sky, showing off their golden sleeves. The weather had been bright, hazy sun bleeding into pale blue skies, a warm glow surrounding the triumphant hurrah of colour. Her and Rupert had taken lazy Saturday afternoon walks through the woods under their rusty canopy, their boots crunching through a carpet of burnt orange. The sun shot through the trees, bolts of warm light pooling on the ground. Squirrels dashed past and ran up trees, their soft tails swishing after them. He'd put his arm around her and she'd let herself go, resting herself against him as they walked along, side by side. Her heart beat faster when she was with him, or thought about him. Her breath caught in her throat and her tummy felt full and warm. She was furious with herself and had pulled back on several occasions, only to be coaxed and reassured by Rupert that everything would be fine. She didn't know how, he was leaving to go to New York in a few months and she'd foolishly gone and fallen in love with him. Her feeling of self-loathing had increased at her stupidity and childishness, falling for a man who was going to leave her, just like Nathan had. *Had she learned nothing?* And this time it was worse. She was a mother. And she *knew* Rupert was leaving.

Yet she was still behaving like a teenager. She despised herself. Still, after many, many nights of soul beating, she decided to try and give herself a break and enjoy the time they had. For she had gotten over being left before, she would do it again. And this time it would be easier, because she had Tilly. And Alex. She would write off any future relationships and treat herself to a new vibrator and be done with it. Or maybe one of those funny little lapping machines that simulated cunnilingus. She'd become quite accustomed to it of late and was going to miss it when he and his tongue flew stateside. He would be on a different time zone and she would eventually move on. What was she thinking, that this young guy with the world at his feet, would give that all up to play house with her and her child? She'd scoffed at herself more times in the last few months than she had in years. She needed to get out of her head and enjoy this dalliance for what it was. Amazing sex, laughter, walks, pub lunches, theatre trips. It was perfect. It wouldn't last when he saw her in Mum mode, running around trying to sort Tilly's lunchbox in her pyjamas, spending the evening labelling clothes and logging on to the school website to buy yet more raffle tickets off the fucking PTA. Saturday's filled doing crafts and cleaning, and wringing the last of the day out in the park. Was he going to be Tilly's step Dad? No. She laughed at herself. *Just enjoy it, be grateful that Mum and Tilly were having such a wonderful time together every other weekend* she told herself. Right now, she could pretend to be the free, relaxed, sensual woman she was feigning to be when she was with him. And best of all, Nancy was happy, and Tilly was getting the best of her. Nancy wasn't going to let Rupert meet Tilly, she wouldn't put her daughter through it for such a short space of time. So she was going to stop worrying about the future, worrying about any pain she might feel. Because she'd felt it before, she'd felt it her whole life. And right now she was 'rom com' happy and she must allow herself to enjoy it.

As Autumn turned to Winter, she started to plan for Christmas. She and Tilly had always loved Christmas, the music, the baking, the scent of cinnamon in the air, the markets, visiting friends, snuggling up together. Nancy and Alex turned the house into a grotto come December 1st, and from then on, only Christmas music rang through their home, jammies were donned and Bailey's was free flowing. They went to a few cocktail parties, squeezing into spanks and sparkly black numbers, quaffing Vol-au-vent's and champagne, wishing they'd had a proper dinner as they stumbled out and into their taxi at midnight. They hosted the 'Christmas Sandwich and Christmas Jumper' party for Nancy's birthday, a week before Jesus' with her family. But other than that, they tried to keep the month as free as they could, to just be home and cosy, the three of them. She didn't know how she would include Rupert into her plans this year. She wanted to be with Tilly and would just have to see Rupert less. It was probably a good thing to start the separation process. He was due to leave for The Big Apple in January, so there was no point hurting herself further by curling up in front of the fire with him listening Nat King Cole. This would provide her with the distance she needed to get back to her normal life with Tilly.

"What are you thinking about?" Rupert asked, that evening at his over dinner.

"Oh, um, Christmas" she said.

"I love Christmas" Rupert smiled.

"Me too" I said quietly.

"What's wrong?" Rupert asked.

"Oh, nothing" she smiled, the same smile she used when Tilly asked her. The kind of smile that didn't reach her eyes.

"Are you worried about what you will get me for Christmas? I have very expensive taste" he grinned, holding his hands up to display the huge kitchen they were sitting in for dinner.

Nancy laughed.

"I don't think I could afford your taste, mate" Nancy teased.

He reached across the table to her and touched her hand, clasping hers, looking straight into her eyes, silently asking her to open up.

Nancy shifted in her seat, uncomfortable that she couldn't think of what to say that didn't make her sound like a lovesick teenager.

She lifted her wine glass to her lips with her free hand, and took a long sip to give her time to think of something.

"No it's just, well I will have Tilly and won't get to see much of you and well, I just feel bad for you" she smirked.

"Ah, well, don't worry about me. I am living in a mansion" he flashed his teeth like a gameshow host.

"With your parents" she interjected.

"With my parents, who are out of the country" he added.

"So I will have to choose between swimming, working out or playing pool…by myself" he mock wailed.

Nancy smirked.

"We will see each other when we can. Alex will watch Tilly when she's asleep so I can come over. I just need to make sure I spend plenty of time with Tills this Christmas."

"I completely understand Nance" Rupert said, smiling and then looking away, stroking and then gently letting go of her hand.

"You know if I had it my way, you would spend the whole of Christmas at mine, with Tilly and Alex" she said, trying to catch his eye.

"But, but you are leaving" she stopped, her voice catching. She cleared her throat quickly and took a mouthful of wine to numb the emotion rising in her chest.

"I know. I know. Fuck, this is such bad timing." he said, dragging his hand through his dark brown hair and pulling on the back of his neck.

Nancy looked down at her plate, the steak he'd cooked, half eaten. She picked up her knife and fork and sliced a piece of rare beef, pronged a piece of fondant potato, mopped it into the creamed spinach, and shoved it into her mouth. It was too big a bite, but she was glad it filled her gob, before she could say something stupid.

"I wasn't expecting this. I mean, of course I'd told the boys that you were mine before we came over to you and the girls in the bar. I'd seen your hesitation to let go when Alex had bought you those shots. You looked sad and worried and I wondered what made you feel like that. Then something changed. Your shoulders dropped and you relaxed, and this free woman appeared. And I wanted to know both of them."

She pushed more steak into her already full mouth and smiled, her cheeks bulging.

He laughed and reached out to touch her hand again. She swallowed and went to put more food in her mouth and he stopped her.

"Stop shoving food in your face to try and ignore what I'm saying to you Nance" said Rupert.

"Listen, I know this is awful timing and I shouldn't be saying this but" he paused. "I'm in love with you Nancy. I know it's complicated and I don't know what any of this means, but if I don't say it, I'm going to explode" he confessed, sighing with relief.

Nancy took the serviette off her lap and took her time to gently wipe the corners of her mouth.

Rupert laughed, squirming like she wanted him to. Her heart pounded, heat rose up through her body and coloured her neck, she took a sip of her wine whilst she considered how much to tell him.

"The problem is" she said slowly. "It's me that gets left behind. So I don't really don't know what you want me to say. I've been here before and look at me, I'm right back here again. I have learnt nothing" she said, head bowed, tears pricking in the corners of her eyes.

He scraped his seat back, and walked round the table, kneeling next to her. He took her face in his hands.

"Why do you do that to yourself? If you were as unkind to your friends as you are to yourself, you would have no one."

"Well, who do I have?" Nancy asked, her tone laden with hurt, a tear escaping from the corner of her eye.

"Alex will leave when she meets someone, Tilly will grow up and have her own life, my Mum will die, who do I have that's mine?"

"Me" Rupert said. "You have me. I won't go to New York, I couldn't now. I only want you Nancy".

"You don't even know me!" she exploded, pushing her chair back.

Rupert looked hurt, knelt on the floor like a little boy.

She picked up the bottle of wine off the side and topped up her glass, picked it up and took a large swig. Her heart banged, confusion ringing in her ears. She was furious with herself that she was in this situation. Again. Furious with herself for losing her temper.

"I want to know you Nancy. But how can I? I know you are trying to be that woman in the bar for me, but I know there is someone else in there. A mother, a friend, a daughter. Someone who does so much for everyone else, so she doesn't have to think about what's really makes her sad."

"Why are you saying that?" she started to cry, childish whimpers slipping out of her mouth. How had he seen through her disguise?

"Why?" she asked crossly. "What could you possibly know about my sadness Rupert? Look at this place? You were born with a silver spoon in your mouth and you are about to go and live in New York for fuck's sake".

He looked hurt. Why was she behaving like this? She hadn't even told him that she loved him too. She sniffed, and forcefully breathed out to calm herself before she said anything else.

"Look, I think it's better if I just call a cab." Nancy said.

"Please don't, Nancy. Just stay, please. Don't leave like this."

She hesitated. She was so angry with herself. How had this wonderful evening turned into this? And he loved her. She wondered if he ever could when they had first got together, and now she knew he did. But this declaration complicated everything. It was better when it was all in her head.

He walked over to her slowly and rubbed her upper arms. Her lip trembled and her eyes filled with tears.

"Come here" he said, pulling her into his arms.

She leant into him, tears cascading down her cheeks. She held her hands up to her face and howled. She didn't know where this was coming from. Maybe the wine, maybe the months of overthinking. Maybe the fact that she loved him too, and that she knew it wouldn't last. He would leave her, just like Nathan had. He had let her down, just like every other man had. Maybe because Rupert knew she was sad inside and it made her feel exposed and vulnerable. She knew she couldn't keep this act up, and that maybe she wasn't fooling anyone, not even herself anymore. She clung to him and sobbed, soaking his shirt. He kissed the top of her head and rubbed her back, making soothing sounds of comfort, telling her it would be alright. After a few minutes, the tears slowed, and she managed to get a hold of herself. She wiped her hands over her face, smearing diluted mascara across her cheeks.

"Yuck, where did that come from eh?" she laughed between choked sobs, hugely embarrassed. She pulled at a piece of kitchen roll on the work top, wiped her face and noisily blew her nose.

"Sorry" she smiled, blowing again.

"There's nothing to be sorry for" he reassured, smiling.

"I'm being so silly, really, I'm so embarrassed" she said, straightening up. She cleared her throat and tried to decide how much to tell him. She took a big breath in and out.

"My life" she stopped, steadying herself.

"Has not always been that happy. I mean, it has, I've been very lucky. Tilly, my parents, my brother etc. But stuff has happened, and I'm not...I don't know. I'm not sure who I am really, I suppose". She cringed at herself, not really sure what she was trying to say.

"It's just, I'm confused. And you're right, I am sad inside. But I feel so guilty for even saying that. It's all in the past and I should be living for now." her voice waivered.

"And I have a child, and you practically *are* a child, and this person you see is not the person I really am, you know. You think I'm carefree and fun-loving, but if you came and lived with me, you'd see a different Nancy. Pyjama wearing, make up free, braless..." she laughed, choked.

"Really?" he grinned.

"It's not as sexy as you think" she joked, pretending to slide out of her bra, and mock flinging across the kitchen.

"Well, I want to know this braless woman. I want to know all sides of you, and to help you see what an incredible person you are. I don't know what this means, or what will happen Nancy, but all I know is I love you, and there's nothing I can do about it."

There was silence, whilst Nancy's eyes danced around the room, trying to avoid eye contact.

"The question is, do you love me too? Otherwise I might as well pack up my broken heart and take it to New York with me and be done with it" he laughed, sniffing and pressing the heel of his hand into his eye socket.

She hesitated. She was fighting with herself.

"I do… I really fucking wish I didn't. But I do" she said through gritted teeth.

"And I don't know what it means, and I hate that it out in the air now, ricocheting off these bloody walls." she laughed.

He laughed too, swiping a tear from his cheek.

"We don't need to work that out right now. Right now, it's just you and me" he said, lifting her chin and kissing her deeply, with his arms wrapped around her.

CHAPTER 16

Present

"Now, Mr Penn has decided not to press charges. He said he understands how people these days are in a hurry, and that he was the one who stepped on the tin." said the police officer.

Nancy felt awful. This kind old man had been subjected to a rage so deep inside her, she didn't even know it existed until today. She nodded.

"Is he alright?" she asked.

"Yes, he will be fine, the nose isn't broken, and he will have a bruised back for some time, but there is no serious damage."

Nancy winced. She'd been so desperate to protect herself, the man's welfare had been way down her list of priorities. She was certainly going to Hell for this.

"I really am very sorry, I never meant to hurt anyone."

"Yes, well next time please try and be a bit more considerate for your fellow man." He gestured towards the manager.

"And Mr Richard's has asked that you find somewhere else to shop from now on. He cannot ban you officially, but we would advise it".

Mr Richard's was obviously loving it. Standing behind the power of the police that he clearly didn't own in his own role.

But Nancy didn't need warning off. She certainly wouldn't be setting foot in the supermarket again. The image of a bloody-faced pensioner laying motionless on the floor was enough incentive for her to switch to home delivery.

She left the manager's office, a few of the witnesses spotting her, rubber necking, clearly hoping she'd have been escorted off the premises in cuffs. She walked briskly to the automatic doors and straight across the car park. She got in her car and drove straight off, pulling out the carpark onto the main road without looking properly, a car swerving round her, swearing at her with its horn.

"Shit!" she gasped, straightening up and driving down the road.

"What the fuck, Nancy!" she shouted at herself.

She drove home slowly, trying to steady her nerves. She pulled into her road and then into the driveway, where she pulled up the handbrake and turned off the engine. She gently placed her head into her hands and then raked her fingers down her face, looking up at the ceiling of the car. She burst into tears, angry, frustrated sobs shaking her body. She wanted to hit herself in the head, smack it off the steering wheel. She started scolding herself in between cries, nonsensical words, shaming and hating herself. She tried to calm down but she couldn't, the more she cried, the more upset she got, feeling more and more furious at herself. "Why did you do that?" she shouted at herself, sobbing.

"So what if you thought it was him? What were you going to do, ram him with your trolley until he died!?" she screamed into the empty car and howled.

She couldn't even remember making the decision to run at him. Before that had happened, she was frozen in fear. Like a little girl.

"Why did this happen to me!?" she cried.

"Why? Why? WHY!?" she yelled, and smacked the steering wheel, agonised cries escaping from her mouth.

Why did he do it? What is wrong with him? What did she do to deserve it? She was only a child. Why didn't she stop him? Why didn't Grandma stop him? She felt disgusted with herself, her brain filled with memories that infected her body and made her skin crawl. She leant forward on the steering wheel and hugged it, her shoulders heaving with each repulsive thought. She wanted him dead. She wanted him, and every other man that had ever done that to a child to be killed. They didn't deserve a second chance. They were the scum of the earth, taking what they wanted from an innocent being, for their own selfish, seedy satisfaction. She wanted to throw up. This is the most she'd allowed herself to think about it in years. Yes, it had always been in her mind, but she'd managed to crush the thoughts and distract herself with other things for so long, she'd forgotten how painful it was to remember. Her cries subsided, leaving her breath catching and lip wobbling like a toddler after a tantrum. Her head pulsed and her eyes burned. She felt like she wanted to crawl under the duvet and pretend it hadn't happened. And that she hadn't just done something awful to a complete stranger. But it had happened and now she was hurting others. She had deal with it. She had to learn to live with it. She just had to decide how.

CHAPTER 17

Then

Age 5

It was December, and Nancy was excited. She'd written her letter to Santa with Mummy's help. She'd asked for an Etcha Sketch and that she wished to be happy. Mummy asked her what would make her happy. She said an Etcha Sketch. Mummy had laughed. Nancy couldn't tell her what she really wanted.

The tree was up, presents were appearing underneath it from aunties and uncles, who were really friends of her grandparents and old people who lived in her street. She didn't care who they were from, she just loved looking at the parcels under the tree, and when her parents were upstairs, she and Robert would look at the labels to see who had the most. When she saw her name on the gift tag, her tummy would twist, and she would feel loved and special.

Nancy loved Christmas, and when she was alone with Mum and Dad and Robert, she felt safe and loved and that everywhere she looked she could see lights and sparkly ornaments. When she thought about Father Christmas coming down the chimney, she felt like her insides would explode. Her Dad was the silliest of all. He behaved like a 6 year old, grinning and bouncing around the house, and Nancy loved him more than she ever had before.

Grandma and Granville always came down on Christmas Day, and they bought a huge red sack, filled with gifts for each of them. Their arrival was always bittersweet. She loved the presents but spent the year before making sure she was never on her own, which meant dragging her Mummy to the toilet with her every time she needed a wee. Mummy had got a bit cross with her, so Nancy had taken to holding it in, which ended up with her getting a bladder infection and Nancy had to have medicine from the doctor to make it better.

This year, she had bribed Robert to go to the toilet with her each time she needed to go, or to get a toy from upstairs. She'd promised to give him her selection box and all of her Christmas Tree chocolates as payment, and he wasn't allowed to ask why. He'd agreed without arguing, and said she could keep her chocolates, and he would just take the Crunchie from her selection box.

She wondered why he was being so nice, then remembered what he'd witnessed the last time they'd stayed at Grandmas. Granville had waited for Nancy to go to her room to get her Polly Pocket and followed her.

"A quick game before we go to the park, Nancy? I'll get you an ice cream".

"Okay" agreed Nancy, sighing and sitting on the bed.

Granville had asked her to lay back, just as Robert had walked in. Granville jumped out of his skin, and Nancy pulled down her dress and sat up.

"What are you doing?" Robert asked.

"Nothing! She was just mucking about on the bed. I'm just looking for some matches. My lighter's buggered" Granville said, and started rummaging through the bedside drawer.

Robert stood there, puzzled. Granville slammed the bedside drawer and they both jumped.

"Where are the fucking matches in this house?!" he spat, red faced.

Both children looked at the ground, shocked that he'd sworn. Twice. He turned and faced her brother.

"You shouldn't just walk into a room in someone else's house Robert. It's just plain rude. I will tell your parents next time you do that. And don't tell anyone else about Nancy being silly, playing on the bed. She's just being stupid, but she will get in trouble with Grandma and your parents if you do. Understand?" he threatened.

"Yes" Robert had said quietly and stepped out of the way for Granville to stomp past.

Both children were red in the face, and Robert looked at her with a furrowed brow. He took her hand and helped her hop off the bed and walked her to the lounge and sat down beside her on the sofa. Granville was in a foul mood, but he didn't touch her again that weekend.

Chistmas Eve finally arrived, and the air was filled with silent excitement. It was a secret they were all in on, and as they went for a walk together in the morning, they smiled at every stranger they saw.

"Morning", Dad nodded and smiled.

"Morning, Merry Christmas!" they would reply.

Nancy loved the opportunity to say Merry Christmas to strangers. She wasn't allowed to talk to strangers. She wasn't allowed to go with strangers. If a stranger tried to take her by the hand, she had to shout, "Stranger Danger!" or "I don't know this man!". Mummy had talked about it often. She even bought her a book, which she sometimes read to her before bedtime. Nancy wanted to ask her Mummy so badly why strangers were so dangerous. It seemed to Nancy that strangers were friendly and polite, whenever she'd met one. Nancy spent time with people who were much more dangerous than strangers, but Mummy didn't know that of course.

They walked up to Pig Woods, made up by Robert after they'd come across a family of pigs once, on their usual woodland romp. It seemed a funny place to come across some pigs, but after he'd named it, it had been one of Nancy's favourite places to go. Her parents had always saved seeing the pigs until last, to motivate them to keep walking when they moaned.

It was a beautiful day, the sky was white, but the sun had snuck through, a golden glow tinting the clouds. The trees were all bare now, and frost outlined each blade of grass that crunched underfoot. In the woods the leaves and twigs crackled and snapped as the children stomped, beams of warm light streaking through the gaps in the branches above. Steam puffed out of their mouths with each breath, Nancy and Rob ran ahead pretending to smoke with twigs, blowing their breath in each other's faces. Mum and Dad walked behind, hand in hand. Mum talking quickly about timings for the Christmas meal and the rest of the things she needed to do today. Dad put his arm round her and kissed her head, then whispered in her ear and she playfully slapped him on his chest.

Nancy wished she could stay up in these woods forever. Well, not forever, because she was scared of the dark and she wanted to get back to watch The Snowman and make mince pies and leave a plate out for Father Christmas. But away from everything, just with the people who loved her, and whom she loved too. She and Robert fought like cat and dog, they were always bickering, teasing and thwacking each other. But on these special occasions, a line was drawn, and they briefly became friends. His silly side was what she loved most. He didn't care what anyone else thought and would get over excited and do anything to make her laugh. Stuff that she would remind and embarrass him with when he reached adolescence. Like right now, running ahead out of their parents eyesight, he pulled down the back of his tracksuit bottoms and ran through the woods flashing his bum. Then he did a roly poly, crashing into a fallen tree. She chased after him, laughing, his bare bottom in the air. He rolled onto his front and pulled his bottoms back up before she grabbed fistfuls of leaves and shoved them down the back trousers. He grabbed her legs and she fell onto her back, laughing. He jumped up and picked a fistful of frosty berries from the bush next to him and shoved them up her nose. They were fighting for breath by the time their parents had caught up with them, telling them to get off the ground and to stop being so silly. It was said with a fond smile, and they knew they weren't in trouble. When their parents had walked past, Ron grabbed Nancy in a headlock and drove his knuckles into her scalp. She wriggled out and punched him on the arm. He turned around, with an evil grin on his face and then dropped it, wrapped his arms around his little sister and kissed her on the top of her head. She squeezed him back and closed her eyes, his cold jacket against her face.

"Love you smelly" said Robert.

"Love you too stinky" she replied.

"Race you to the pigs!" he said, pushing her into a pile of leaves.

CHAPTER 18

Then

Age 28

Nancy sat on the edge of the bath, watching the timer on her phone. She couldn't bear how long it was taking for the minutes to quietly tick past. She impatiently pressed the home button, and scrolled through her emails, deleting a bunch of marketing messages, pausing to read an email from the school, reminding them of all the Christmas activities through December. She re-read the email maybe three times, and still couldn't absorb what crap they'd asked her for this year. There were diary reminders for all the fund raisers, so she opened her calendar and wrote in dates for the Christmas Fair, Santa's Grotto, their Christmas plays and the Carol Concert, setting alarms and reminders to bring in costumes, pocket money and donations to the raffle.

The alarm rang out, two minutes had passed. She drew in a nervous breath and looked in the window of the plastic stick. She couldn't remember what the lines meant, it had been five years since she last used one and she'd forgotten what the instructions had said no sooner had she disposed of the packaging. She pulled the box out of the bin and checked the back. She wanted to see one line. She did not want to see two. She looked at the white stick with the blue cap. There were two lines. Not one. Two. She swallowed and breathed in at the same time, inhaling a droplet of saliva into her lungs and started coughing her guts up.

"Are you okay Mummy?" Tilly asked from outside the bathroom door.

"Yep!" Nancy croaked, still coughing and trying to catch her breath.

She swallowed and tried to calm herself and took a few handfuls of water out of the bathroom tap. She breathed heavily, leaning on the basin, water dripping from her mouth. She looked up at herself in the mirror. *What the fuck are you going to do now, you fucking idiot?* Her mind whirled. A baby. Another baby. With a man, who she loved, but who was moving to New York City. *You absolute tit.*

"Mummy are you having a poo?"

"No" she replied through gritted teeth.

"I would just like five minutes to myself, once in a while, if that's okay with you Tilly?"

"Sorry Mumma" said Tilly, and walked back downstairs.

Guilt slapped her round the face. *What was she going to do? Did she even want another baby? Could she afford it?* She couldn't tell Rupert. It would ruin his life. He would want to stay. She wanted him to stay. But not like this. People would think she was trying to trap him. He would think that too. What if he went anyway? Of course he would, look at Nate. Men had that freedom; inseminate and leave if they wanted to, like they did in the wild. She always thought the human race were going against nature, forcing men to play 'house', when they really wanted to fuck and fuck off. She felt sick. Her head was spinning, and each thought was catching like fire, making her head thump. She flushed the toilet and washed her hands. She put the test in her back pocket and pulled her jumper over her jeans to cover it. She unlocked the bathroom door and walked out on the landing, straight into Alex.

"What's going on." Alex asked, although it wasn't really a question.

"What do you mean? Nancy said, keeping her eyes down and trying to sidestep her.

Alex took her by the shoulders.

"Tell me the truth. You've been acting weird all week".

She stared back at Alex, biting her trembling lip. She reached around to her back pocket, pulled out the pregnancy test and held it up to Alex's face.

"Shit!!"

"Yeh, shit" said Nancy.

"Shit, shit, shit!" said Alex.

"Yes, we've established the situation's shit" said Nancy.

"Sorry. Shut the fuck up Alex" she said to herself, leading Nancy into her room to take a seat on the bed, the mattress bowing under her bottom. Alex sat down next to her and put her hand on her thigh.

"Sorry I'm being such a twat. I'm lost for words. I knew something was up when you were turning your nose up at my famous fish pie. And you kept saying the wine was vinegary" Alex said.

"What am I going to do Alex?" Nancy asked her best friend, looking down into her lap, eyes pooling with tears.

"Come here. Look, you've done this once and you can do it again. And this time you've got me from the start. I will be here, and you will never be alone, do you hear me?"

Nancy leant into her friend, resting her head on her shoulder and sobs emanating from her chest. She made a sound she was embarrassed by, a painful groan escaping through her lips, which seemed to be drawn directly from her helpless heart. She turned to wrap her arms round Alex's neck and howled. Alex stroked her hair and kissed her cheek, wiping her tears away.

"How did this even happen, I thought you were on the pill?" Alex asked.

"I am. But I took two packets in a row so that I wouldn't have a period" Nancy said, scolding herself for being a sex-hungry whore.

"I took the break and had my period, but I must have misjudged when to start taking it again. You know what it's like in the early days, you can't keep your hands off each other and I just lost track of the days."

Alex rubbed Nancy's back, staring down at the same spot of nothingness on the carpet.

They sat in silence for a few minutes, Nancy snivelling and blowing her nose into a tissue Alex had passed her.

"Are you okay Mummy?" Tilly appeared in the doorway.

"Mummy is fine my darling" swooped in Alex.

"Alex just showed her a video on You Tube" Alex still referred to herself in the third person, when talking to Tilly.

"It was a baby deer making friends with a rabbit. Real life Bambi it was, and you know what a soppy sausage Mummy is. How about we all put our jammies on and watch a movie. A happy one. And get a pizza, my treat."

"Yay!" squealed Tilly.

"Can I pick the film? And the pizza toppings?"

"Course" smiled Alex, ruffling Tilly's hair.

"You go and get changed and Mummy and I will be down in a minute."

"I'm fine my darling", Nancy reassured Tilly.

"She's being silly Tilly" smiled Alex and they all laughed.

"Off you pop then!" shooed Alex and pushed the door to. She walked to Nancy and squatted down, so that she was looking up at her.

"Right. We are going to go and have a lovely, cosy evening with Tils. And you are going to try not to worry. You can do this. We can do this. And the best thing is, you've done it before, so there are no surprises. And your Mum is an incredible support. You have a great job and you have this house, and you have me. And I will never leave you Nance, never ever, not never, not on your Nelly."

Nancy looked at Alex through her tear-filled eyes and had never loved her more. She was so grateful to have a friend like her. She was family. Why would she ever be scared when Alex was around? She would save worrying about telling Rupert until tomorrow. After all, until about ten minutes ago, she didn't even know she was pregnant. Nothing had really changed. She was pregnant before she'd taken the test. She just knew about it now. So, she was just going to try and not run away with herself and live for the moment, cuddling her daughter, dangling pizza into her mouth, whilst watching Saturday night tv. A lovely, unrealistic plan, she thought.

CHAPTER 19

Two Weeks Later

She'd been distant with Rupert, replying briefly to his messages, if at all. He'd asked her if she was alright, and she'd assured him she was, just tired from work and Christmas preparations. She hated lying to him; it had kept her up at night. She wanted to tell him so badly but hated the thought of shattering his American dream. If he stayed, he would wake up in five years, exhausted, full to the brim with resentment, and a little bit fat. She would be older and exhausted, and he would leave them. What was the point of ruining that many lives? She couldn't do it to him and she couldn't do it to herself. If he'd have lived down the road and commuted into the city for work, and had been older, it would have been different. But he was young with the world at his feet. Trapping someone with a pregnancy, even an accidental one, was a bad idea and could only end in disaster. She'd been there before, and the ending wasn't pretty.

She wouldn't tell him. He was leaving in January anyway, so she could use Christmas to distance herself, occupying Tilly, and even if she had started to show by the New Year, she could blame the post festive bloat that the rest of the population would be suffering anyway. He would go and she could have the baby, and he would never need to know.

However, when night fell and she was alone in bed, the guilt of keeping the secret weighed heavy on her heart and she couldn't sleep. She was losing hours every night, thrashing about, hot and bothered, as if the secret was swaddling her in a thick, itchy blanket.

She wanted to tell him so desperately, to have him swing her around to dramatic romantic music and kiss her under a blossom tree. He'd get down on one knee and he would promise to take care of them for the rest of their lives. They'd be married in the morn and then she would give birth at home, in no more than three pushes. They would both cry and hold each other, and the credits would roll, the audience sniveling in their seats; they may even be a slow, appreciative clap.

But life wasn't a movie, and as much as she longed for this ending, she knew it was unrealistic. She'd put her heart and soul into her relationship with Nate, and wholeheartedly believed he would come back, especially at the beginning. She'd emailed him almost every day giving him updates of the size of the baby and what appointments she had coming up. She had to wait for him to get to an internet café to log into his inbox and reply, so she wasn't worried when she had to wait for days to hear from him. As her bump had started to grow, she took photos and attached them to the emails. He seemed excited at first, but by the time the dark line of the linea nigra started to show on the swell of her belly, she was hearing from him less and less. She tried not to worry and knew that he was reaching the end of his trip and was likely to be up a mountain, sleeping in a hostel or hut, with no means of making contact. He'd complained about it whenever he did get the chance to call. He was due to return when she was just over seven and a half months' pregnant, but just two weeks before that, she received an email from him in the middle of the night. She'd been lying awake anyway, the baby laying in an awkward position, elbowing her bladder. She'd gotten up to go for yet another wee, then went downstairs to get a drink and to see what she could pick at in the fridge, before lumbering back to bed. She'd left her laptop open from the night before, refreshing it to see if she'd had a reply from

Nathan, to any of her many emails over the last week. She hadn't had anything and had finally given in and gone to bed.

She took a pot of olives out of the fridge and popped a few in her mouth, their garlicy vinegar coating her tongue. She took a swig of milk and swallowed, her latest craving hitting the spot. She looked over at the laptop, still glowing.

Temptation overrode her and she went over to the screen and refreshed her emails. She waited, the egg timer somersaulting slowly in the centre of the screen. It refreshed, and an email titled 'I'm Sorry', appeared in her inbox.

Her heart skipped a beat, the baby lurched in her belly and she stroked the surface of it, shifting uncomfortably from foot to foot.

She swallowed nervously and heaved her large bottom onto the bar stool. She double clicked on the email and it opened in a new window.

"I don't know what to say" was the opening line. Her face burned and a thumping sounded in her ears. She read the rest through her blurred lens, silent tears splashing onto the keyboard.

He'd met someone. They were in love. He wasn't coming back. And he was sorry. She slammed the laptop shut, breathing heavily, adjusting to the darkness in the kitchen. She placed a hand on her large tummy, stroking it in circular movements. Her mind whirled. She was going to have to raise this baby alone. It would have no Dad. Her heart felt like a wall being stripped of wallpaper. She stood up, stars dancing in her eyes. She used the breakfast bar to support herself, as she let her knees go, sitting down on the tiles and leaning against the fridge. She looked up at the ceiling and shouted, swore, banged her fists on the floor with every realisation that he wasn't coming back.

Nancy laid in bed, reliving the pain, the feeling of betrayal, the gut punch of abandonment. She'd felt a fool. Superfluous. An unwanted anchor, cut from a ship to sink to the bottom of the ocean, lying motionless on the seabed. How had she ever believed that he would return to her. How could she have been so stupid? Because she wanted to believe it. She'd had to. And now he was living in Oz with the love of his life. She never heard anything from him, other than the monthly 'ping' on her phone when he would transfer his token guilt money for Tilly. She often wondered if he would ever come back and want to see her. Would he turn up in ten years and want to be a father?

Would Rupert, if he ever found out about this baby? She threw her arm over her eyes and pressed her face into the crook of her elbow. She couldn't bear to relive the pain again. But she should also give him the choice. Give him the option to go anyway. She would be fine. She, Alex, Tilly and the baby would be fine, more than fine.

But she loved him. She couldn't lie to him, even if she couldn't keep him. He needed to know the truth, and she would tell him to go anyway, and that he needn't feel guilty. He could go and live his life, and she would never turn him away, if he wanted a relationship with their child in the future.

She would speak fondly of him to their child and help them find him, if they wanted to. It wouldn't hurt like it did with Nathan. He had promised to come back and she had gone into it blindfolded, expecting a different outcome.

This time, she could be honest and manage the situation for herself. She wouldn't be deserted, stranded, left flailing. She had to tell him, or she would hold onto yet another secret that would ruin her life.

CHAPTER 20

The Next Day

"Hello?"

"Um Hi, is Rupert here?" asked Nancy, wincing under her hood, rain beating against her face.

She stood at the door of his parent's house, a well-dressed woman, in her late 50's, who she assumed to be his mother, looking quizzically at her.

"Who, may I ask, is asking?" she requested.

"Oh sorry, I'm Nancy, Rupert's…. friend" she lied, pulling the hood over as far as it would go.

"Oh Nancy! I've heard so much about you! Not as much as I'd like though!" she said.

Nancy smirked.

"I'm sorry, but Rupert's not here. He is at his office Christmas party at the Savoy and they're putting them up for the night".

Nancy swallowed, embarrassed that she didn't know this and also that she hadn't been invited as his Plus One. Perhaps if she hadn't been a cold fish, trying to push him away the last few weeks, she would have been.

"Please come in, the weather is ghastly!" said the woman, stepping onto the porch and pulling Nancy through the front door, before she had the chance to refuse.

"Oh" said Nancy, surprised at the woman's gesture.

Inside Nancy stood on the mat, coat and face dripping, her leggings soaked through.

"Oh, look at you! Let me get you a towel. I'm Audrey, Rupert's Mother, by the way."

"Oh, thank you Audrey. Sorry to be such a nuisance" said Nancy, using her poshest voice, then blushed, seeing Alex in her mind, shaking her head in disappointment.

Nancy unzipped her sodden coat, and peeled it off her skin, hanging it in the boot room, to the left of the porch. She was absolutely soaked, and fidgeted, wondering what the hell was she doing here. She'd been sitting in the car for ages, trying to psych herself up to knock on the door. Only Rupert's car was in the driveway and the lights were on. She was about to talk herself out of it, but before she could convince herself, she turned off the engine, bolted to the front door and knocked. It was obvious now, that Rupert had gone out without his car and his parents were back from their trip, their car most likely in the garage. She was furious with herself. And she was even more furious that she'd come into the bloody house.

"Here we go" said Audrey, wrapping a towel around her shoulders, the smell of powder fresh laundry comforting her. It was Rupert's smell.

"Now, we've got the fire going in here, why don't you come in for a minute and warm up?"

"Thank you, just for a minute" Nancy said.

She couldn't believe what she was doing. But she had been to the house countless times over the last few months, so she didn't feel like she was in his parent's house. In a way she felt like they were in her house, and then smiled to herself at the brazen thought, like she could ever afford a place like this.

Nancy sat down on a wing-backed chair in front of the crackling fire, flames licking the firewood, warming and lighting her face golden, yellow and orange. She immediately relaxed, feeling comforted by the heat and the glow.

"Now a drink, something to warm you up? Brandy? Whiskey?" Audrey asked.

"Oh no thank you. I'm driving" declined Nancy quickly, even though she would have loved one.

"Something a little less strong? I'll open a bottle of Pape". It wasn't a question.

She walked into the kitchen and Nancy sat there, staring at the throbbing orange embers. The flickering flames devouring the logs, hungrily engulfing the darkening wood. She could barely blink, hypnotised by the confidence of the fire, its intention set without an element of doubt. Wood snapped and sparks jumped. Smoke exited obediently through the chimney, leaving the beautiful scent of blown out birthday candles behind. She was so ensconced in the sight, she almost forgot where she was.

"Here we go" said Audrey, as she came back into the lounge; one of three. This one was actually her favourite and she cringed inwardly as Audrey sat back down into the very chair that Nancy had ridden her son on, a matter of weeks ago.

Nancy accepted the drink, staring wistfully at the rich, burgundy liquid, its 'legs' clinging to the edge of the glass.

"Well, good health!" said Audrey, raised her glass and took a long, elegant sip and placed her glass down on the side table.

Nancy mimicked, enjoying the taste of the wine for the first time since she'd found out she was pregnant. She placed her glass down on her coaster also, to avoid the temptation of throwing it back.

"So, how do you and Rupert know each other?"

"Well… we met on an evening out and have become good friends" Nancy said, avoiding eye contact and shifting uncomfortably in her chair, trying to block out the images she could see around the room where she'd shagged Rupert. What on earth was she doing here? She could hear Alex scolding her.

"Well that's lovely" smiled Audrey.

"And what do you do?" she asked.

Another person asking her that on a Saturday night. Unbearable.

"I work in travel and leisure." Nancy nodded to reassure her it was a good job. Not a stockbroker, by any means, but she was happy with it.

"How lovely" said Audrey, taking another lengthy sip of wine.

Silence descended whilst Nancy scrabbled for something to say. She couldn't think of anything, so she picked up her wine glass and took a deep sip of the delicious wine. She closed her eyes, enjoying the relaxation flooding over her. She would just have the one glass; it was good for the baby for her to be relaxed. She'd been told that once by a friend who was married to a doctor.

"Your home is lovely, truly" Nancy said, smirking at herself for mimicking Audrey's beautifully spoken English.

"Why thank you Nancy" she smiled. "I'm assuming you've been here before, since you knew where Rupert lived".

"Once or twice" Nancy lied, and looked down into her wine glass as she took another sip.

"How was your trip? Rupert said you'd been on a cruise" Nancy said quickly, excited she'd found a topic to spark conversation.

"Oh well, it was incredible. Beautiful islands, the food was fabulous, and we had a lovely cabin too. Have you ever been on one?"

"Oh no I haven't actually. But it sounds like I might have to!" Nancy exclaimed, laughing and swilling her wine round in her glass.

"Won't you stay for dinner?" asked Audrey enthusiastically.

Nancy quickly refused.

"Honestly, no thank you, I only meant to pop in to see Rup-"

"Oh, but you must, otherwise it's a completely wasted journey. Come now"

She rose from her seat, picked up her near empty glass and walked into the kitchen.

Nancy mouthed "for fuck's sake" to herself and followed, bringing her near empty glass with her also.

Audrey was laying another place at the kitchen table, the table where Rupert had regularly laid her down on, instead of placemats, and eaten something, other than supper. She looked down at the grey tiles to try and hide her embarrassed face.

"Come and sit down, my Dear. Let me call Stephen down." She picked up her phone, pressed the screen a few times with her index finger and placed it back on the worktop.

"Honestly, you really don't have to feed me, I feel bad"

"Nonsense, I always cook enough to feed the 5000, so you will be doing me a favour" she winked.

Nancy decided she was rather fond of Audrey. The kind of Mum you want. Luckily for her, the kind of Mum she had. Scary to strangers, but once known, a strong yet soft, caring and capable kind of woman. The kind of woman you want on your side. The kind of woman Nancy was trying to be.

Just then, a man, she assumed to be Stephen, walked into the kitchen, looking down at his phone screen, He wore jeans and a thick jumper, that zipped from the chest up, and an expensive watch. He had a full head of thick grey hair, blow dried to the side and a good, strong nose. He was handsome, and Nancy could see where Rupert got his good looks from.

"This is Nancy, she's a friend of Ruppies and she's staying for dinner".

Stephen looked up from his phone, brows furrowed.

"Oh. Hello." he said.

"Hello, I'm really sorry, this is a bit weird isn't it, shall I go?" Nancy said to Audrey, feeling as though she couldn't speak directly to Stephen.

"Don't be silly Dear, you are more than welcome. Stephen, Nancy popped round to see Ruppie but obviously he is out at his Christmas dinner and she was soaked through, so I invited her in to dry off and well, here we are" she smiled, catching him up.

Stephen stared at Nancy. Eyes scanning, brows furrowed. There was a moment of silence. Nancy shifted in her seat. He was staring at her like he knew her, but he didn't know from where. She looked back at him, trying to think where she could know him from, but other than him looking like Rupert, she drew a blank.

"Come and sit down dear" said Audrey.

She pulled out a chair for him and went back to the stove, stirring whatever was in the pan. It smelled delicious and Nancy's stomach growled. It smelled like roast dinner. Stephen took his place at the head of the table and reached for the wine. He went to top up Nancy's glass, but she quickly covered it with her hand.

"Oh no thank you, I'm driving." She said with a smile.

He didn't say anything but filled up his wife's glass and then his own.

"Here we go" said Audrey, carrying the cast iron pot to the table and lifting the lid. Steam billowed out of the dish, and Nancy peered in to see what smelled so delightful. All she could see was a layer of sliced potato, crisp and bubbling.

"Creamy chicken hotpot" Audrey announced, whilst placing a dish of buttered peas and carrots next to it.

"Yum-mee" said Nancy, gathering the saliva that pooled in her mouth and gulping it down.

"Pass me your bowl dear" said Audrey. Nancy almost shoved it into her hands.

She took a large metal serving spoon and cut a large portion and lifted it into Nancy's dish, followed by a serving of vegetables. She placed it in front of Nancy, beaming as the steam engulfed her face. Through the steam she could see Stephen staring at her and Nancy cleared her throat, realizing where she was.

"So, Stephen, what do you do?"

"I'm a Stockbroker" he said bluntly.

"Yes, yes I knew that, Rupert told me and he's obviously following in your footsteps" she smiled encouragingly.

"That's right, off to New York, to start his new life" he smirked before putting a forkful of food in his mouth.

Nancy gulped and cleared her throat, emotion travelling down her jawbone. It was evident he saw her as a threat.

"Yes, I know! How exciting for him. New York, wow! New York, New York eh? Start spreading the news…" she sang. There was a moment of silence, so she carried on to fill it.

"We're leaving today" she continued, and quickly shoved a forkful of chicken in her mouth and told herself to shut the fuck up.

Audrey smiled and cleared her throat, offering Nancy some more wine.

"Oh no thank you!" Nancy said, clamping her hand over her glass.

Stephen took a long slow sip from his glass, looking at her over the rim of the glass, and placed it back on the table.

"Where are you from Nancy?"

Nancy swallowed her mouthful and took a sip of water.

"Hampshire. I lived with my parents and my brother near-"

Stephen's glass smashed onto the tiles.

Audrey and Nancy both gasped in unison and sprung up from their seats.

"Shit!" swore Stephen.

They all crowded around the glass and Stephen signaled for them to step back. Glass had sprinkled in tiny specs as far as the island, and a blood red pool was expanding and running through along the grout, changing direction as it reached each junction.

Audrey rushed to fetch the kitchen roll and Nancy scanned the room to see where a broom and mop might be kept.

"I think you should go."

"Stephen, don't be so rude!" scolded Audrey.

"Honestly, its fine, I shouldn't have stayed" said Nancy, embarrassed and a little confused as to why Stephen dropping his glass meant she had to leave. She got up from the table quickly and her head spun, blood rushing away from her face and her stomach churning. She tasted salt in her mouth and looked down at the chicken, it no longer smelling delicious. Since she'd fallen pregnant, she could be gobbling something delicious one minute and the next she felt like she'd just eaten dog food.

"Excuse me" she said, clapping her hand over her mouth and running to the cloakroom by the front door. She lifted the lid of the toilet and threw up the wine, hotpot, peas and carrots, barely digested. She sat on the floor breathless. Shit. She pulled herself up to her feet, using the towel rail and looked at herself in the mirror. She really didn't even know herself anymore. What the fuck was she doing here? And why was Stephen being so hostile towards her? I mean, she knew why really. She was a threat to his prodigy, heading off to New York to continue his work, keeping their family name on the tips of the tongues of rich clients wanting to expand their wealth even more. But he looked at her like he actually recognized her and not just that she was a threat to Rupert's future. And when he asked her where she was from, he'd dropped his glass.

"Nancy?" there was a gentle knock at the bathroom door. It was Audrey.

"I'm fine, I'm sorry I'm just not feeling very well. Thank you so much for dinner, I will let myself out, don't worry. I'm sorry for interrupting your evening. And for the glass" she said through the door, even though she wasn't really sorry for the glass.

"Can I get you some water?" Audrey asked.

"Honestly, no thank you. You have been more than kind. I will let myself out" she repeated, willing Audrey to leave her alone, so she could slip out.

Nancy swilled her mouth out and spat into the sink. Colour was returning to her cheeks, the way it usually did once she'd gotten over her morning sickness. She hated it being called morning sickness. For her it cropped up at the most ridiculous and unwelcoming moments.

Nancy opened the door, ready to grab her wet coat and bolt for the door, but Audrey was standing there waiting, along with Stephen.

"Oh!" said Nancy, surprised.

"I'm really sorry. Again, thank you so much for having me. But I'd better go."

Stephen stared at her, differently this time. Fear and worry swept across his brow, his jaw clenched, his colour pale. His eyes were wide and moist. He rubbed his bristle and took a deep breath, as though he was about to say something, but just exhaled deeply instead.

Nancy lightly pinched the skin under her nose with her index finger and thumb, removing the droplets of sweat that had gathered on her upper lip.

The standoff lasted but a moment, but felt like it ran in slow motion, eyes flickering between one another; suspicion, accusation, guilt but no one knew for sure why, other than the person hosting the emotion.

Nancy side stepped to her right which broke the trance, and Stephen and Audrey's heads turned to follow her to the door, grabbing her dripping coat and pulling the door behind her.

CHAPTER 21

Afterwards

"What the fuck were you thinking?" asked Alex, just as Nancy knew she would, when she walked through the door, soaked and panicking, confessing where she'd been.

"I know, I know, just give me a minute won't you."

"I thought you'd decided you wouldn't tell him. They will undoubtedly tell Rupert about this and it will evoke all sorts of questions about why you were there, and *you* can't lie! You'll tell him, he'll stay, and he will resent you."

Nancy took every point from Alex's mouth like a bullet to the chest, but she knew she was right. What the Hell was she doing, trying to tell him? Thrashing about in bed at night, was the worst time for overthinking, and acting on the thoughts that sprung up in the darkness rarely ended well. It was a matter of weeks before he flew to New York to start his new life, and she was not going to crush his entire career by telling him he was the father of her unborn child. His world would be amazing over there; an incredible apartment, money, women, an exciting career and a lavish lifestyle. By telling Rupert about the baby, she was essentially stealing all this from him, like a common thief. And she hated stealing, apart from the occasional odd item that snuck through the self-check-out, without being scanned in the supermarket.

Alex reached out and squeezed her tight. Nancy needed it and being held by Alex always made her feel better. The way Alex engulfed her in an embrace, her hands pressing against her back and squeezing her tighter and tighter made her believe that everything would be alright someday. She didn't know how, but just that she had to believe it.

"Listen, you can do this. We can do this. And even if I meet a bloke that I allow in my life, he can fit in with us."

Nancy burst into tears. How did she deserve this, this true love and support from her friend who would dedicate herself to their life?

"But what if I meet someone?" Nancy sniveled, pressing her wrist into eye socket.

"Good luck meeting someone, with two kids and me in tow" she smirked.

They both fell about laughing. Alex always knew how to cheer her up and see the lighter side of things.

Nancy gathered herself together, sniffing and drying her eyes on her sleeve, taking a big breath in and releasing a huge sigh.

"Right, that's enough. I will be fine. We will be fine. You are completely right. Thank fuck he wasn't in!" she breathed.

Nancy realised how close she was to ruining his life.

"Yeah, but don't think there won't be questions raised since you had dinner with his parents, caused a big scene and threw up in one of their twenty fucking toilets. Why do you need so many toilets anyway? Only three arses live there!"

Nancy laughed.

"There aren't twenty…" she defended and then realised that actually, there were still half as many.

"How about, just say you went there to call things off before he went to New York, so that there would be less upset all round, and to wish him every success in all his endeavours. And you were sick because you had a sick bug, and you probably shouldn't see him now before he leaves, in case he gets it and ends up shitting himself in the First Class lounge."

Nancy smiled, but her stomach twisted at the thought of not seeing him before he left. Perhaps never seeing him again. Apart from when she looked into his child's eyes every day.

Alex stood up and kissed her on the head, announcing she was going into the kitchen to make them a picky tea, which was usually whatever cheese they had kicking round in the fridge, some crackers, grapes and a dollop of chutney. Nancy just wanted to eat something quick and delicious, watch something lighthearted and go to bed. It had been an exhausting day which hadn't gone to plan in any way, and she wanted to hit the hay and put it behind her. She hoped that she wouldn't wake up in the night and unravel her plan not to tell Rupert. Right now, she felt it was the right decision for all involved. Left to her own devices in the dead of night, she would lose all confidence in herself.

They ate their cheese plates, and Alex drank a bottle of wine, getting more and more confident in the decision as the evening went on, which comforted Nancy. When the film finished, Alex hugged her goodnight and walked the five doors down to her house in her onesie, slipper boots and coat. Nancy trudged upstairs and flopped into bed, closing her eyes. The last thing she saw before she drifted off, was Stephen's face looking at her like he'd seen a ghost.

CHAPTER 22

Then

Age 9

"Come on, let's go to my room" Alex said, tugging her upstairs by her arm.

Nancy looked behind her as she was being pulled up the stairs, her parents standing at the bottom, chatting to Alex's parents.

Nancy had come to Alex's for a sleepover. They'd been planning it for weeks, but as the day grew closer, Nancy's desire to go had waivered.

They sat down on the carpet, picked up a Barbie each and started dressing her in the tiny clothes Alex had laid out on the floor. Nancy's hands shook as she tried to put Winter Barbie's arm through the sleeve of her ski suit, listening to her Dad laughing at something Alex's Dad had just said. Alex was chattering away, doing high pitched voices for her doll whilst Nancy was trying to swallow the lump in her throat. Nancy's vision blurred the dinky dresses and thimble sized shoes splayed out in front of her.

"Well, we're going to head off now Nance!" Dad called up the stairs a few minutes later".

Nancy's heart stopped. They were leaving. She didn't want to stay.

"Dad!" Nancy shouted, making Alex jump. She threw the doll down and ran to the door.

Nancy pelted down the stairs into his arms, and pressed her wet, embarrassed face into her father's coat.

"Hey hey what's this?" Dad asked, chuckling to make light of it in front of Alex's parents.

Nancy didn't say anything but held on tighter, interlocking her fingers behind him so he couldn't escape.

"Sorry about this, let me just talk to Nance in the other room" Dad apologised.

Dad led Nancy to the other room, shying her face away from Alex who had now joined them.

"What's the matter love?" Dad asked in the kitchen, kneeling down in front of her.

"Dad please don't make me stay! Please, please, please!" she cried, wringing her trembling hands in front of him.

"I thought it was you that was desperate to come Poppet, you haven't stopped talking about it for ages!" he smiled.

"I know, I know, but I can't. Please Dad, please!"

"Well Mum and I have got tickets to a show. How about we go and call you afterwards, and if you still feel the same, we will come straight back and get you."

Nancy lifted her arm to her face and covered her eyes, only her wobbling lips on show. Dad held her, stroking her long hair. Mum joined them, kneeling down and holding Nancy tight, whispering 'it's alright' in her ear.

Once Nancy had tired, she pulled away.

"Okay" she whispered. "What's Alex going to say, I feel so silly Mum". Nancy said, another tear dripping from her eye.

"Listen, if Alex is your best friend she won't mind, she will just want you to be happy, okay?"

"Okay" said Nancy, feeling embarrassed and hot.

They both kissed her on the head, and Alex poked her head through the kitchen door.

"You okay Nance?" she asked tentatively.

"Yeh" Nancy smiled, sniffing. Mum wiped Nancy's face and they stood up.

"I'll look after you" Alex said, walking over and putting her arm around her shoulder.

Nancy leant into her, feeling safe and understood, even though she couldn't possibly understand.

"Let's watch a video. And if you want to go home afterwards, that's cool. And if not, we've got chocolate cereal in the morning Mum let me have because you are staying".

Nancy smiled, and felt calmer.

"You'll call me after Mum, promise?"

"I promise" Mum smiled, crossing her heart with her finger.

Nancy had stayed up and sat by the lounge phone to wait for her call, and she had. Mum asked her if she wanted them to come back, and she did, but Alex looked so happy asleep on her lap that she said she was fine. Even though she wasn't. Nancy shakily hung up the phone and stroked Alex's hair and watched the rest of the film. She couldn't bear the thought of Alex waking up in the morning without her. She would stay and eat chocolate cereal.

CHAPTER 23

Then

Age 29

Christmas had been and gone in a blur of rich indulgent meals, sickness and sleepless nights. Tilly had had a wonderful Christmas. Nancy had bought her a beautiful wooden kitchen, and Alex a big tub of plastic fruit and vegetables, a basket and a serving platter. She'd squealed when she opened it, and cast all other presents aside, in order to cook up a storm for her Mummy and Alex. They'd watched her, delighted at the joy the gift had brought to her, and in turn, them. She opened the oven door and thrust the baking tray in, setting the timer and telling them their breakfast was nearly ready. Nancy placed a knowing hand on her tummy and felt the warm glow of what was to come inside. Tilly would love a sibling. She asked Nancy all the time and the thought that Nancy could give her this gift made her feel very fortunate. Yes, it wasn't under ideal circumstances, but it was still going to make Tilly very happy, and that's all that mattered.

Rupert had tried to see Nancy over Christmas, but following Alex's advice, she had kept him at arm's length, keeping her diary packed with Christmas activities and socials, and, for when she wanted to just relax at home, a pocketful of excuses on hand as to why he couldn't come over. She hated hurting him like this and was in turn hurting herself. She wanted more than anything to just tell him and he be overjoyed and then they'd move in together and live happily ever after, but she knew how this would play out. The love that she and Rupert shared was real, but it was new. New love always felt incredible, like it could defy the odds, create miracles and overcome the most impossible of challenges. It felt like it was a partnership that knew no bounds, and anything could be achieved, simply because you were standing side by side. She'd felt it before with Nathan, she knew how this feeling could lead her into a place where she was going to have her heart ripped out and blended into liquid. She'd heard it a million times in every romantic film she'd ever watched, about how if you don't put yourself out there and take risks for love, then you are not really living. Nancy wanted to argue that, because recovering from your heart being metaphorically beaten within an inch of its life, didn't feel a lot like living either.

It was only a week until Rupert left. He'd sent her the link to the apartment he'd picked. He'd done it online in the end and had a realtor out there who'd managed the whole thing. As it was only a rental, Nancy supposed it didn't really matter if he didn't like it, because he could just get somewhere else a few months later. From the pictures, there didn't seem anything not to like, a large open plan living area with kitchen and lounge looking out onto Central Park through floor to ceiling windows. Two huge bedrooms with king size beds and en suites, beautifully decorated in pale dusky grey throughout, light, modern and painfully cool. Jealousy punched her in the gut but the opportunities that lay ahead of him affirmed she was making the right decision.

The schools had gone back. Drop offs in the rain, with heads down, people rushing from their cars to the gate and back. 'Happy New Year' was banded back and forth between parents donning Lycra active wear, not only to facilitate their new fitness resolutions, but because it was the only thing that actually fitted them following the festivities. Nancy got home and hung her wet coat on the radiator and walked into the kitchen to make her coffee. She placed her new Christmas mug under the spout, placed a decaffeinated pod in the coffee machine and pressed the button, watching it drip its rich, bitter scented liquid into the cup, knowing without the caffeine it would do nothing to perk her up. Stupid baby, she thought, and then immediately took it back, crossing her heart and begging God to ignore what she just said. She walked over to the dining room table and opened her laptop and fired it up. She logged on and watched her inbox fill up and sighed. She deleted any emails that looked like spam and took the total of 104 down to 75. A slight improvement. Nancy went back to the coffee machine to pick up her coffee and saw a face at the window.

"Shit!' she held her hand over her heart and stared at the man at her window, a thick head of grey hair, blowdried neatly to the side, in expensive looking casual clothes and a strong, straight nose. Nancy breathed a sigh of relief as she realised it was Rupert's father, Stephen. This was closely followed by a tightening in her stomach at what on earth he was doing at her house. She walked to the front door and opened it.

"Stephen, hi. Is everything alright?"

"Yes, sorry for just coming by. I just wanted to talk to you. Can I come in? Rupert is fine by the way" he said, holding his hands up in reassurance.

"Oh good" breathed Nancy, still bemused why he was here.

She stood back from the door and welcomed him in. He stomped his boots on the mat, discarding water droplets and mud off his boots.

Nancy closed the door behind him and she faced it for a moment, her heart and mind racing. Had he come to warn her off? To apologise?

"Um, can I get you a drink of anything? Tea? Coffee?"

"No no, I won't stay long. Thank you" he said.

Nancy gestured towards the lounge and she followed him in, looking up to thank the Lord that she'd run the hoover round last night.

She sat opposite him, nervously, palms sweating, her mouth so dry that her tongue suctioned to the roof of her mouth.

He tapped his foot, his knee shuddering. He rubbed his palms together like he was trying to warm himself against an imaginary campfire.

"Listen, there's no easy way to say this. I almost didn't come…"

Nancy's stomach felt like it was going to fall out of her arse. What was he going to say? Whatever it was, she knew it wasn't going to be good.

"Aud doesn't know that I am here. Neither does Rupert. And it must stay that way okay?"

Nancy nodded, and then immediately regretted agreeing to staying silent before she even knew why.

"Are…are you pregnant with my son's baby?"

Time stopped. Silence screeched in her ears.

She opened and closed her mouth like a fish, like the ones that swim around slowly in tanks at a Chinese restaurant.

She went to speak, she didn't know what to say, but nothing but a croak came out. She coughed to clear her throat and swallowed whatever saliva was present and tried again. Her mind danced between indignantly denying it and turfing him out, and bursting into tears.

"Are you?' he asked again.

Nancy looked down at her hands grasping together on her lap.

"Yes" she admitted.

As soon as the words were out there, she instantly regretted them and wished she could grapple at the air in a bid to put them back in her mouth.

Stephen's head was in his hands, rubbing up and down his face, his jaw tightly clenched. He rubbed his face until it was bright red, then they ended up in his hair, pulling it up like he'd been electrocuted. Nancy's heart thudded like the sound of a runner's trainers on a treadmill.

He finally looked up, and looked around the room as though he was searching for answers.

"I'm sorry" said Nancy finally. "But I never meant for this to happen. And I'm not going to tell Rupert, if that's what you are worried about. I am going to let him go to America and live his life. I won't ruin it for him, he need never know" she said earnestly.

Stephen had tears in his eyes. He tamed his hair down and tried to straighten up, his lower lip trembling until he coughed and licked his lips, pressed them together and swallowed his emotion down into his belly.

"Does anyone else know about this?"

Nancy went to lie, but thought better of it.

"Just my best friend, Alex. But no one else"

"Let's keep it that way shall we"

Nancy nodded, tears starting to roll down her cheeks.

"I didn't do this on purpose" she said, like a child.

She wondered why she was being so subservient. It was a mistake. And she was the one being left high and dry. Weeks of guilt and doubt leaked out of her, she used the sofa cushion to shield her face, embarrassed and relieved all at once.

"I know. But there is a lot at stake here. Rupert's future, among other things."

"What...other....things?" she asked between sobs, lowering the cushion.

Stephen sighed, a deep reverent sigh that saddened his whole body. His eyes danced back and forth, his mouth opening and closing into a terse grimace to stop whatever he really wanted to say from coming out.

"It's... the thing is...well look, you've obviously been through enough. And Rupert tells me you have a daughter already and the story behind that. My heart goes out to you"

His words were of empathy, not of pity, and it made her cry even more. She cried for Nathan, she cried for Tilly, she cried for Rupert and their unborn child. She cried for herself, feeling pathetic and furious that her life had turned out this way. She cried for the weeks she'd been holding this in, for the fact that she was being blackmailed into further silence, but mostly for the approval from Stephen that keeping this to herself was the right thing to do.

"Are you going to keep it?" he asked.

"Of course, how dare you-"

Stephen held his hands up defensively.

"I'm not saying you should or shouldn't. I was simply asking you, before I carry on".

Nancy took a tissue from up her sleeve and dried her face, blotted her nose and listened.

"I respect you for letting Rupert go. And it sounds like you have been through enough. I want to help you."

"Help me? How?" Nancy sniveled.

"I want to make sure you will be alright. I need you to give me your account details and I will set up a monthly payment for you and the child until they are eighteen years old. You won't need to worry about finances."

He paused.

"However...no one is to know about it, our family name is never to be mentioned and you are to defer any questions about who the father is. It would do you good to mention another man to your friends and family now, for when you can't hide your pregnancy anymore."

Nancy couldn't believe her ears. She tried to remind herself she wasn't going to tell Rupert anyway, and this way the fear of how she was going to cope financially was gone. But being told this was what she was going to do felt different. She couldn't change her mind once she agreed, and it made her throat constrict. There were still times in the middle of the night where she fantasised of telling Rupert and he would take her in his arms and tell her everything was going to be alright. That he would stay, that he never wanted to go to the US anyway, and they would raise their children together. But then she would think of Nate and what he did to her and the dream shattered, painful pieces of their life smashing onto the floor, her on her hands and knees sweeping up the shards with a dustpan and brush, all alone. Rupert would never stay, and if he did, he would eventually leave after years of resentment and guilt-fueled rows. She could make a life for her and her children, with this money, though she didn't know how much yet, could set them up and no one would get hurt. She would see pictures of Rupert in fancy cocktail bars with leggy blondes on social media and she would be jealous, but satisfied that she did right by him, by her children and by herself. And Stephen clearly didn't want Nancy or his grandchild in his life either. It hurt, but she didn't even know this man. And if he could use his money and power to be so calculating, so controlling and manipulative, did she want him or Rupert in her life anyway?

Nancy sat there silent for a while, trying to compute what he was offering. She cleared her throat, tears welling in her eyes.

"So let me get this straight. You will pay me every month until this child is 18, and in return, I will never tell Rupert or anyone else that he is the father of my child. I will design a dalliance with an imaginary man and tell my friends and family that he wasn't interested when I told him, so I am going to raise the baby alone."

"Correct" affirmed Stephen, rubbing the bridge of his nose with his thumb and his forefinger.

"I hate to ask this, but can I ask how much?" she winced at the question, already feeling like somehow she'd deliberately fallen pregnant in order to squeeze money out of this wealthy man. She knew it wasn't true, but the moment the thought entered her mind she felt as though she believed it.

"£5,000 a month, starting from next month. There will also be an account that the child will be able to access when they are 21, with enough money for a car and to buy their first property.".

Nancy stared at him.

"If you agree to this, there will be a contract written up for you to sign. You yourself will receive the sum of £100,000, in exchange for my family name to be completely removed from this situation, that you never make contact with Rupert or anyone in our family again. The child will take your name and will never source a paternity test. I want you to forget that you ever knew us, and this money should give you the opportunity start a new life for yourselves. It will obviously be explained fully by my legal team when you meet with them next week."

Nancy sat there on the edge of the sofa, unable to comprehend the offer. She desperately wished Alex was here, to help her understand what was happening and what she should do.

"Do I have to decide right away?' Nancy muttered. The decision seemed obvious, but she felt like she was making a deal with the devil. That as soon as she accepted, she would be damned to a life filled with guilt and shame, lying to her child and its father for the rest of her life. Every time the child asked after its father, she would lie. And the man she loved would be living on the other side of the world, completely oblivious that he had a child with a woman he once loved.

"No, but I will come back tomorrow for your answer. But I urge you to accept, for everyone's sake. You've been through enough and it's the least I can do."

Nancy looked up; her brow furrowed. She stared at Stephen confused and he stared back, his eyes full of guilt and apology.

"What the hell does that mean?" asked Nancy.

"Well I just mean, you know, with your last fella leaving you to go travelling. Rupert will do the same."

"You don't know that!" Nancy exploded, shooting up of the sofa.

"How do you know? We love each other!" She choked on the words. "How about we call Rupert now and tell him the truth? Tell him about the baby and how you are paying me to keep it from him? So he will never know that he has a son or daughter and it will be all your fault!" she cried.

Stephen rose to meet her eye level.

"I'm sorry young lady but you were obviously planning on doing that before I even came here. I am just offering to look after you and the baby to make your life easier" he said firmly.

"Like you care about making my life easier! You just want to avoid embarrassment and make sure your son turns out just like you!" Nancy screamed.

She didn't really know why she was reacting like this. He was right, she wasn't going to tell Rupert. And this meant that their life would be incredible. £100,000. Plus £5000 a month. She could go part time and they could move to a bigger house. They could go on amazing holidays together and create incredible memories. She could look after Alex. They would be safe, and no one would ever hurt them again. She could live with what she'd done. She would just do lots of yoga and praying and it would all be alright. The alternative of declining Stephen's officer and struggling financially seemed pointless now. And the other option of declining and running to Rupert with the truth would cause more upset that she could never undo. She would be responsible for ruining so many lives, and at what cost? He would most likely go anyway and she would have lost this opportunity forever. She couldn't believe she was thinking like this, like some kind of honeypot golddigger, greedily and selfishly thinking about how to look after number one. The difference was, she wasn't looking out for number one at all. She was looking out for number two and now number three. They deserved the best, and if she had to deal with torturing herself for the rest of her life so that her children could have a secure and a happy childhood, then so be it. Every mother in the world would understand. Protecting one's young is instinct. Nothing else mattered.

Nancy looked down at her feet, sniffing.

"I'll come back tomorrow for an answer" he said again.

And with that, Stephen walked out of the lounge, through the front door slamming it behind him, leaving Nancy standing tears dripping onto her slippers.

CHAPTER 24

2 Weeks Later

Nancy stared at her account. She'd always wondered what it would be like to see a large sum of money in there. She'd always lived pay cheque to pay cheque, rarely struggling so to speak, but never really thriving either. Nathan had paid his way what he was told to by the CSA. Thanks to having a reasonably well-paid job that allowed her to mostly work from home, and with her Mum helping out with childcare, Tilly only attended nursery twice a week, therefore keeping her outgoings to a minimum. When Alex had moved in and paid her rent, she had been able to relax a bit more, and save what she paid them for holidays and weekends away together. She always tried to treat Alex when they were away to meals and cocktails by the pool, as she felt as though Alex's money had paid for these luxuries. And perhaps the fact that Alex had moved in with them had saved her; Nancy felt as though she should be paying her. Alex was impossible to spoil, and goodness knows Nancy tried. But for every meal Nancy tried to pay for, Alex would flap her arms and grab the card machine, shoving her card in and pressing the buttons, then wafting the waitress away before Nancy could even open her mouth to argue. Nancy had tried different approaches, like trying to pay for the meal halfway through on her way back from the toilet, or even putting her card behind the bar on arrival. It often turned out that Alex had got there first by calling ahead and giving her card details over the phone. Alex was comfortable, but not because she had come from money or had an exceptionally well-paying job. She was a hairdresser in a high end salon in town, and even though she was the Senior Stylist now, they paid her the standard rate and the only extra money she earned was from selling products to clients and doing friends' hair in the evenings. The problem was, she was always so knackered from being on her feet non-stop for 12 hours that she had started to refuse extra work. But she didn't have any children to pay out for, and obviously Grayson had made sure she would be alright.

But now Nancy was gawping incredulously at her current account. The £500 of her own money being dwarfed by the £100,000 of Stephen's. Of course it wasn't from him. She'd been gifted it by some unknown uncle of Nathan's who'd passed away, and Nathan had wanted her to have it, and that was the story she was legally obligated to tell. She found it incredible how powerful people seemed to work above the system. Nancy struggled to change the name of her bank accounts, let alone make it look like money was being sent from someone else. She blinked, staring at the figures, like she'd made a mistake and gazing at the screen had caused the numbers to stretch. But it was all there as promised. For one greedy and selfish moment, she wondered if she should have negotiated for more. She shook her head and told herself to shut up. She was looking at more money than she would have ever dreamed of seeing next to her account and sort code, and there would be more coming in every month for the rest of her baby's childhood, not to mention a huge whack in an account set up for the baby for the to access when they turned eighteen. Nancy would keep this information from the child. Knowing that they could buy their first flat and car outright as a teenager would do them no good whatsoever. It would lead to a life of laziness and entitlement, careless sex and drug taking, being rude to teachers and stomping out of the house into the night. No, her child would never know this. And Nancy would split the money between the baby and Tilly. Tilly shouldn't miss out, they were both her children equally, and she didn't want this baby to be treated any differently because they had a rich grandfather who paid them to not exist.

She'd not seen Rupert before he'd left for New York. He had tried, almost everyday to talk to her, to see her. She'd ignored him as much as she could, and replied bluntly if she couldn't. She felt numb and cruel, selfish and calculated. But he was better off without her. Whatever love he thought he felt for her was surely null and void now she'd done what she'd done, and it made it easier convincing herself she was saving him from a life of enforced responsibility. On the day of his flight he'd sent her a message.

'Hey you. Just in the departure lounge waiting for my flight and thinking of you. I'm not really sure what happened between us. Timing was just out, I suppose. I want you to know that meeting you was the best thing that ever happened to me. Maybe there will be a right time for us one day, at least that's what I choose to believe anyway. It's the only way I'll manage to get on this plane and not run back to you. I wish you and Tilly every happiness in life, and if you ever need me, I'll be there. Be thinking of you always. I love you xxx'

She hadn't replied. How could she? She had fought with herself not to bomb up the motorway to the airport, like they did in the movies, and tell him she loved him too. She hoped after a few weeks in America, he would forget all about her and move on. She wished the same for herself. She had no choice but to try.

She made the transfer, and moved the £100,000 into the new savings account she'd set up. She made a vow not to even touch it, and a week later, as promised, £5000 landed in her account on the 1st of the month, gifted by the widow of Nathan's deceased uncle, who had more money than she knew what to do with, apparently. She took Tilly, her best friend Olivia from school and Alex out to their favourite pizza place that Friday night, where they had one of those sticky playzones in the corner of the restaurant, so kids could roll around screaming and their parents could enjoy a glass of wine without interruption. The pizza was alright, a bit doughy and you almost always had a tummy ache afterwards, but Tilly loved it, and therefore so did Nancy. When Tilly and Olivia were out of earshot but in her eyesight, Nancy turned to Alex.

"Right, I have something big to tell you. And it is a secret, the biggest one I have ever told you, or ever will okay?"

"Nance you've already told me you're preggers" Alex smirked.

"Sshh!" This place was very popular with the nursery Mums as somewhere to hit after school for a much needed easy tea.

"And no, much bigger than that"

"Bloody hell, I'm listening" smiled Alex, putting her wine down and leaning in.

"Right, I am contractually obliged to not to tell a soul"

"Contractually obliged?" repeated Alex, baffled.

"But I've never kept a secret from you in my whole life and I'm not about to start now. But this is huge. The big shit, the real deal. This is not like the time when you told Sam and Soph over dinner that I got fingered by that guy from accounting at the Christmas party" Nancy smirked.

Alex leaned back and laughed loudly, a few diners looking up at her cackle.

"Seriously, what I am about to tell you, cannot go any further. It can't be mentioned, joked about, alluded to in anyway, or I could lose everything if anyone were to ever find out."

"What the fuck's going on?" asked Alex.

"Listen, its nothing illegal so don't get your knickers in a twist. It's just something and you have to promise me, promise me with all your heart, that only you and I will ever know about it. Well, and the other person that knows about it, but I'll tell you about that in a minute" Nancy waffled.

Alex leant over the table and held Nancy's shaking hands.

"I promise. You know me, I would never tell a bean. Unless it's about fingering again then you're on your own. The world has a right to know."

"Ha. Ha" smiled Nancy and looked at Alex dead in the eye. Alex returned the stare back, and they interlinked pinkies on both hands, and pressed their thumb pads against each other's.

"The most sacred vow anyone can swear to. If broken you must suffer serious consequences" they said at the same time, chanting their mantra like they had since they were children.

Nancy proceeded to whisper to Alex about Stephen's proposal, checking over her shoulder several times. She told her about the money, including the generous monthly installment to support them through the child's life.

Alex sat there open-mouthed for most of it and when Nancy rounded up the story, Alex took her wine glass and tipped almost half the contents into her mouth.

"Fuck me" she breathed, a little too loudly, families nearby scowling at her. She didn't give a shit.

"I know".

Nancy's stomach hurt. She trusted Alex more than anything when it came to serious stuff, but now the secret was out there, it was harder to control.

"But this is a legal agreement Alex. If Stephen or anyone finds out that I told, I would be breaching the contract, and the money would stop. No more monthly income, no deposits and cars for the children, and I'd have to pay back the lump sum too".

"Listen, I will take this to the grave. I wouldn't do anything to jeopardise this for you and Tilly. And the baby of course. Shit..." she exhaled again, and finished the glass in another deep swig. She replenished her glass, and stared into space for a moment.

"Well, I think....bloody fuck, I think it is bloody brilliant. Fucking hell Nance you were going to have the baby anyway, and now you won't need to worry about money at all! And your kids are going to be set up for life!"

She grabbed the laminated menu and scanned the drinks section, looking for champagne.

"Fuck's sake, of course a place like this doesn't serve Champagne. Let's get some shitty prosecco and pretend" she grinned.

She waved to the teenage waiter and he came over to their table, looking bored out of his mind.

"Prosecco por fa vor", she said to him in her best Del Boy voice, who looked at her like an idiot who was genuinely trying to speak Spanish.

She wafted him away, and held Nancy's hands across the table.

"Look, I know you cared about Rupert, I do. And this must be really hard for you. And I know saying 'don't worry' won't work because you will, you will worry, you will feel guilty for the rest of your life knowing you. But don't. There are men all over the world with children they never knew existed. Or do but don't want to know."

She raised her eyebrows and pursed her lips, alluding to Nate.

"This is the best possible outcome for all involved. You'll be taken care of, Rupert can go and fulfill his destiny, Dad gets his son to carry on their family business and throws you a few breadcrumbs to let him go and keep yourself to yourself. And when the kids ask about their father's, we will tell them they were fuck wits so they were raised by two strong women who are not Lesbians, despite what some people may think".

Nancy eyed Alex.

"Okay, so *Rupert's* not a fuck wit and we won't raise them to be man haters. Just to be independent and strong, knowing they can depend on you and me. And most of all, on themselves."

The Prosecco arrived, and two glasses. Nancy poured her coke into her glass.

Alex poured the fizz into her glass and they held their glasses up.

"To the future"

"To the future" Nancy repeated, sipping her coke and trying to ignore the guilt pumping through her veins.

CHAPTER 25

Then

Age 5

The rest of Christmas had come and gone in a lazy haze. Robert had kept his promise that he wouldn't leave her on her own on Christmas Day. He had orchestrated a sleepover in his room for her on Christmas night when Grandma and Granville were staying. His room was actually a loft conversion reached via some very creaky stairs, so anyone walking up them would alert everyone in their very small house. Nancy couldn't have loved her brother more. He looked like a valiant knight to her now, and all the bickering and fighting that had ever gone on between them paled into insignificance. They'd opened their presents as usual, the squeal of surprise echoing round the room as they opened some of the gifts they'd wishfully circled in the Argos catalogue back in November. A Tiny Tears and a talking computer for Nancy and Game Boy games and a Manchester United poster for Rob. It had soon been time to tidy away ahead of the Grandma and Granville arriving, and the sparkly magic that had filled Nancy's heart sunk deep down into her tummy and turned dark and heavy, filling her stomach with dread and ruining her appetite for her turkey dinner. It sat like a loaf of stale bread in the pit of her stomach, refusing to budge.

When they arrived, Rob stood by her side holding her hand, and after they had dutifully kissed Grandma, he yanked Nancy into the lounge to get out of kissing Granville. Mum had shouted after them of course, but Rob ignored her, and fortunately Mum was so busy with timings of the meal, let them go without reprimanding them. Granville had tried on many occasions to talk to Nancy but Rob had interrupted or pulled her away to play.

Whenever Nancy needed to go somewhere, she lightly tapped Rob on his arm, and he followed her like her shadow. She could see Granville getting increasingly fidgety, eyeing Robert with disdain. After a few hours, he was clearly frustrated.

'Do you two have to go everywhere together?' he remarked irritably.

The other grown-ups had looked at him briefly with their brows furrowed and then continued to nibble and chatter on the sofa.

After dinner, Nancy needed to use the toilet, so she lightly touched Robert's arm and they both excused themselves to go upstairs. Nancy's Mum was well into her post Christmas meal relaxed state, where the pressure of entertaining and getting the meal to the table was no longer on her agenda, and Dad regularly topped her glass up and gently kissed her on the head in appreciation as he cleared the table and brought out dessert and cheese. They were all stuffed to the gunnels but could always find room for another mouthful. Nancy was having a wee upstairs, Robert guarding outside, when she heard another voice.

"I need to go to the toilet"

"Well Nancy's in there at the moment' said Robert boldly.

"None the less, I am desperate".

"There's another toilet downstairs"

"You are going to make an old man walk all the way back down when there is a toilet right here? I don't think so"

He nudged Robert to the side, and opened the door.

Nancy was standing right by the door, snuck under Granville's arm still holding the door knob. He grabbed her roughly by the arm, and she yelped.

"Ow!" she winced.

"You just be careful you two. Or I'll tell your parents how rude you've been. Just think how upset Grandma will be with you, and your parents will punish you for being the little shits you are" he growled through gritted teeth, his grip tightening on Nancy's arm until it really hurt.

Both children looked up at him through watery eyes, Robert's teeth clenched in frustration and hate. Granville's grip on Nancy released.

"Now run along you two" he smiled, roughly patting them both on the head. He squeezed Robert temples and the clip on Nancy's bow dug into her scalp. Robert took her hand and walked her back down the stairs. Granville didn't touch her anymore that day.

That was the last time they took a risk like that, and when it was finally bedtime, they went into the bathroom together to have wees and brush their teeth with the bathroom door firmly locked. Mum didn't like it when they did that, but they would rather have had a scolding from her and be safe. When they unlocked the door, Granville was standing there like they'd feared, but they ducked and ran straight upstairs to Robert's room, shut the door and pushed his chest of drawers against it. They decided if there was a fire they could climb onto the roof and they could wait there until a fireman saved them. They slept with ears cocked. Any creak and they both lifted their heads off their pillows immediately, eyes dashing around in the darkness. Robert had suggested they both sleep in onesies because they were cosy and safe. Nancy hadn't argued, even though she got too hot sleeping in one.

When they woke, they clocked that the chest of drawers remained in place and they both breathed a brief sigh of relief. They came downstairs and Mum had already laid the table, and was frying up the leftover vegetables and potatoes for bubble and squeak, their usual Boxing Day breakfast. Nancy could smell the salty waft of bacon and her tummy growled. She wondered how on earth she could possibly be hungry after all the food the day before, but she was. Grandma was helping Mum, and Mum looked hot and bothered. She was probably looking forward to a sit down after yesterday's hosting. Granville sat at the table with the Radio Times, circling programmes she presumed he wanted to watch. His small glasses were balanced on the end of his nose, his dark green cardigan straining over his belly, his yellowing shirt underneath, his beige trousers riding up his fat legs. He crossed his ankle over his knee, and tapped his slipper against the leg of the table. He looked up as the children came down the stairs together, and grumpily looked back down into the magazine. Nancy and Robert made themselves useful, taking stuff in and out of the kitchen to the table; pickles, mustard, sliced white bread and a closh of golden butter. Granville looked up every time they placed something on the table and they quickly retreated back to the kitchen to help Mum and Grandma. Mum called upstairs for Dad, and when he came down, they all sat down to eat their breakfast. They chatted about the day before, sighed that they couldn't believe it was all over after all of the build- up, but agreed they were looking forward to some relaxing days at home before the New Year. Granville said nothing, he just ate his breakfast quickly. He finished first and leant into Grandma and whispered something in her ear. Nancy looked around to see if anyone saw but they were too busy stuffing their faces. Not even half way through her breakfast, Grandma placed her knife and fork down on the plate and exhaled.

"Goodness, I think my eyes were bigger than my belly" she exclaimed.

Her parents looked up, eyes scanning to see what they had missed.

"I will just go and get our things together, and then help you tidy up, Jane"

"Everything alright?" Dad asked, a serious expression on his brow.

"Yes, yes of course, I am just feeling rather full and we have to unpack and I have to put the gammon on for tea, amongst a million other things".

She excused herself and rose from the table, Granville following after, and they climbed the narrow staircase of the terrace house. Mum sat there red faced and furious but Nancy and Robert held hands under the table, their palms sweaty with anxiety and relief. They had done it.

The next few days had drifted on by; playing with their new toys, bickering over board games, and the adults nodding off during the afternoon film on the television. It had been fun, albeit slightly boring. If she knew what was about to happen next, maybe she would have savoured the time more.

It was almost bedtime. They were bathed and in their pyjamas, dressing gowns and slippers, wet hair combed into side partings. They had been granted half an hour's playtime downstairs before they went up for stories, and the mood had turned childish. A tickle fight had broken out with their father the lounge, and they were hoarse from squealing and shuddering with adrenaline, attacking him from all angles. What happened next, would change their families life forever. Nancy had been on Dad's back, arms wrapped around his neck whilst he turned the colour of beetroot, Robert pretending to punch him repeatedly in the stomach. Dad had reached round, and grabbed Nancy, pulling her over his shoulder and onto the carpet, pinning her arms down with both his knees and tickling her under the chin. She screamed in morbid frustration. It tickled and she was laughing, but she absolutely hated it. Dad continued, lifting up her top and blowing raspberries on her belly. She screamed louder, laughing and hating, tears rolling down her face as she fought the giggles and the fury. Dad came up for air and looked at her face, wet with tears, red with anger.

"Oh come on Nance! You always do this, beg me to play tickle fight with you and then end up crying!'

Nancy lifted her hands to her face, covering the shame that was radiating from her, sobbing uncontrollable sobs.

"Hey… what's wrong poppet?' he said, pulling her hands off her face. "Did I hurt you, I'm sorry'

"It's not that. It's just what Granville does and I don't like it" she wailed, her heart thudding against her tiny rib cage.

"Well it's only raspberries on your tummy poppet. But if you don't like it you should say"

"They're not on my tummy, Daddy"

Dad stiffened, and sat up on his bent knees.

She knew he'd asked her a few questions after that, but she couldn't really remember what they were. She remembered her shoulders being held firmly, told she wasn't in trouble, but she needed to tell him exactly what she meant. She couldn't really look at him, she just stared at the large wooden cabinet behind him, which contained their family photo albums, the posh plates Mum used when they had guests, and in the drawers, batteries and instructions for electronics they no longer owned. Mum joined them, both of them looking unusually serious. Nancy answered as best she could, but all she could think about was what else they kept in that cabinet behind them. She tried to list all the things she could think of but just kept repeating the same items over and over again. She snapped out of her daze when Dad stood up, running past Mum to put his shoes on. Mum grabbed his arm but he shook her off and ran out of the house. Mum was calling after him, but he was gone. She turned around, ashen-faced, her hands shaking. She walked over to Nancy and scooped her up and held the back of her head, gently bopping her up and down. Nancy closed her eyes and nuzzled into her mother's neck, breathing in her beautiful, heady scent. It was a combination of soap and her perfume that made Nancy's tongue relax in her mouth and her jaw unclench, her body and mind lay weightless in her mother's arms. Nancy was tired. She hadn't realised how tired she was. Relief exhausted her, a huge yawn escaped from her, though the thumping pulse in her stomach refused to let her find peace for long. Robert walked over and held onto their mother's body too, her hand reaching down to include him. Robert placed a hand on Nancy's back and they swayed from side to side, Mum shushing them with a lullaby they'd never heard before until she sniffed, turned away from them and wiped her face. "Let's get you both to bed, eh?"

123

CHAPTER 26

Present

"Muuuuuummmm! She's won't get out of my room!!!" Tilly wailed, irritation scratching down Nancy's spine.

"Fuck me" Nancy exhaled, shoving clean washing into Lottie's drawer.

"Lott! Stop annoying your sister!" Nancy shouted.

"I'm not! I just want her to play with me!" she whined.

"I'm talking to Olivia, Mum! Get out Lottie!"

She heard a scream, as Tilly obviously pushed her out her room and slammed her door. It wasn't a whinging scream, it was blood curdling. Nancy dropped the washing she was holding and bolted to the door and looked across the landing to see Lottie thrashing about with her fingers trapped in the hinge of Tilly's door. Lottie was silently thrashing, panic and pain pulsing over her face. Nancy sprinted to her, yanking the door handle and pushing it open, releasing her white fingers and pulling her tightly into her chest, waiting for her to catch her breath. She found her voice, looked up to the ceiling and let out a gut-wrenching wail, angry and full of pain and panic. Nancy took her hand and shoved her fingers in her mouth, sucking them. Tilly was on the other side of the door, white and distraught.

"Lottie Lou! I'm so sorry I didn't mean to hurt you. Mumma I'm so sorry!' she wept.

Nancy kissed and comforted Lottie, and wiggled her fingers around to see if they were broken. Lottie had no problem moving them, so Nancy assured her she would be alright. Nancy's heart raced and she was sweating, trying to hold back tears herself. When the girls were hurt, she felt physical pain and terror herself, as though her own fingers had been slammed in the door too. She reached up for Tilly, and held both girls on her lap tightly, stroking their heads and wiping their tears away, whispering words of comfort to calm them down. She used their soft hair to mop up her own tears, that crept out as she replayed the accident in her mind.

"Now what have I said about slamming doors"

"I'm sorry, I'm so sorry Mummy. Lottie, I'm sorry will you ever forgive me?" she wailed.

Nancy tried to keep her strict scary face on whilst she begged for forgiveness, to ensure the lesson was properly learnt. Tilly cried more as the shame sunk in, wishing she could go back to a time when she hadn't hurt her baby sister. Nancy's heart bled and she reached out for Tilly and held her in her other arm, cradling them and pressing her lips against their heads.

Lottie forgave quickly, and held Tilly in her arms. They pressed their foreheads together and closed their eyes to show they were friends again, like they always had since they were little. An ora of light shone over their heads in unbreakable bond that only Nancy could see. Her heart swelled and she thanked God for the gift of her beautiful babies. Nancy went and fetched a plaster and dressed Lottie's fingers. Then they ran off downstairs together, asking for permission to build a den using the sofa blankets in the basket in the lounge, to fetch a snack and watch a movie. Nancy granted it and with a squeal they ran downstairs, planning with excited gasps as they created new ideas to have more magical fun together. She paused for a moment, wistfully gazing after her daughters, trying to lock the memory deep into her psyche so that one day when she was weeping about the forgotten years, she would be able to recollect that sweet memory and force herself to remember that she was a good Mum. She often felt she wasn't, no matter how hard she tried, she always felt she could have done a little bit more. She envied those mothers who completely lost themselves in their children and their desires and dreams. She had tried, but her own haunting past and memories cast a black shadow over her ability to delve completely into their innocent joyful hearts. That and trying to keep a tidy-ish house, see friends and run off the crisps and wine she consumed every weekend. *Did that make her selfish?* She thought it most likely did. But she also didn't want to be one of those Mums who, when their children flew the nest for university, would have nothing left but to call them 45 times a day to make sure they were eating vegetables with their pesto pasta and that they weren't burning the candle at both ends. Of course, she would be doing that, but she'd like to think she'd only call 30 times, in between day drinking with Alex and staying in bed past 6am.

She returned to finish folding the washing, pressing the last of it into Lottie's drawers which were bulging with unworn hand-me-downs. Lottie didn't share Tilly's love of fashion, and almost everything Nancy saved for her remained unworn in the wardrobe. Lottie wouldn't let her give any of it away, in case she changed her mind, but the chances of that happening were as likely as Nancy getting abs. Lottie was a tomboy through and through, and lived for hoodies and joggers. She couldn't bear anything uncomfortable, and made Nancy cut out the labels of every item of clothing that dared to touch her skin. Her daughters were like chalk and cheese in some ways, but they also had many undeniable features which fortunately inherited from her. She was forever grateful for this, and although she could see both the girls' fathers in traits of their personalities and sometimes in their eyes or the way they would look at her, she could mostly see herself. Whether that was nature or nurture, she did not know, nor did she care. She was just pleased that she didn't have to be reminded of the feeling of crushing abandonment every time she looked at her girls, even if Lottie's father was oblivious to what he'd even left behind.

She finished and straightened up, holding the small of her back, feeling ancient. She picked up the empty laundry basket and took it downstairs into the utility room and placed it on top of the washing machine ready for the next load, which was rotating to a halt, ready for the next feed of dirty clothes. She never felt on top of her jobs. She felt organised and powerful for a fleeting moment once or twice a week if she was lucky, before a wave of washing and unfinished chores crashed over her, casting her onto the shore. She would scrape herself off the sand, and wade straight back out into an ocean of relentless demands, before a wave would knock her off her feet again. She tried not to complain. Who else was going to come in and save her? Even if she had a man, she would just be doing more washing, he wouldn't necessarily lighten the load. Sometimes she fantasised about what life would have been like, if Nathan had come back. He had been reasonably handy around the place. He was lazy of course, a dreamer, always gazing into the distance and planning their next adventure together. The thought of him made her throat catch, and she gulped deeply and inhaled simultaneously, choking on her saliva. She spluttered, and marched to the sink to sip from the glass she'd left by the tap. She managed to soothe the burning in her throat in a few gulps and shook her head in a bid to shake the memory far away. She then laughed to herself. How was he actually handy? He put up the shelves in their place, and took the bins out every week, only if reminded. He organised all their trips and all she had to do was pack, which was something she probably took for granted. But other than that, what else had he brought to her life? A bit more money maybe. She raided her memory and a reel of photographs from their life unrolled, the two of them snuggled up on the sofa, laughing, having sex. She swallowed again, and her lip gently trembled, and her eyes brimmed with tears. She wasn't actually crying for the lost relationship. It had been fine, and of course she loved him, but she knew he hadn't and never could have truly touched her soul. He was an island, a man who used her as an accessory. She was a loyal puppy who followed along behind him, in awe of his dreams and passion for life. She'd become so eager to be everything he needed, she rarely thought about what she wanted. Of course, she wasn't going to argue about the travelling, she loved it and it made their life exciting and spontaneous. But now she thought of it, he had never asked her which part of the world she wanted to see, or even on a smaller scale, what film she'd like to see at the cinema, or even what she would like to watch on the television. She watched what he wanted, or they watched things in separate rooms and it had become so normal to her, she rarely questioned it. She chose ease over argument more and more as their relationship progressed, until she didn't even recognise herself anymore. She'd become subservient and fearful of displeasing him, and her self-esteem had sunk to an all-time low. She knew she wasn't crying about the lost relationship; she was crying over allowing herself to sink and disappear, all in the name of love. Not to mention the abandonment. She didn't think she would ever truly get over that feeling, the feeling of being dropped from a height, like when you fall in a dream and jolt awake. And no matter how much she'd cried, stomped and drunk-dialed her evenings away, there was absolutely nothing she could do to make Nate change his mind. It had been embarrassing. She was full of shame and felt worthless. This was exactly why she had sent Rupert away without telling him about Lottie. How could she risk such a brutal attack on her soul again? If what happened with Nate still got to her like this, all these years later, how could she possibly recover from a second dose of neglect? Nate left her and there was nothing she could do. But she chose what happened with Rupert. It was her choice. And that was the way she wanted to live her life. Even if she ached every day of her life for it. She grabbed her sleeve and brushed it across her wet face and cleared her throat. *Enough. Why was she raking over past pain? It would get her nowhere.*

She straightened up, walked over to the bin and heaved the full bag out onto the tiles, and tied the handles together. She lifted the bag to the door, slipped on her slippers and opened the door to take it out to the dustbin at the end of the driveway. She lifted the lid and heaved the bag into the bin, pushing the lid down to crush it on top of the rest. A car pulled up at the junction, right in front the house and Nancy looked up. The driver's profile looked familiar. The wind blew and Nancy pulled her cardigan round her body, straining to see the drivers face through the tinted window. The driver turned their head to look left and then right, trying to find a gap in the flow of cars. As they turned their head towards Nancy, they locked eyes. Nancy frowned; it was that girl again. The one who'd knocked on her door and knew her name. Nancy took a step forward, folding her arms across her chest. With that, the car quickly pulled out onto the busy main road and disappeared into the flow of traffic.

CHAPTER 27

The Next Day

"Namaste"

Alex and Nancy sat crossed legged on the grey fluffy carpet, hands pressed together in prayer and reverently bowed forwards.

A tingling shimmer showered over Nancy's sensitive skin, and she shivered, the blonde hairs on her forearms standing to attention. It felt like a beam of sunshine was illuminating her face, and she felt warm, peaceful and safe. She sat for a moment, trying to bathe in the feeling, until Alex brought her crashing back to reality.

"Well that was fucking lovely! I can't believe I just thought yoga was for women who refused to shave their pubic hair."

Nancy smirked, keeping her eyes closed, hands still firmly pressed together. She was determined to keep swimming in the twinkling water, glittery droplets settling on her skin, golden breath delving deep into her gut and flooding her veins. But she was being shaken by the shoulders by Alex and she gave in.

"Bloody hell Al, it's like doing yoga with Lottie!" Nancy groaned.

Alex laughed, jumping up. She got Nancy into a headlock and held her tight to her chest, smacking loving kisses all over her head.

"I'd advise you to do yoga alone if you don't want to be interfered with" warned Alex. "I can't help it when I see you looking all happy and peaceful, I just want to schnuffle you!" she said in an animated voice.

Nancy laughed and reached up and wrapped her arms around her best friend's neck, and used her to pull herself up to standing. Alex moaned as her back strained with the weight of Nancy dangling off of her. They both laughed and hugged, like no time had passed. They were 12 year old girls again, when their whole lives revolved around one another. She breathed Alex, from the moment she knocked for her to walk to school, to the time Alex would drop her off, after walking home, laughing, arm in arm. Sometimes Nancy would carry on walking with Alex to her house, and then walk back, just so she could steal another 10 minutes of her time. They'd never even had an argument, not once.

Alex was the one person who knew Nancy better than she knew herself, who could see into her soul, who knew how she was feeling before she did. She had endless patience and tried to help her understand her feelings. She asked her how she was at random times of the day and wanted to know the real answer. Alex loved Nancy for exactly who she was. Nancy didn't know how, seeing as she didn't have a single clue who the fuck she was herself.

They released one another, Alex ruffling Nancy's hair once more and marching off into the kitchen to make their coffees and Nancy followed.

"So how are you feeling?" Alex asked, placing a mug under the coffee machine spout and pressing the red button.

"Fine, you?" Nancy replied.

Alex cocked an eyebrow like she always did.

Nancy felt a tightening in her throat, her lower lip trembling, eyes filling with fresh, salty pools of tears. Alex was at her side.

"Hey, hey what's this? I knew something was up!" She kicked herself. She'd been watching Nancy over the last few months, knowing there was something on her mind but every time she asked, Nancy brushed her off.

Nancy clung onto Alex, tears streaming down her face, lifting her head away from her shoulder so she could take desperate gasps of air in between sobs. Alex sushed her gently, stroking her hair, just like her mother had when, well, when she was little.

"Argh, where did that come from?" laughed Nancy, hurriedly wiping her hands across her face. "Sorry about that, must have been the yoga making me all sensitive. I'll be a fucking vegan next, you watch" she said before blowing her nose into a tissue that Alex had passed her from the kitchen side.

Alex led her into the lounge and beckoned her to sit on the sofa.

"Really Al, I'm fine, please" as Alex pushed her friend by the shoulders to sit down.

"Talk to me Nance. It's me."

Nancy resisted, trying to shuffle to the edge of the sofa, to stand back up. Alex placed a loving but firm hand on her knee. She remained seated.

"Al I'm fine, maybe it's almost my time of the month or something". Nancy blew her nose again.

"Listen, I know you are suffering. I can see it in your eyes. I know you are going to hate me, but I have booked you a session with a therap–"

"Alex! No, bugger off I'm not doing it again" Nancy said, shaking her head.

"Listen to me. He's not a shrink, he is just someone you can just talk to who can help you sort through all the things on your mind. You seem to have the weight of the world on your shoulders and you can't carry on like this. It's no way to live".

Nancy started howling then, a surrender to the pain she felt inside. She bent forward, laying her chest on her upper thighs and just shook with sadness at every sob. Alex rubbed her back and made soothing sounds of comfort. When Nancy was all cried out, she sat up and blew her nose again, laughing at herself.

"Look at me, what a mess eh?' Nancy sniffed.

"I know you won't like what I'm about to say, but you listen to me and you listen good. You have been through a lot in your life. What happened in your past."

Nancy stiffened, her stomach lurching, palms sweating, heart racing like a lab rat.

"You've never dealt with it. Then there's Nate, Rupert, the girls, you are carrying so much guilt, shame, responsibility, how can you expect to have a kind voice inside? I mean I try to be that voice, but you can't even hear me over all those other twats in there."

Nancy laughed, and returned to a wobbly, sorrowful frown.

Tears kept pooling and silently cascading over the rim of her lower lids. She stared at a stain on the carpet and thought she would get the Vanish out after this. In fact, she would do a big clean today. Make it spick and span. She'd had a cry now. Time to push this feeling back deep down where it belonged.

They sat together in silence for a few minutes in the end, Nancy desperately trying to think of anything else than what Alex was trying to make her think about, but Alex waited patiently, expelling soothing sounds and comforting touch.

"It's just…" Nancy choked on the words.

"It's alright Nance, just let it come out"

"I don't know what it is. It's like a dull ache that permanently lives deep inside me. I hate it and am lost without it all at once. Whenever I am momentarily relieved from it, being with you and the girls, running, yoga, I feel guilty. I am briefly relieved from the pain and torture that splays across my stomach lining, before I am once again engulfed in suffering, like I don't deserve to feel any way but agonised. I'm so fucking tired" she howled.

Alex kept her hand on Nancy's back, rubbing up and down the length of her spine and shushing her, whispering *it's alright* with each stroke. Eventually Nancy started to calm down and rubbed her exhausted, wet eyes, leaning back on the sofa, drained.

"You are tortured Nance. I know you think if you stay in this state of misery, then you will be punished, as you believe you deserve to be for not telling on Granville, for not being enough for Nate, for lying to Rupert…'

Nancy stared at the carpet stain through her aching, red eyes, hardly blinking, trying to ignore what Alex was saying.

"I know you don't want to, but I do think you should go to see this therapist" Alex said gently.

"No thanks. Raking everything up, I'll just be more upset everyday" Nancy said, shaking her head.

"What if I told you that you might feel better? I did" assured Alex.

Nancy looked up.

"You saw someone? You?"

"Yes, don't act so surprised" Alex chuckled.

"I was just so full of hate and anger after Gray left me. I just couldn't believe that I'd ever be happy again. There was a dark cloud over everything. Every time I laughed at a party I felt like an actress, playing a part."

"I wish you'd told me! I could have helped" Nancy said.

"You did, believe me. Giving me a home, giving me a family, drinking endless glasses of wine with me, talking about it over and over, egging his car. Believe me, you saved me."

They both laughed and cringed at the memory of a moonlight attack, drunkenly launching eggs at Grayson's car in the driveway of Alex's old house one night after several bottles of wine whilst Tilly was at her grandmothers. Not one of Nancy's finest moments, but the mob mentality had taken over.

"But I needed professional help, someone who wouldn't just understand me, but someone who knew how to force me to find myself. To get to know me. To forgive me. To forgive him. To heal and move on."

They sat there in silence for a few moments, listening to the dull murmur of cars driving along the main road outside, the washing machine running in the utility room.

"Okay." Nancy finally breathed.

"Ata girl" said Alex, putting her arms around her shoulders and pulling her in for a cuddle.

"I will sort it all out for you, you just need to turn up, so you can't over think it and put your head in the sand" Alex said gently into her ear.

Nancy started numbly over her shoulder at the stain.

CHAPTER 28

Then

Age 6

"So, how did you feel when he did that to you Nancy?"

Nancy sat, ankles crossed, thighs pressed together, sweaty palms clamped together, hunching forward, trying to line her forearms up with the join in her lap. She said nothing.

"Nancy?" the counsellor pushed.

Words that made no sense rose in Nancy's chest and she pressed them back down again. She liked the silence that ensued after the lady asked her a horrible question. Nancy was in charge. She didn't have to speak. No one could make her. So, if she could just concentrate all of her attention into pressing her forearms together and getting them perfectly in line with her pressed together legs, then the lady would leave her alone.

"Nancy, I want you to understand something extremely important okay?"

Nancy dug her nails into the backs of her clasped hands.

"This was not your fault. Not in any way."

Nancy's throat constricted. She was being choked by pain, fury, shame, guilt, disgust.

A groan of agony emulated from Nancy's little throat and she slammed her face into her hands. She wanted to scratch her face off, she wanted to yank her skin off her flesh, she wanted to cut off everything he'd ever touched on her body and watch it burn. She wanted to burn him. She felt bile rise in her chest, she wanted to punch something. Her temples throbbed and her face was full of hot, blazing blood. She pressed her fingers into the top of her scalp. She felt disgusting and she hated herself. Nancy tried to rein herself in, she tried to stop thinking about it so she would stop crying in front of this stranger, but she was hysterical and her head pounded, which only made her cry more. The counsellor rose from her seat, walked a few paces to her desk and picked up the box of tissues and took them over to her. She gently touched Nancy's shoulder, and she looked up through bloodshot eyes to gratefully take a tissue. She wiped her eyes and blew her nose, and clutched the tattered tissue in her fist, little cries reverberating out of her mouth. She must have been there for quite a while, and spent most of it refusing to talk. She hoped they were nearly out of time and she could run to Mum in the waiting room. The lady returned to her seat with a sympathetic frown. Nancy wished she could swap places with her. Be the person helping everyone else with their problems, instead of having the problems herself. That's what she would do when she grew up, so she didn't have to talk about hers. But then she thought how sad she would be if she had to go home every night and worry about the way these poor children felt, and decided against it. She would be a primary school teacher instead. That looked fun.

"I want you to know, and this is very important, that you are a child. And it is the responsibility of adults to behave properly. If they don't behave properly, it's their fault, not yours. So no matter what you think you did, or what he told you to do, you did not deserve this, you didn't."

The inbreath caught in Nancy's throat, not believing a word the counsellor said. She wanted to, she wanted to so badly, but she couldn't. She believed with her whole heart that it was her fault. He'd told her so. Doing cartwheels in the lounge in a dress, forgetting to close her legs when she was watching the television, not telling Mummy, thinking it was a fun game, because he told her it was. It was all her fault and she knew it, no matter what anyone else said. Her molars squeaked as she clenched her jaw. She was disgusting. She would feel disgusting for the rest of her life. She wished she was dead. She wished he was dead. She wondered how long she would have to wait until then.

CHAPTER 29

Then

Age 7

"There's Grandma's car!" exclaimed Robert, pointing at the silver mini metro parked at the multistory car park.

Her mother stiffened, grabbing Nancy's forearms like she'd been naughty, and shoved her behind her, her eyes darting like a deer looking through the grass for a lioness.

There was a hushed conversation between her parents, walking like penguins trying to protect their egg from a biting storm.

It seemed no one was actually in the car, so her parents told her they'd decided to make a quick dash to the shops, and head back home. Her parents seemed to relax, and so did Nancy, running ahead with Robert to climb on the walls either side of the walkway towards the shops. Her parents hung back, twittering, arguing too quietly to hear. What where they arguing about? Nancy felt important, but for all the wrong reasons. Like she was ruining everyone's fun.

They'd come to the shops because Mum had wanted a new coat, but Nancy knew that they would come home with more than just that, they always did. They sat there, bored, on the chairs outside the changing rooms with all the other Dads, but not with their Dad. He was running back and forth from the shop to the changing room where Mum waited, fetching other sizes of the clothes she'd picked, and new items he thought she might like. They would go on like this for a while, and Robert and Nancy would entertain themselves by kicking each other and secretly laughing at other people around them. She thought her Dad was normal, but when she looked around at all of the other Dads around her, she realised he was special. The other men were fed up of waiting for their wives, and their faces said it all. Their Dad was thrilled to be helping his wife. They were having fun together. That's what she wanted in a husband, when she grew up.

Mum emerged eventually with quite a few items draped over her forearm, holding the rejects in her other hand. She passed them to Dad to hang on the rail by the exit but he pulled out the black velvet off the shoulder bodice hiding within. He held it up with a questioning look, and she thumbed through the clothes she was keeping, signifying she already had too much. He hung the bodice up in front of her and mouthed 'wow' and she grinned. He hung it over his arm and took the rest of the clothes from her. He leaned in to kiss her cheek and whispered in her ear and as he pulled away, Mum flushed, her eyes sparkling, a smile sitting in the corners of her mouth as she watched Dad walk over to the till to pay. She tapped both Nancy and Robert on their heads and they followed her over to the shop exit to wait for Dad. Nancy nuzzled into her mother, and she bent down and kissed her on the top of her head, whilst Robert was face down in his Gameboy.

"You have the best Daddy ever, did you know that?"

"I know" Nancy smiled, looking over at Dad at the counter.

He joined them at the exit.

"Shall we?" he said in his poshest voice, before leaning in to kiss Mum once more. They walked out onto the street into a sea of shoppers, bustling along, heads down, coats wrapped high around their necks to protect them from the cold and bleak January weather. They were swept along in the stampede, Mum's hand coming down in front of Nancy's face for her to hold. Mum put a protective and guiding arm around Robert shoulder, so that he could carry on playing his computer game without looking up. Dad, who was tall enough to see over the crowds, beckoned Mum with his head to follow him back in the direction of the car. *Phew, they were heading home*, Nancy thought. She didn't want to be dragged around any more shops. She wouldn't believe it until she was actually buckled into the car though, Mum always found one more shop to stop at after the 'last one, I promise'.

She stayed close to Mum, plastic and paper bags bashed Nancy in the face as they overtook fellow shoppers. A pram rammed the back of her heels. She knew better than to make a fuss. You were more likely to get a 'watch it' than an apology at her age. She was staring at the back pockets of the people in front when all of a sudden, her mother stopped dead, tugging Nancy's arm to a stop, a man from behind running into her, knocking her slightly.

"Oh good place to stop lady!" he cursed, weaving round them.

Nancy looked up to see her mother's face, ashen.

"Pete!" she shouted to Dad, who stopped a few steps in front too. They looked in the same direction, frozen to the spot, unsure of what to do. She looked to Robert to see what was going on, but he was still ensconced in the game. Mum let go of Nancy's hand for a moment, but turned her round so they were facing one another and pressed Nancy's head into her coat. Nancy could feel the metal of Mums zipper indenting into her skin. But Mum's hand remained firmly on her ear, the other hand covering her eyes. Nancy was too scared to ask what she was being shielded from, her heart drumming, mouth dry. She closed her eyes and clung to her mother, awaiting direction. All of a sudden, Mum was bending down to scoop her up. Nancy wrapped her legs around her mother's hips and her arms around her neck. She buried her head into her shoulder, eyes still squeezed shut. Mum held her under her bottom and walked quickly in the other direction, Robert following her closely like a duckling. He had put his Gameboy away. Dad swore at a few people who called him names, and he used their shopping bags to guide a path for his family. Nancy clung to her mother all the way back to the car. She was strapped in, and kissed 3 times each by her parents. They drove back in silence, looking out of the windows, Dad holding Mum's hand tightly on the gearstick.

CHAPTER 30

Then

Age 30

She'd slept well a baby, waking only once or twice for a feed as, she'd got older. Nancy couldn't have been more grateful, after the restless nights she'd had with Tilly left her weepy and hopeless most days. She wasn't sure if she'd have even slept anyway, and at least the baby gave her someone to blame for being awake through the darkest hours of the day. On the 4am feed, she looked down at Lottie's innocent face, brushed with new silk skin, her tiny, well thought-out lashes resting lightly on her under-eye, whilst she drank gently from Nancy's breast. Nancy was both enveloped in both love and fear. She couldn't imagine life without her. She was terrified of life with her in it. Her heart groaned at the thought of anything bad happening to her. She scolded herself for bringing something so perfect, so innocent and vulnerable into this hateful world. She thought of all the other babies, toddlers and children around the world who could eventually break Lottie's heart or hurt her, when they were most likely innocents themselves right now. Nancy's heart was sore, it ached for peace. She feared tragedy, how she would ever cope if anything horrendous happened to her children. She swallowed the bile that rose in her chest like an eruption of burping lava, coating her esophagus, causing her to rub and press against her chest bone, wincing.

She placed Lottie back into the moses basket and rocked her back and forth until she was sure she had definitely drifted off. She laid her tired head down on the pillow, thoughts of the past immediately rushing in. She closed her eyes, rage descending. What if someone did to her babies what Granville did to her? How had Mum and Dad coped knowing what he'd done to their little girl? They'd ended up getting divorced when she was at the end of her teens after a year or two of problems, that Nancy didn't want to understand. It had been painful, but, being twenty at the time, she'd drunk through it, filling as many days of the week as possible with a party. But she'd always wondered, if it was her fault, always anxious about being away from them, that they'd hardly had any time for themselves. They'd never complained, but Nancy knew what they had sacrificed so that she was happy. Yet she'd never done what she really wanted to do, for fear of upsetting their lives further, and that was to have Granville punished for what he'd done before he died. She wanted to tell Grandma how much she'd hurt her before she missed the chance. She wanted her to be sorry. She wanted him to be sorry.

She replayed the night after Nancy had told Dad about what Granville had been doing to her, him vanishing out the door. She recalled the sound of him running down the gravel path and their car screeching out of their road, her Mum panicking, calling after him. Mum had held her tightly for absolutely ages. No tears had fallen from Nancy, but her shoulder had been awfully wet from the ones that fell from her mother.

She knew Granville been arrested the day Dad disappeared, after Nancy told him. Her parents had told her when she'd asked as a teenager. They hadn't pressed charges apparently, because a psychiatrist had told Mum and Dad that Nancy was unlikely to remember. She was due to start a new school and they didn't want people to know, didn't want her to be treated differently. He'd denied it anyway, and as there was no proof or statement from the victim, he was free to go. He'd gone back home afterwards, but his bag was on the doorstep. Grandma had thrown him out and he'd had to go and live somewhere else. Mum and Dad had been there for Grandma, said they would share their life together for always; holidays, Christmasses, weekends. They were to live it as a new family of five. But after a while, Grandma decided she didn't want a life with just them, that she missed Granville and asked him to come back to live with her. They'd stayed married and their lives were once again irreversibly flipped upside down.

Mum and Dad had kept a reluctant, strained relationship with her after that, and we only saw Grandma occasionally on her own. She came down for birthdays, she came down for Christmas morning but had to get back to Granville. He dropped her off so she could have a glass or two of sherry but waited outside to collect her. As they got older, Grandma had taken them out for the day. Ice skating, swimming, cinema, bowling. She loved it. They always got a McDonalds too. She loved her other grandparents dearly, her mothers parents, more, absolutely. They were sweet but old fashioned in comparison. They didn't drive and cared more for taking her to church, buying her educational books or frilly frocks, and to take them to cafes for tea and sandwiches. Nancy loved it, her time with them was innocent, quaint, sweet and safe. But Grandma was fun.

As the years went by, Nancy had grown into a young woman, and thoughts of confusion, disgust and hurt roamed her body and mind. She couldn't talk about it, not even with herself. She couldn't even write it. She pushed it down, deep down until it caused a permanent ache at the top of her tummy. And that's where it lived. Set up camp, only ever to be temporarily washed away with vodka, only to be rebuilt on a larger scale the next day. She'd simply borrow the happiness from tomorrow.

Nancy rolled over onto the other pillow, trying to settle. *What if either of them died before they were punished?* She wanted them to suffer, but just in her imagination. Despite what they'd done to her, she didn't want to inflict pain back. She wanted them to be sorry of course, to beg for forgiveness, but she didn't want him to rot in jail on her watch. Nor did she wish for her Grandma to blame her or give Dad even more grief every time he somehow displeased her.

Dad sometimes told Nancy that Grandma would moan about her to him, if Nancy hadn't sent her birthday card on time, or the fact Nancy wouldn't let her meet the girls or have a photograph of them. Nancy had felt so furious. Grandma was lucky Nancy had even given her the time of day after her betrayal of accepting Granville back into her home and life. Nancy needed to punish her, both of them, in order to move on. But how? She turned over again and a wave of tiredness washed over her. She drifted into a fitful sleep, dreaming that Grandma and Granville were laughing about her, whilst they ate their dinner.

CHAPTER 31

Then

Age 20

"You may now kiss the bride!" announced the priest as the happy couple embracing as husband and wife.

The congregation clapped and cheered, women on the front row blotted the corners of their eyes with screwed up tissues, the rest quickly gathering their order of service and belongings, eager to get to the reception to consume the first of many alcoholic beverages.

The guests followed the newlyweds down the aisle and out into the graveyard for photographs, the most important family members were beckoned to line up next to the bride and groom. The guests chatted and laughed, and complimenting each another's outfits. They made their way outside the church, and excitely threw confetti over the newlyweds before they were bundled into a Rolls Royce, waving excitedly to their friends and family.

"See you there!" the bride called out the window. Ladies hobbled and gents crunched over gravel to get back to their cars to follow.

"Well wasn't that nice, first of my Grandchildren to get married off" said Grandma from the front seat, as they all got in. Nancy sat in the back with Robert and his fiancé Andrea, her father in the driving seat.

"Yes" they all agreed in unison.

"Claire is such a good Granddaughter"

Nancy flinched. *Did she just say that?*

"She emails me every week and calls too. She is so sweet and considerate".

Nancy's mouth went dry. Her tongue velcroed to the roof of her mouth.

"Chris too. Although he will obviously have more on his plate now. New wife, no doubt a baby on the way before we know it. But he still always takes the time to contact me and have a good chat."

She felt Robert bristle next to her. Nancy couldn't even look at him. Blood flushed her face, her temples pulsed. The audacity of Grandma speaking so proudly of their cousins and the way they treated her. The way that Robert and Nancy would have treated her if she hadn't chosen Granville over them. Robert still hadn't told Andrea about it all as far as Nancy knew, and she probably wondered why the hell everyone was being so hostile.

Dad yanked the steering wheel round, and spun off the gravel, making a few of the old dears nearby hold their handbags up to their chests in horror.

He drove much too fast down the country lanes back to the hotel they were staying at, where the reception was being held. He put the radio on, and drummed the steering wheel obnoxiously. Grandma held onto the handle above her on the passenger side.

"Slow down, goodness you drive like a teenager".

Dad continued at the same speed for a few moments, clenching the steering wheel, knuckles white, before gently tapping the brakes to bring them below the speed limit, and turning off the radio. She could see his furious expression in the rearview mirror.

Nancy stared out the window, watching the trees, bushes and houses with small doors rush by. Everyone must be so happy out there. The squirrels, the birds, the people who live in those cottages. Rage and hurt bubbled beneath her surface, the car silent with tension. A laugh rumbled in her throat which she managed to swallow back down and disguise as a cough. How was *she* the dreadful granddaughter? Why wasn't this woman sorry? If anything, she should be giving her special dispensation for not keeping in contact. How could Grandma sit there and praise her cousins for serving her so well, when she hadn't served Nancy when she needed her most? Grandma didn't deserve Nancy's time or energy, yet she still got it. She still bought her birthday and Christmas presents, cards, she took her to hospital appointments, invited her to family parties and acted like nothing was wrong. But no, she wasn't going to call for idle chit chat like her cousin Claire did, who was oblivious to what Grandma and Granville had done. Nancy didn't want to know about any of this. Nancy didn't want to know. Not until Grandma could tell Nancy at least 100 reasons why she chose a paedophile over her.

CHAPTER 32

Present

Nancy stared at her phone. She'd typed Rupert's name into the Facebook search engine, careful not to write it and post it as her status and let the whole world know she was thinking about him. She knew she shouldn't press the spy glass. She wouldn't like what she saw. But she was 3 glasses in, and reason had been packed into it's spotty red hankerchief, hung off a wooden pole and trudged off into the distance. She clicked, and she was on his page. Photographs of him loaded. She scanned the dates, who was tagged, where they were tagged. It was mostly group photographs, none of which Rupert had posted himself. He had just been tagged in them. He hadn't posted anything since Christmas, a round robin message to wish everyone a Happy Christmas, so that he didn't have to spend the day replying to each individual message. There were handsome men in the photos, Rupert's arm around them posing in Central Park, by the Statue of Liberty, in glamorous looking cocktail bars. There were women, beautiful women in the photos too. Pearly straight teeth and flawless matte skin, clearly American she thought. Nothing she could ever compete with. She gulped, realising she was letting saliva pool in her mouth. She took a large swig of her wine, finishing the glass. She reached over to the side table and replenished her glass, wiping the red drip that pooled around the base on the thigh of her pyjama bottoms. She scrolled some more, until she came across a photo of the two of them, a long way down the page. Filtered of course, she'd been hungover from staying up late drinking wine with him the night before, shadows under her eyes from the little sleep they'd had after rolling around on the floor together. But she looked so happy, her head against his chest, tucked under his chin, cheek pressed against coat, his arm around her shoulders, squeezing her in tight whilst holding the camera up above his smiling face to take a selfie. She swallowed, remembering the smell of his aftershave, the feel of his arm tight around her, the way he'd kissed her after they'd taken the picture. He didn't just let go of her like Nate did after taking a photo with her. She and Nate looked happy in their photographs, but no sooner had the flash gone off, he'd let her go, moving on to the next thing. She took a deep painful breath in, her heart sore. She clicked off Rupert's page, and looked at the gorgeous picture of the girls on the home screen of her phone. Tilly, looked just like her fortunately, but Lottie looked more and more like her Daddy, now she was looking at his picture. The same mischievous smirk. She placed her phone face down on the sofa and took another large sip. Would he ever return? Would she ever be able to tell him what she'd done? What his father had done to keep her and Lottie out of their lives? She would lose the money if he knew, surely. But if she ever saw Rupert when she was with Lottie, he would know in a heartbeat she was his. And if she said to Hell with the money, and chose Rupert instead, would he want to be in Lottie's life? No, she thought. He would despise her for her lies, the deceit. He'd be furious that she'd plotted against him with his own father, would make a half-arsed attempt to be in Lottie's life and then Lottie would have Daddy issues because of it. Right now, Lottie knew where she stood in life, her mother was all she needed. If Nancy introduced him and he didn't want to know, they would all be in for a world of emotional and financial pain. She shook her head over and over, affirming her decision to leave him out of it and get on with their lives. She yawned, picked up her glass and got off of the sofa, commending herself that there was still a small glass left in the bottle. She walked into the kitchen, placed the bottle next to the oven to finish off when she was cooking the next night. She placed the glass in the dishwasher, added a tablet and ran it. She turned off the lights downstairs and clicked on the landing light and ascended the carpeted stairs. Her phone pinged. She looked at it and didn't recognize the number. Pinged again, and again. Nancy's brow furrowed, it was late, almost midnight. She paused half way up the stairs and unlocked the phone to read the messages.

Nancy...

You can't ignore me.

I know.

Nancy's heart hammered as she stared at the messages on the screen. She replied.

Who is this???

The three dots appeared signifying they were typing, but then they disappeared. Nancy stared, breathing heavily, willing the dots to reappear. They didn't.

CHAPTER 33

1 Month Later

"What brought you here today Nancy?"

Nancy looked down at her cold, clammy hands, interlocked together as if in prayer. She played with her rings, twisting and pulling at them and noticed a piece of dry skin below her cuticle on her pinky. She lifted into her teeth and gnawed until she successfully pulled it from her finger. She pressed her tongue against the sore left behind, the taste of metallic blood seeping into her mouth. She continued to bathe the wound in her saliva, until he cleared his throat gently. Nancy didn't look up, just searched her hands and nails for any other snags in need of extraction. The therapist tried a different tack.

"From what you said on the phone, you experienced something in your childhood, that you would like us to discuss together".

Nancy fidgeted, her pulse quickening. Her hands felt like they'd been washed in a basin and left undried. She rearranged herself in the chair, crossed her legs the other way to get comfortable but still felt as though she'd been sprinkled with itching powder. She'd come after dropping the girls off at school and had dressed like she had her shit together to try and fool herself and the therapist. She'd tied her dark blonde hair into a neat bun, tucked a cream blouse into a pair of smart black cigarette trousers and donned a pair of slip on loafers. She was sliding around inside the shoes, her feet sweatier than her hands and they only stayed on her by gripping at the sole with her toes. She wished she had worn cosy joggers and trainers. Something soft and comfy so that she could have just run out of the room in should she need to. Nancy cleared her throat and sat up in her chair, reached over to the side table next to her to take a sip out of the plastic cup of water that she had brought in with her from the waiting room water cooler.

"I'm sorry this must have been the most silent this room's ever been eh?" Nancy laughed, fidgeting again.

"Just take your time" he said.

Alex had found her a therapist at the same practice she'd been to, some new age place, where the receptionist looked only a little older than Tilly. She'd been assigned to Doctor 'G', who specialised in childhood trauma. She's spent more time in the week building up to the sessions wondering what the fuck the 'G' stood for, than actually worrying about the therapy itself.

Nancy stared at the carpet for what felt like a lifetime. She could hear the traffic down below, muted by the closed windows and the height of the building. She imagined everyone circling the roundabout outside the counsellor's office had not a problem in the world, apart from being late to a meeting or irritated by the traffic. She knew within, this couldn't possibly be true, and she was being a self-indulgent, narcissistic prick thinking that her problems were bigger than anybody else's. She kicked herself for thinking like that. It was simply that she just felt alone. Like she was the only one that was childishly burying her head in the sand, unwilling and unable to speak, even in the safety of a professional's office. No one dragged her here. Well, Alex kind of had but she had driven herself here and sat in this chair without her hands tied behind her back. She cleared her throat.

"I don't really know what to say." Nancy spoke into the air, her words hanging in the quiet room.

"Why don't we start with your childhood? Would you like to tell me who was involved in the thing that's hurting you?" he said calmly, pushing his black, thick framed glasses up his nose and crossing his legs.

Silence played loudly in the room, Nancy gathering herself before she spoke.

"My Grandma. And her husband, who's not my real grandfather, by the way. And she's my Dad's Mum" Nancy explained.

Nancy breathed out, her lip trembled, her eyes on the carpet, vision blurred. She felt relieved, like she'd started an essay she had been putting off, followed by feeling horribly vulnerable. She'd pulled at the thread now. The door was open and this man could come in and move things around. Her stomach twisted, throat tightened, she felt fidgety in her knickers, she wanted to claw at her skin.

"And did he hurt you?"

Nancy's vision blurred further. She pulled at her fingernail.

There was silence whilst she gathered herself.

"Yes" she whispered, a tear dropping onto her lap.

"And did she hurt you?"

"No" Nancy replied.

"Well, not physically" she added.

"Did he sexually abuse you?"

The question echoed in the air like it has been asked in a tunnel under a railway bridge.

Nancy cleared her throat and recrossed her legs.

She nodded, wanting to peel her itching, filthy skin off her bones.

"How old were you when this happened Nancy?" he asked.

"Three" said Nancy, gritting her teeth and making two fists in her lap.

He wrote something on his note pad.

"And when did this take place?

"When I used to stay at my Grandma's when my parents went away for weekends or nights out." Nancy sniffed, another tear dripping onto her trousers.

"And where was your Grandma?" he asked.

"She was there. In the kitchen mostly. He used to do things to me in my bedroom at their house. He'd tell Grandma we were making surprise presents for her, things like that. And then come back in the night too".

Nancy used to the back of her hand to wipe away the tears that had fallen onto her cheek. She reached for the tissue box next to her water on the table and blew her nose loudly.

"Sorry" Nancy apologised.

"Don't apologise, you are doing really well. Just take your time" he smiled gently. He had a kind face, short dark hair and large eyebrows. He looked like he was in his thirties, so he couldn't have been that far into his career, but he seemed to know what he was doing, like he was born to do it. She preferred him to the lady she'd seen when she was little. She'd seemed so scary, like she was really cross or something. This guy looked like nothing phased him. The things she'd told him hadn't seem to make him angry or sad, so maybe he could help her feel the same way.

She grabbed a few tissues and tapped her face, and twisted them round and round in her hands. She could feel him looking at her, and the longer the silence went on, the more awkward she felt, and the harder it was to start talking again. He crossed his legs again, his bright blue eyes behind his specs, resting gently on her. She felt hot, and she wanted to go.

"What he did to you…" he said into the quiet room.

Nancy stiffened.

"…was not your fault Nancy."

Hot salty tears rolled and rolled. Nancy continued to stare at the carpet. She covered her face and silently sobbed, shoulders sagging, furious fingertips pressing hard into her hairline. She wrung out her lungs, took a large breath in and on the exhale, a loud, animalistic groan emanated from within. She wailed; an embarrassing, desperate cry filling the quiet room. It was all she could hear. She was so aware of herself, but she couldn't stop. She kept her wet face planted firmly in her palms, hot, headachy, tired. She wished her Mum was with her so she could speak on her behalf. She would tell him to leave Nancy alone and drive her home to bed. She didn't want to talk anymore, not that she had talked much anyway. She just wanted this ache to go away. For someone to please take it away. She just couldn't do it.

CHAPTER 34

Then

Age 15

"That'll be £6.22 please".

The gentleman handed over a crumpled five pound note and thumbed several silver coins into her outstretched hand.

Nancy's heart beat under her Nirvana t shirt, not that she knew any of their songs bar their main hit, and she hoped no one would ever strike up a conversation about it with her. She hated working out the customer's change under pressure. She'd heard the shop owner was going to buy and install a new till soon, which would tell them how much change to give, but for now she had to work it out herself. She placed the note in the till drawer under the clip, and looked down at the coins in her hand, immediately forgetting what she'd charged him. She counted the coins in her hand and tried to remember which note he'd given her. It was a fiver wasn't it? Or was it a tenner. Sometimes customers liked to be clever and give a larger note and some coins so they could get a smaller note back in change. He could have done that. The gentlemen huffed, sliding his folded paper under his armpit and taking the celephane off the cigarette pack he was trying to purchase.

"Is there a problem?" he asked, his wild eyebrows raised, stale smoke emanating from his breath.

"No, sorry" flustered Nancy.

Think! Okay, he gave you a fiver, two fifty pence pieces, and two twenties. She owed him 8p.

She took the change out of the register and handed it to him. He stated at it.

"You are missing another ten pence" he snarled.

"Sorry!" Nancy sweated, and grabbed another silver coin and handed it to him, red faced.

He walked away, muttering under his breath, placing a cigarette in his mouth and lighting it as he pinged through the shop door onto the pavement, the bell announcing his exit.

Nancy felt tears of embarrassment pricking in her eyes. She wasn't bad at maths, she was just bad at maths under pressure. She hated this job, she wanted to quit. But she earnt £21 a week for two evenings and a Saturday morning, and when she got the change right, it was quite fun. Robert had a paper round at the same place and earned the same amount but had lug newspapers up a hill before school in the pissing rain, so she thought herself quite lucky to be inside without a strap digging into her shoulder. Plus, Alex used to come by the shop at midday on a Saturday when she finished, and they'd go off and spend the rest of the weekend together. Alex hadn't been happy when she first got the job, they liked to walk out of school on a Friday with youthful freedom coursing through their veins until the inevitable dread of Monday morning loomed on a Sunday evening when they remembered they hadn't done their homework. But Nancy had promised it was only short term and that she would always spend the rest of the weekend with her, at least with a bit more money to spend on McDonalds and cider.

It was Tuesday afternoon and the shop was now empty, so Nancy decided to go out to the stock room and grab some boxes of chocolate bars to stock the shelves. This would maybe absorb twenty minutes if she took her time, and there would almost be time to push the hoover around, bring the signs and newspaper stand in from outside, and start shutting up the shop. She loved that part. She walked from behind the counter, her low-hung flared jeans dragged along the floor, loops of chains hanging off her chunky black studded belt. Her midriff was showing, it always did. She flicked her dyed red hair out of her face, her heavily kohl lined eyes scanning the shelves to see what needed replenishing, as she walked past the shelves to the back. She stood in the stock room, boxes of chocolate bars and sweets stacked floor to ceiling. It was a bit scary back there. No surveillance, only on the shop floor. The creepy owner had pointed that out to her on her first day of the job. He was one of those men whose midriff always showed too. He didn't have a stomach like Nancy's though, his strained out the bottom of his tiny t-shirt like an overfilled water balloon. He had put his arm around her shoulders when he told her, her shoulder sucked into his wet, hairy armpit, the peppery stench catching at the back of her throat. She was polite so she didn't pull away but made sure she never went out the back when she was there on her own with him in the shop. She hardly drank anything in the afternoon beforehand so she wouldn't need the toilet which was back there too. She stayed on the shop floor, on camera and only went out the back if his wife was working too.

She decided she was hungry and was allowed to help herself to one chocolate bar a day. The heady scent of sugar and plastic made her stomach growl. She wondered how many bars she could inhale before she realised she was full. Mum was making her favourite creamy chicken pasta bake for dinner. She must save herself and bring the chocolate bar home with her for pudding, it wouldn't taste as good if she had a large bar of Galaxy now.

Nancy selected 5 boxes, and stacked them on the windowsill, then carried them under her chin back to the shop floor. There were still no customers, so she squatted down, ripped the boxes open and started to stack. She was on the second box, when the doorbell pinged, announcing a customer's arrival. She sighed inwardly, stood up straight and turned to see no one was there. She walked round behind the counter and looked at the camera which flicked between 4 different views of the shop floor. No one there. She looked up and strained her neck to see if anyone was down one of the aisles. She couldn't see anything. Huh. Did she imagine it? She looked down at the CCTV again, which changed views every 20 seconds or so. Nothing.

"Hello Nancy"

"Argh!" Nancy jumped out of her skin, hand on her chest.

"You scared me, sorry Sir I didn't see..."

The colour drained completely out of her face.

It couldn't be. It was. No it wasn't, was it? It was.

"Forty Silk Cut, a lighter, 2 lucky dips and this paper" he croaked, tossing The Daily Star onto the counter.

Nancy's hands trembled, stiff, cold and white. Useless. She turned and looked for the Silk Cut. She'd been told to memorise the layout of the cigarettes. Smokers didn't like to wait. But all she could see was a blur of blue, white, gold, red and black.

"Down the bottom dear" he rasped, his voice crawling over her cool pale skin.

Nancy bent down and picked two packets of silk cut up, and placed them on the counter.

"And a lighter. The red one"

She turned and bent down again, reaching behind to retrieve the plastic red lighter and placing it on the counter.

"And two lucky dips" he said with a grin, revealing his slimy yellow teeth.

"For tonight?" she whispered, to which he responded with a nod.

Nancy took two wobbly steps to her left to the lottery machine, put her ID key in, and pressed lucky dip twice, and the tickets printed.

She shakily placed them onto of the cigarette packets and started to type the prices into the till.

She hadn't swallowed since she'd seen him, but there wasn't much to swallow.

He put a twenty pound note down on the counter and she picked it up, desperately trying to figure out his change so he could leave.

"Haven't you grown?" he said.

She felt bile rising in her throat but swallowed it back down.

158

She worked out the total goods and opened the till to retrieve his change. She placed it on the counter and slid it towards him.

"I think I am missing a fiver, missy" he smirked.

Nancy looked down at the coins and realised she'd forgotten to add the note to his change. She flipped the clip up and slid the fiver out of the till and placed it next to the coins.

"Sorry" she said, eyes down on the money, her throat thick.

"That's okay. I forgive you" he smiled.

Her temples bulged like a bubble in a frog's throat.

He placed his hand on top of the money and lottery tickets and slid them into his other hand at the edge of the counter, and slipped it into his trouser pocket. He removed a cigarette from the packet and put the box in his inside jacket pocket and zipped up his beige coat.

"Well, I'll be seeing you. Oh, and it would be good if you could make more of an effort to keep in contact. Your poor Grandma has suffered so" he said, placing a cigarette between his stained teeth, before he walked out of the shop lighting it, the bell dinging behind him.

CHAPTER 35

Present

She didn't sleep. A large proportion of the twilight was filled with tossing, turning and staring into the abyss. She finally fell into an unexpected deep sleep around 5:30am, just as she was deciding she should just get up. It was fitful, filled with broken dreams of chasing, running, screaming, crying. People without faces, but with the intent to hurt her. She woke a few hours later, dribble in the corner of her mouth, the sound of the television downstairs and the clink of a spoon against a bowl, the girls having breakfast. She wiped the drool from her face, propped herself up on her elbow and reached over to her bedside. She necked half a pint of last night's water, slightly stale but thirst quenching. She placed it back on the coaster and laid back down on her pillow, catching her breath after gulping. She counted the wines and she decided she didn't feel too bad considering; the painkiller she'd popped in the night had obviously helped. It was Sunday, she had no plans other than cooking a roast and taking the girls out for a walk. She had to get their stuff ready for school and tidy the kitchen, before flopping on the sofa in front of a film, with big bowls of popcorn and crisps. She exhaled. A perfect Sunday. On her inhale, she felt agitated, anxious, an unclear memory prodding her. The messages. Her heart rate increased, jaw clenched, headache returned. *Who was that?* She grabbed her phone to see if they'd replied, but they hadn't. *I know.* Nancy felt like she'd swallowed a brick. Did they know about Lottie? About what Nancy did? Were they going to tell Rupert? Had Stephen paid someone to threaten her, so she would tell someone, breaking their contract and she would have to give him the money back? Or did they want a cut? Stephen was a wealthy man. They would know he paid her well in exchange for her silence. Had she watched much television, or could that actually happen? Nancy laid there, her mind spinning. She took a breath in and started to type.

CHAPTER 36

Then

Age 8

Nancy woke, knowing what day it was before she'd even opened her eyes. She was almost standing before, she was even conscious. It was her birthday and she'd been excited for it since they'd put the tree up. She was able to count down in chocolate, thanks to her advent calendar, which made waiting slightly more bearable. Nancy was impatient, a trait inherited from both her parents. She stumbled to the bathroom for a birthday wee, washed her hands quickly, dried them on her pyjamas and ran into their bedroom. 6:05 on the digital alarm clock. She knew it was a bit early for them, but they surely wouldn't be mad on her special day.

"Mummy" she whispered loudly.

"Muuuuummmmmyyy" she increased the length and volume.

"Mmm?" murmered Mum.

"Are you awake?"

"Mmm" she confirmed, eyes shut, motionless.

"Happy birthday poppet" croaked Dad from the other side of her, and she hopped from one foot to the other at the acknowledgement.

"Happy birthday baby" Mum whispered, eyes still closed. Her arm reached out and scooped her into bed under the duvet, and kissed her cheeks.

"My baby girl is getting so big"

Nancy's skin shivered with excitement. She wondered what presents she would get, what special treatment she would receive, what special dinner and what cake she'd been made. She liked to be surprised, so even though she had specified what she would like a few weeks ago, she had tried to forget as soon as she had asked for them.

"Lay here until your brother comes down and then we can open some presents" Mum whispered, awake now. Nancy climbed on top of her mother and threw her arms around her neck and they cuddled, Dad next to them with an arm over her back. They laid their for a while, Nancy feeling protected and adored. She loved them both so much. Not long after, Robert wandered into the bedroom, dozy from sleep.

"Happy birthday Smelly" he yawned.

Birthdays were a huge deal in their family and whoever's day it was meant they were treated like royalty on their special day. She loved her own birthday but loved other people's more, where she could spoil them and make a big fuss, make them feel special, the way they made her feel on her day.

She sat on the bed and opened a few presents, a new doll, some chocolates, a book and a board game from Robert for him to thrash her at. Then her parents gave her a box, about the size of a book, wrapped in pink ballerina paper, with a knowing smile they could hardly contain.

"Open it" Mum said.

Nancy slid her finger under the cellotape and pulled the paper off, a plain cardboard box underneath. She fiddled for the opening, pulling at the edges until something gave. She looked in and couldn't believe her eyes. Had they won the lottery? She tipped it out on to the duvet. It was a Walkman. An actual Walkman. Yellow with black headphones. She looked up at them, dumbfounded. They replied by gleefully nodding.

"Thank you, thank you, thank you!!!" Nancy squealed, kneeling up and lurching forward to embrace them.

"I cant believe it, a Walkman! This must have been so expensive!"

163

She was pressing the buttons on the edge, clicking play, stop, rewind and forward and the mechanism making a quiet whirring with each click.

"There's something else" Dad said with a smile, and pulled a small cassette box shaped gift from his side of the bed, wrapped in the same pink paper.

He handed it to her, and she tore it open. There they were, Gary, Robbie, Mark, Howard and Jason, cuddled up in open cream shirts and matching shell necklaces, laughing at nothing. The Everything Changes album. She felt utter joy and excitement in her belly. She couldn't believe her luck.

"The Take That Album too?! You are the best parents ever!" she cried, hugging them once more.

She frantically opened the cassette box, opened the Walkman and slid the cassette in and clapped it shut. She pressed play and quickly popped the headphones on her head.

"Girl, come over here, let me hold you for a little while, and remember, I'll always love ya…"

"Forever moooorrreeeee!!!" Nancy practically shouted the next lyric.

She jumped off the bed and started dancing around the bedroom, singing the lyrics she'd learnt, after seeing them on Top of the Pops.

Her parents exchanged a smug glance, their gift delivering pure and utter joy to their daughter on her special day.

Mum hopped out of bed, gathered the torn wrapping paper into a ball and told Robert to get ready for school. She held up five fingers to Nancy and mouthed five minutes. Nancy nodded, whilst singing completely out of tune, unable to hear anything but the music belting into her ears.

After a lovely day of being spoilt at school by her friends, Nancy came home to her birthday dinner of lamb chops, mashed potatoes and peas, with mint sauce. Grandma came too as she did every birthday, on her own.

"We love lamb chops, we only have them on special occasions really, but we do love them" said Grandma.

Everyone nodded and smiled and looked down at their plates trying to ignore the mention of 'we' once again, cutting what little meat they could away from the lamb bone.

"Nancy will have to show you her new Walkman after dinner, Mum" Dad said, changing the subject.

"Oh yes that sounds lovely Nancy, can you listen to all your favourite music on it?

"Yes, Grandma. I only have one Take That tape, but that's all I would ever want to listen to anyway" Nancy smiled.

"Well maybe you could add another to your Christmas list? We would love to get you another to listen to when you are bored of Take What"

Robert scoffed. Nancy, Mum and Dad kept sawing at the lamb, getting frustratingly little off the chop. Dad clattered his knife and fork down, which made Grandma and Mum jump, and picked up the bone with his hands, and started to gnaw at it. Mum went to scold Dad but thought better of it when she saw he was hot and bothered enough already.

Mum bought the cake out after dinner, a chocolate gateau as per Nancy's request. She loved it because it was more chocolate cream than sponge. Once they'd sung to her, she squeezed her eyes tight and wished to be happy and blew out her candles.

After dinner, they got down and the adults had cleared the dinner plates away, Nancy opened her gifts from Grandma. A dressing gown, a Barbie and two more board games. She thanked Grandma for her gifts. She could imagine playing lots of games with Mum and Dad over the Christmas holidays. Nancy and Robert were told to go upstairs and put their pyjamas on afterwards, as they had school the next day. They moaned of course, and dragged themselves up the stairs to get ready for bed. Nancy had almost changed, when the house phone rang. She pushed her head through her top and ran down the hallway to the landline in her parent's bedroom.

"Helloooo?" Nancy answered. She wasn't supposed to answer the phone like that because it could have been a customer for Dad, but she thought, seeing as it was her birthday, she would be forgiven.

"Hello Nancy. Happy Birthday dear" croaked a familiar voice.

"Thank you" Nancy politely replied, feeling sick.

"Is Grandma there? I was going to set off to pick her up now, if you have finished your birthday celebrations. Did you have a nice time?"

"Yes, thank you" Nancy replied, looking at her feet, her skin crawling and her stomach twisting.

She walked downstairs and handed the phone to Grandma.

She looked surprised at first and then realised who it would be.

"Oh hello" she smiled.

"Yes, yes, I am just finishing my tea. Why don't you set off in 10 minutes, we will be done by then. Yes. Yes. Okay love. See you soon"

She hung up. Mum and Dads faces were pale, Dad's jaw tight, Mum frowning.

"Well, night then" Nancy said.

"Night darling" Grandma said, holding out her arms.

"Did you have a lovely birthday?"

"Yes, thank you. And thank you for my presents" she answered politely.

"You are welcome. I will see you next week on Christmas morning to do this all over again!" she squeezed her tight and popped her feet back on the floor.

She walked over to her parents and gave them both a hug and a kiss and walked upstairs to bed. She climbed under her duvet and pulled the cover right up to her chin. She laid there, listening to the muted chatter downstairs. She pricked her ears, but couldn't make out what they were saying. Until their voices got louder.

"What? How else is he supposed to know when to leave?" she heard Grandma say.

There was more muffled conversation, and a door slammed. Her parents talked, voices slightly raised, Nancy could hear her mother crying. Oh no. She couldn't bear it. If her mother was upset, then how could she ever possibly be happy? She held her breath and listened. She heard the door to the front room close. She couldn't hear anything now. She laid there still for a few minutes, her mind whirring as to why her mother was crying. She stared into the darkness, her eyelids eventually growing heavy and drifted into a fitful sleep where she was at Grandma's in her bedroom, and not alone. Her perfect birthday had literally ended in a nightmare.

CHAPTER 37

Now

"How you feeling kid?" Dad asked

"Like I want to drink the bar dry" Nancy smirked.

Dad chuckled, and slid a tonic water across the table towards her, sans gin.

"Mmm hits the spot" she smacked her lips sarcastically.

Dad laughed again and sighed. They both stared at the same cardboard coaster on the round wooden table, that wobbled slightly on the busy beer scented carpet.

She'd sent the girls to her Mum's for the afternoon, and they'd skipped off happily, always elated to spend time with their Nannan who gave them unlimited attention and biscuits.

"He's not going to set fire to the house and we'll be trapped in there right?" Nancy asked, half smiling, half panicking.

Dad cracked a quick laugh.

"He's a really old man now, Nance. It takes him five minutes to get out of a chair, I think we could crawl out before he burned it down."

She looked down, but a slight weight lifted off her shoulders. Being trapped and burnt alive in his house, along with many other dramatic scenarios, had kept her awake until almost 5am.

"Still..." she said quietly, raising her brow.

"I'm not going to let anything happen to you Nancy" Dad promised, staring earnestly at her.

"I know" she said, still staring at the beer mat.

"I just keep getting that feeling of imposter's syndrome, you know when you are watching a film and shovelling popcorn into your face, like I'm watching someone else. I can't believe what I'm about to do"

"I know love" Dad reached over and placed his hand on hers. She resisted the urge to pull away, and looked up at him through her eyelashes, her lip starting a tremble.

"I'm so sorry, Nancy" said Dad.

"Dad. Stop" she said.

"I mean it. I'm really sorry this happened and I wish I could take it away. I wish I'd never gone on holiday with Mum and never taken you there. I wish Grandma had never remarried. I wish my Dad hadn't died. I wish I'd handled it differently" he said, his voice cracking.

Nancy took her other hand and placed it on his, sandwiching his hand between hers.

"Listen" she said.

"None of this was your fault, or mine, or anyone's but his. And hers. And we've all done our best, so don't ever apologise to me ever again. What are you apologising for? For loving me? Protecting me? Trying to help me? Keep the peace? You've done everything you could Dad, and you are in an impossible situation. But today we are going to hopefully get an explanation or an apology or something to help us move on."

"How are you so strong?" my Dad laughed, a tear escaping his eye and splashing on to the table, which he quickly swept away with his hand.

"I'm not Dad. But I've blamed myself for a really long time. And it's shit. And I don't want you to do the same. We were just living our lives, and they hurt us. And hopefully, today, they will tell us why" Nancy said, squeezing his hand.

"Well let's get going before we change our minds eh?" he winked and drained the last of his orange juice and lemonade. They stood up and silently walked to the car to drive to the house she hadn't set foot in since she was five years old.

CHAPER 38

Then

Age 10

"Here's just £170 because you passed Go but landed on Old Kent Road with two houses, which is mine, so I've kept £30?" questioned Nancy, as she slowly counted out the notes in Grandma's hand.

Grandma nodded encouragingly and congratulated her on her mental maths. Then she pretended to be annoyed that she'd been caught on the space and Nancy giggled. Nancy hated maths lessons, but she loved Monopoly, so she was always encouraged to be the Banker by her parents or Grandma, so she could practice. She found it really hard to do and hoped she'd never have a job where she had to give change.

They carried on playing, working their way round the board. Nancy owned most of the cheaper properties, and had put houses on a few. When she played with Robert he dominated the game, told her she was only allowed to own the browns, pinks and blues, and he would own the rest. She'd allowed this, until she cottoned on to what he was doing. She loved the victory, if she landed on Mayfair before he did. She didn't want to buy it, it was too expensive, but she was in a bargaining position to let her buy other forbidden properties, like the reds, as way of compromise. Same with the Stations. She would buy one of them, so that he couldn't own them all and fine the maximum fee if she landed on it, and then get him to give her too much money or more properties than the station was worth so that he could own all four. She loved that she'd gone from the manipulated to the manipulator. He still was in charge, he was older and male, and never let her forget it, and the game would still be over if he decreed it, usually by flipping the board and thumping her. But she finally had a small amount of power she had previously been denied, and she was giddy about that. She liked that other people were happy to own more expensive things than her, and she sat happily with her cheap and cheerful roads and streets and plenty of green in the bank.

"I just need a wee, two secs" Nancy said, standing up and walking across the carpet to the bathroom.

"Shall we take a little break? My legs have gone to sleep" said Grandma, holding onto Nancy's bed post to pull herself up to standing, hopping from foot to foot, wincing.

"Okay" Nancy shrugged and left the room.

When she came back, Grandma was sitting on her bed.

"What shall we do now?" Nancy asked, looking in her cupboard at her other board games.

"Anything you like. Just set it up whilst Grandma stretches her legs. Maybe something we can play on the bed"

Nancy selected Crocodile Dentist, a game where you extracted a plastic crocodiles teeth, one at a time, hoping you didn't pull the tooth that made it snap and scare the life out of you.

Nancy was setting it up, clicking each plastic tooth into the slot in its red, plastic gums, when Grandma quietly cleared her throat.

"Would you like to see Granville?" she asked.

Nancy froze. Silence thudded between them. Nancy didn't know what to say, so she kept clicking the teeth into the crocodile's mouth.

"He wasn't well Nancy. But he has seen a doctor and they have made him better."

Click. click. click.

Nancy's ears were ringing and the crocodile was blurring. Why was she saying this? She wasn't allowed to talk about him. There had been a 'hoohah' a little while ago, because whenever Grandma was round, she told stories of what they'd been up to, using 'we' all over the shop. She'd finally said something to Mum and Dad, who told Grandma to stop it. It hadn't stopped completely, but it improved. Still, every 'we' that was thrown into the conversation cut Nancy like a knife each time.

Had Mum and Dad put Grandma up to this? Said that it was okay to ask her? Was he coming back, even if she said no? Would she have to go and stay up at their house again?

Click click click.

She'd run out of teeth, the crocodile's mouth wide and full to the brim of pearly whites.

"He really is very sorry. It only happened once, and it was an accident".

That's not true thought Nancy. It had happened lots of times. She'd had a least two birthdays' whilst it was happening. Her throat thickened and she struggled to swallow down the pain and confusion that was rising in her chest. But she did. She swallowed her pooling saliva, taking the shame, hurt, betrayal and confusion down to the pit of her stomach, where it would live permanently for the rest of her life.

"Can we play now?" Nancy asked, still staring down at the game.

"Yes dear. Let Grandma know what you think, hmm?"

CHAPTER 39

Present

"Bloody hell…Dad, it feels like the world's going to fall out of my arse".

He laughed.

They were sitting in the driveway of her Grandma's house. Facing the bungalow where it happened, in view of the window to the bedroom where it had all taken place. The reason they were here.

"I feel like my legs don't belong to me. I don't know how I am going to walk to the door" Nancy said quietly.

"Listen, if you don't want to go in, we can drive off right now. Back to the pub and order ourselves multiple Gin and Tonic's and forget all about it" he smirked.

"Ha" she said, staring forward without focus.

There were a few beats of silence between them.

"No" she said, after a while.

"I've got to do this" she said flatly.

"Okay then. It's going to be alright. I will be right by your side and if you want to go, just give me the nod" he winked, and pressed the red button on the buckle to release her seatbelt. It slid up and across her body, releasing her from the seat. She desperately wanted to grab it and jab it straight back into place, locking her in her place, safe and secure. She felt like she'd just had her socks quickly pulled off by the toes, leaving her exposed and irritated.

Dad opened his door, and walked around the car to open hers. She looked up at him, unable and unwilling to move. He reached in and took her hand and she reluctantly swung her heavy left leg out of the car, followed by the other, which twisted her body to face out of the car. She sat there for a moment, unable to find the energy to stand. She was in flight mode, and knew in order to fight, she would have to tell herself why she was here.

She'd been seeing Dr G for months now. She'd wasted most of the expensive sessions crying her eyes out, wailing, murmuring nonsense and feeling worse when she left than when she arrived. She hated going, she hated being in the room, but to have him actually ask her how she was feeling about things she had pressed deep down into her gut, and listen without judgement, felt wonderful. Not that she had said anything worth listening to, most sessions she sounded like an injured sealion alerting its colony that it was beached on a rock. But if she managed to utter a few quiet words, or answer a few questions with simply a nod or a head shake, she felt she was taking huge steps, as opposed to sitting there, with a soaked face and lap, surrounded by scrunched tissues.

"Who are you most angry with Nancy?" Dr G had asked.

She hadn't said anything, just twisted the tissues round her knuckles until it hurt.

"Is it him? Your Grandma? Your parents?" he'd suggested, pen poised.

Nancy flinched at the mention of her parents. They'd done nothing wrong.

She held the silence, fearing if she spoke she would cry, and she'd only just caught a hold of herself.

"Her" Nancy whispered, looking at her spot on the floor.

She gritted her teeth and wound the tissues round, until her fingers went white.

"That's understandable. You trusted your Grandma and she betrayed you. To me it seems like you don't hold him in any regard.

He was not a real relative. You did not love him. But you loved her. And you still do. But she has not treated you with the respect, love and care you deserve Nancy" he said firmly.

Silent tears dripped onto the back of the hand in her lap, her teeth grinding together, tissue-bound fingers almost dropping off.

Nancy had continued to stare straight ahead. She was not sobbing, but tears were leaking out of her, like a tap that hadn't been fully turned off. Her jaw hurt, her heart hurt. It felt like it was breaking, although she wasn't fully sure it had been whole in the first place.

"How did you feel, when you were told that she was taking him back?"

The question blurred her vision. She was tired. Exhausted. She felt like laying down in a large bed with fresh sheets and feather-filled pillows. She wanted Mum to pull the duvet right up to her face, she would breathe in the cotton fresh scent and rub her nose against the soft material. She would be kissed on her forehead multiple times and she would close her achey eyes. *Love you poppet*, she would whisper and she would fall into a sleep and when she woke, this would all have been a bad dream.

Nancy stifled a yawn, and apologised. She took her hand up to her mouth to cover it, and left it there, brushing her lips and pinching at her cupids bow. She took her other hand and reached over to the small brown coffee table, picking up her plastic cup of water and taking it to her lips for a few sips. She returned it to the table, but the cup leant half on the coaster and tipped over.

"Shit" Nancy swore, and jumped up. She grabbed some tissues out of the box to mop it up.

"Don't worry, it's only water" Dr G assured her.

"I'm so sorry" Nancy said, grabbing more tissues, attempting to mop the flood of water on the table, which was now spilling over the edge and cascading down on the carpet.

Nancy continued to use the tissues to absorb the spill but they were cheap and thin, and did little to help. Dr G grabbed a cloth off the window sill and walked over to her, and quickly mopped the mess up, wringing the cloth out on his desk plant.

"There we go" he said.

Nancy swept up the wet tissues and placed them in the bin on the other side of her chair and returned to her seat. The distraction had not only made her forget the question but that she was ever really upset. She smiled at Dr G and breathed out.

"Sorry about that" Nancy apologised, embarrassed about her previous emotional state.

"I don't know what came over me"

He smiled sympathetically.

"I just asked you about when you were told that your Grandma had forgiven Granville. When she let him come home? When she chose him over you? How did it feel to know that your Grandma who you loved and was supposed to love you, chose to live with someone, despite knowing what he'd done to her little granddaughter? Why do you think she did that?" he asked.

The questions hung in the air.

"I don't know" Nancy said.

"But I want to ask her"

Nancy was still sitting on the edge of the car seat with the car door open. She pressed her feet down into the floor and used the door frame to pull herself up to standing. Dad cupped her elbow but she gently shook him off and closed the door behind her. Her legs felt like they would give way beneath her, but she steadily walked forwards towards the front door, to find out the answers she'd been searching for all of her life.

CHAPTER 40

Present

The door opened, but whoever had opened it, stood behind it, so it looked as though it had been opened by a ghost. Was it her or him? She didn't know. Dad took a step forward through the door and stomped his boots on the mat, making sure they were clean before he stepped off it. He took off his coat and hung it on the wall in front and turned back to look at her, still frozen to the spot on the step outside. The last time she'd been here she was a young girl. She had walked past it every day on her way to and from middle school, her stomach twisting hoping she wouldn't bump into either of them. On several occasions she'd seen him, walking back from the corner shop with a paper under his arm and a fag dangling off his lip, so she'd crossed the road and kept her head down, walking as fast as her skinny little legs would let her. He'd called 'hello' to her once, and she'd cried in the toilets as soon as she'd got to school and missed registration. She'd told her parents and he hadn't done it again. She'd have walked another way, but the long way added at least another half an hour onto her already long walk through some scary woods. Plus, her friends walked the short cut and she couldn't and wouldn't bring herself to tell them, or anyone else for that matter, why she didn't want to go the same way.

She was a grown woman now, decades had passed since then, but she still felt the same fear and disgust as she had throughout her childhood whenever she'd come close to the place. She felt the need to pat herself down to remind the little girl inside her, that she was an adult on the outside. And that adult had decided to come back for answers, for an apology, for an explanation, for an expression of regret. She didn't know what she wanted really, or if there were any words that could even make everything feel better, but she had to try.

Nancy lifted her shaky leg and stepped through the door onto the mat, her Dad waiting for her. The leg still standing on the porch threatened to buckle, and she steadied herself on the door frame. She pulled her leg through the door to join the other, and she swiped her trainers a few times like Dad had, before she stepped off onto the carpet. She shook off her coat and handed it to Dad, who hung it on the coat hook next to his. Nancy didn't turn to her right to see who was standing behind the door, she just kept her blurred vision on Dad, who didn't break eye contact. He smiled bravely at her, and started down the hall towards the living room, beckoning Nancy to follow. The smell was the same. It was both comforting and upsetting. How could somewhere so haunting, still evoke sweet memories for her? She remembered running down the hall in her slippers on the soft carpet towards the kitchen, to argue over which plastic cup of squash they would have. She would always choose pink or yellow and Rob would pick blue or green. There needn't have ever been an argument, seeing as they never crossed tastes in colour, but somehow they'd managed it, whoever got to the kitchen first selecting the drink that the other would have wanted, just to be annoying. The front door shut behind them, and Nancy fought the instinct to turn around to the sound of the latch clicking in the door frame. Behind her was either her Grandma or Granville, and behind either one of them was the door to her old bedroom. She held her gaze in front at the back of Dad's spikey grey hair, and tentatively followed him towards the kitchen, turning left just before they reached it, into the lounge.

The same floral pattern covered the sofas, and the same busy carpets were underfoot. Nancy reluctantly looked up to see an old man sitting in his armchair at the far end of the room, next to patio doors that led out to their conservatory. So it was Grandma that opened the door, she thought.

He sat there in black jogging bottoms, that had ridden up his legs, socks and slippers on his feet. He wore a plain dark grey t-shirt, his round belly resting on his upper thighs. His silver hair still swept into a side parting, though there was a lot more baldness he was trying to cover with it now. His nose was still bulbous, and had turned a shade of deep purple, seeping across his cheeks like a whore's rouge. Capillaries were bursting beneath the skin, which was no longer just pitted but cratered. She despised him. Firey rage coursed through her veins, as she sat down in the sunken arm chair next to her Dad, who perched on the sofa, where Grandma joined him. Nancy pulled herself forward so she sat on the edge of the chair, and stared at Dad with moist, childlike eyes, waiting for his direction, waiting for him to start this, so that it could end as quickly as possible. She and Granville were at opposite ends of the room on matching arm chairs, the sofa with Dad and Grandma on running against the wall between them. Nancy had been terrified that he'd feel threatened and try to attack her, but seeing him slumped in his chair now comforted her, that he wasn't going to have the energy to strangle her or lock her in the loft. He couldn't even pull the legs of his trousers down to meet his fat ankles.

There was a thick silence, whilst everyone adjusted themselves in their chairs, unsure what to do next, until Dad cleared his throat. Nancy's stomach dropped.

"So..." Dad said, hands clasped together tightly in his lap, his face red with awkwardness. The realisation of where Nancy was, who she was with and what they were about to discuss hit her, and she felt as though she had floated out of her body and was watching a dream unfold below. Like she wasn't really there and this wasn't really happening. How could it be, it was something she'd thought about for years and years, of course, but she never dreamed she would have the guts to put it into action. Yet here she was, pale and sweaty, terrified and fierce. It wasn't a dream. She was about to hear what both of them had to say for themselves.

"Nancy wanted to come here today to ask you some questions and hopefully get some answers that she's waited a long time for". Dad's voice cracked, nerves and emotion laced in the sentence. He was being so very brave, and she felt so loved that he was doing this for her, even though it would most likely spoil whatever was left of his strained relationship with his mother.

There were a few seconds of silence, Nancy's mind went blank. She'd forgotten all of her questions. She had written everything she wanted to ask down on a piece of paper that was in her back pocket. She was going to have to stand up to take it out, but her knees felt like sand. She reached behind her, slid her hand into her jean pocket, and pulled out the piece of paper that had been folded four times over to fit. She held it in her hand, unopened. She felt better now she had a script should she need it.

The sound of a throat clearing interrupted her thoughts, which consisted of thick phlegm being coughed up, and swallowed back down, making her grimace. It was the sound of an age-old smoker who constantly had a chest infection, which they insisted was nothing to do with their forty a day habit.

"I just wanted to say…" he started, his husky voice raking over her skin.

"That I'm sorry alright? I shouldn'ta done what I did to ya, alright?"

His lame apology sat in the silence of the air.

"Okay?" he asked, impatiently.

Nancy had always been a sucker for an apology. She found it hard to deny someone forgiveness if they had the decency to apologise. She had seen many times in film and tv, even in Alex, when someone had most sincerely apologised and they'd rebuffed the person's effort, rejecting their vulnerability and expecting more. Less words, more action, to show that they really regretted doing wrong by someone. But even if it was half arsed, Nancy would accept it quickly, hug it out and move on, relieved to be out of the theatre of conflict and into a more peaceful place, even if nothing really changed. Nancy apologised even when she believed she wasn't to blame. She didn't really care how she got there, as long as the result was forgiveness and friendship, even if it meant she went to bed mealy-mouthed that she had said sorry when she probably needn't have. People took advantage of her, holding out on sorting problems, knowing she would take care of it and most likely take responsibility. It had only contributed to her lack of self-worth and her desperation to be liked, but she had no idea how to break the cycle.

But on this unique occasion, the empty apology stank. And Nancy could feel the fury bubble up in her throat. It was not only the worst apology she'd ever received but for the worst infliction of selfish, disgusting behavior.

"No it's not 'okay'" she burst, mimicking his tasteless wording.

Her voice echoed in the silence of the room. She wasn't at all sure what she was going to say, she was scared of herself but for once, she let herself go with it.

"It's not 'okay' at all!" she practically shouted.

"Why did you do it?" she yelled, already disgusted at the thought of what he might answer.

"I was jealous alright?" he said, indignant, sitting forward in his seat, jaw jutting out.

"Jealous??" Nancy thought her eyebrows would disappear into her hairline.

"Yeh. Jealous of how much your Grandma loved ya, and wanted to spend time with ya".

Nancy guffawed.

"That literally doesn't make any sense" she scoffed, shaking her head and looking at Dad.

Grandma piped up.

"I think what Granville is trying to say is that he felt left out and wanted to be involved that's all"

Nancy wanted to slap her in the face. Well, she didn't, she wouldn't, she was her Grandma after all. But she wanted to scream at her and smash something at the very least.

"So, let me get this straight" Nancy mock chuckled.

"You were jealous of your wife's grandchildren, so you did that…
to me." Nancy said, her voice thick with emotion and disgust.

"Yeh" he said.

"Granville wasn't used to sharing me, Nancy" interjected
Grandma.

"Hold on, hold on, hold on, I'm sorry" Nancy said, shaking
her head, now laughing with rage, hands in front of her to halt the
conversation.

"Let me get this straight. You did what you did because you
were jealous of any attention Grandma gave me and Rob? Were
you trying to get her attention? Did you want her to find out so she
would notice you? What was it? I'm just asking, because I haven't got
a fucki- sorry, haven't got a clue what you are on about" she laughed,
becoming hysterical.

Nancy's mouth was open, her teeth exposed, eyes wide. She had
promised herself she wouldn't lose her temper and lose traction by
swearing at them.

"Fuck that for a game of soldiers" Alex had said, when Nancy
had told her she'd avoid losing her shit, and a small smirk itched the
corner of Nancy's mouth thinking of what Alex would say right now
if she were in the room too.

"Listen alright!" Granville growled out of nowhere, getting
everyone's attention. Nancy wanted to kill him right then. Who
the fuck did he think he was, shouting at her for asking perfectly
reasonable questions about why he'd singlehandedly desecrated and
devalued a small child's self-worth?

"I've said I'm sorry, what more do you want!?' he yelled. His
shoulders were back, his chest pushed up and out. His eyes were
furious, his fists clenched on the arm rests of the flowery chair.

"How dare you shout at me!?" Nancy glowered.

"You've made a half-arsed apology for ruining my life and expect
me to just leave it at that? And your reasoning doesn't even make
any sense! You don't even deserve to be free! I should have called the
police and you'd be in the jail!" she shouted, wincing immediately

that 'the jail' had slipped out of her mouth, instantly reducing the impact of her threat. She could hear Alex laughing.

"Oh and is that what you would have wanted was it? Your Grandma all alone?" he taunted, face red, pushing himself away from the back of his chair, yet unable to scooch his fat, weak carcass forward to the edge of the seat.

Nancy couldn't believe it. She hadn't really thought how he would react. She actually couldn't believe that *she* was being scolded by *him* and indignant fury bubbled and swelled inside her. She stayed silent for a moment, gathering herself, adamant she wouldn't lower herself into a slanging match, losing all value in her words. Her ears were hot, her temples thudded. She felt guilty. How in the world was she feeling guilty? Like she was a bad person for even implying she would do anything as selfish as sending a paedophile to jail, leaving her innocent Grandma all alone. The Grandma who had chosen to take her husband back after she knew of the unspeakable things he'd done to her baby granddaughter.

Nancy took several deep breaths. She couldn't even look at her father.

She unclenched her molars, lowered her aching shoulders and straightened up in the soft armchair. She tilted her head side to side to click out the tension in her neck.

"I think it's safe to say I don't think what I wanted ever came into consideration, did it?" Nancy said in a low voice, keeping her eyes on him.

She slowly moved her eyes to her Grandma, holding the question in her gaze. Grandma readjusted herself in her seat, but she certainly wasn't squirming.

"I don't really see why we have to go over this dear" she said, her words hanging in the air.

"Are you honestly telling me that you wouldn't have done the same if you were in my position?"

CHAPTER 41

Then

Age 24

"I'll be back before you know it" said Nate, pushing more cheap t-shirts into his huge, khaki backpack, and attaching his camping mat to the bottom of the bag.

Nancy sat there on the corner of the bed whilst he packed, her arms wrapped around her middle, shoulders slumped forward, brow furrowed.

"It's only for a few months, I'll be back by the next scan" he reassured her, slotting deet into the netted pocket on the outside of the backpack.

"I know. I know, I know! You are right" she exclaimed, bouncing on the bed and snapping herself out of her funk, smiling positively.

"You are right" she repeated.

"And it is totally fine, I would only be sitting around here eating weird food and puking anyway, you will have much more fun in Thailand and I will feel less guilty for falling asleep at 6:30pm every night" she laughed, cuddling her protruding tummy.

He laughed too, picked up his crumpled notepad and looked at the list she'd written him to see if there was anything he'd missed.

Nancy's insides twisted. She wanted to ask him something, but it sounded insane in her mind so she was certain it would sound a lot worse aloud. Don't be silly, she told herself.

"Anything you think you've missed?" Nancy asked, trying to be helpful.

"Nah I don't think so. As long as I've got tickets and passport eh?" he said, repeating the catchphrase they said before every trip they'd ever made.

Nancy smiled, her eyes burning and filling up. A telltale tear spilled over and she wiped her face which caught his attention.

"Oh don't, Nance. Don't start crying. Are you trying to make me feel guilty?" he asked.

"No!" she said, furious that any glimmer of emotion she dared to show was received like this.

"I'm allowed to be sad Nate" she grumped.

"I know, it's just, it makes me feel bad, and that's not really fair, is it" he said.

Fury coloured her face. Her back teeth pressed together. Don't fucking come back, she thought. Then she felt guilty for even thinking it, and the tears ramped up again. She placed her head in her hands to cover her embarrassment.

"Oh for goodness sake. We've been over this. I will be back in two months, you will hardly notice I'm gone okay? Really you are being silly, and kind of selfish." He placed a obligatory hand on her shoulder whilst she silently sobbed into her palms. The worst thing was, he thought she was crying because he was leaving her, and she was at first. But now she was crying for the way he was treating her, like she was a clingy child, an infatuated teen, like a nuisance. She was the mother of his child. She was so cross, with him and herself for not screaming at him, but crying pathetically instead. But all it did was make her feel more desperate to hold on to him. If he could treat her like this when she was showing him how much she cared, she couldn't bear the thought of how disinterested he would undoubtedly be if she told him to fuck off right then and there.

"Right" he said. "Enough now. No more tears, okay?"

She sniffed deeply, and wiped her hands over her face several times and breathed out, her whimpers catching in her throat.

He carried on shoving the last of his things in his bag, his toiletries and a comb on the top, and pulled the draw string tight and secured it with the toggle, before clipping the top of the bag down.

"Nate" she said, quietly, looking down at her lap.

"Yes?" he sighed impatiently.

"Nothing bad is going to happen to the baby is it? Like it did to me?" she almost whispered.

"This is hardly the time to be asking me this sort of thing Nancy is it? We're about to get in the car to go to the airport" he huffed, his face red and impatient.

"Sorry" she said.

"I'm just worried that's all" she said, still looking down, feeling sick and pathetic.

"Look, you are bound to have a lot of thoughts at the moment. But you need to just let it go. You need to just move on. I don't want to think about it and you shouldn't want to think about it. So let this be the last time we talk about it okay? Going over it is just bringing up the past and making it worse. Why don't you see a counsellor whilst I'm gone and then when I come home, we can turn over a new leaf and have a fresh start" he smiled, placing his hand on her hand, resting on her tummy.

She tried to smile back, but she felt numb. She felt alone. She felt lonely. She felt angry. She felt like she wanted to reach up and slap him over and over on his face, head, chest, to spit at him. But once that moment had passed, she felt deeply and wholeheartedly sad. She was lost. She was ignored, invisible, misunderstood, unsupported, uncared for and unloved. And she'd known it for a long time. He loved travelling more than he had, or ever would, love her. He had little to no respect for her. Why would he, when she didn't even respect herself enough to fight back against this treatment that he pretended to be love.

"Now. We have about 10 minutes before we head off to the airport. Why don't you give me a little going away present eh?" he said, kissing her on the crown on her head.

She looked up through tear filled eyes, her lip wobbling, as he gently pushed her shoulder back on the bed.

She obediently laid down, and he reached up under her skirt and pulled her knickers down to her knees, like he always did. She stared at the ceiling, palms facing up, lifeless, resigned.

He pulled his shorts down to his ankles and which rested on his shoes, climbed on top of her and after a handful of abrupt dry thrusts, collapsed on her, breathing heavily into her neck, telling her he loved her.

CHAPTER 42

Present

"Are you honestly telling me that you wouldn't have done the same if you were in my position?"

The question just sat there, on an invisible shelf between them.

"I'm just saying that when you get married, you stand by your husband no matter what. But you haven't ever been married Nancy dear, so maybe you just can't understand that" she said.

Her mouth continued to open and shut like a clowns at the final crazy golf hole, the one where the ball goes in and returns to the kiosk never to be seen again. She swallowed and cleared her dry throat, and spoke clearly.

"I may have never been married Grandma" she started. "But I know what is right and wrong. And marriage doesn't protect anyone from that" trying to steady her voice, the woman's words playing loudly in her ears. She couldn't understand what she'd just heard.

"It happened to me you know" Grandma said, after a beat.

"When I was about fourteen. It was horrible but it's life, you move on, you get on with it" she shrugged.

"Hold on, so it happened to you, and you have no sympathy towards me, even though you know how it felt to be taken advantage of like that?"

"I do have sympathy towards you Darling. I just think, well, Granville's apologised, and you are a grown woman with your own family now. Well, children. I think it's just time to move on".

Dad stayed quiet. His fists were clenched, staring straight ahead.

"Tea?" she said brightly, picking up the teapot and filling 4 cups on a tray, adding milk to each, and placing a plate of biscuits in front of Granville and another plate in front of Dad and Nancy.

"And what about you?" Nancy croaked.

"What about me? she asked, suspiciously.

"What about an apology from you" Nancy said, staring straight at her.

Dad lent forward to reach for the sugar bowl and knocked it onto the floor.

"Oh you silly oaf!" she exclaimed.

"Sorry, I've got it, don't worry Mum" he said, kneeling down onto the carpet to collect the scattered cubes. Nancy continued to stare at her Grandmother whilst Dad knelt down and picked up each sugar cube and placed them in his large palm. He then took two, and dropped one into his mother and step-fathers cups.

"Oh that's disgusting!" she frowned.

"It's fine, I could tell you just hoovered, don't fuss" he said, matter of factly.

"I had actually" she smiled proudly.

"See, it's fine" he said, placing the rest of the cubes on the tray. He returned to his seat, pale, shiny, staring straight ahead once again. Nancy looked at him but he refused to make eye contact.

"Anyway, where were we?" said Grandma, somewhat flustered.

"I said, what about an apology from you Grandma"

"Yes. Well, I am sorry for what happened to you dear. But like I said, he wasn't well. But the doctor made him better, see?" she said, lifting her tea cup to her lips and taking a sip.

Nancy smiled to herself.

"I wouldn't really call that an apology. Do you understand how tainted my life has been because of this? Thanks to Mum and Dad I had a very happy life and still do, with my beautiful children, family and friends. But because of what he did, and the fact that you chose him, when you *knew* what he'd done, well that has caused me a lot of unhappiness Grandma. And it's impacted on my life, more than you could ever imagine. And Dad's too. And Mum's. And Rob's. So I need to ask you. Knowing that now, knowing how painful my life has been because of this, if you had the chance to do this all over again, would you do it differently? Would you have left him and been with us?"

The question was out there. The question Nancy had wanted to ask her Grandma since she was a little girl.

"No" Grandma said.

Nancy couldn't believe her ears. She looked at her father, exhaled a laugh of disbelief and returned her gaze to her Grandma.

"Can I just ask again, just to make sure I have got it right in my head" Nancy said, holding her hands up in front of her, speaking more slowly this time.

"If you had your time again, and you knew how broken I've been for the last thirty years, would you have chosen differently, would you have chosen me, us?"

The question, clearer this time, hung in the air.

"No" she repeated flatly.

The word sat like a knife that had been stabbed in her heart and was left hanging out of her. She wanted to pull it out but was scared it would bleed forever. So she left it there, the weight of it pulling on her chest bone. No. No. No? She couldn't believe it. Granville had said nothing since his outburst and to Nancy he'd disappeared into the wallpaper, a pointless extra in the room, like an ugly ornament that had no purpose. No. She wouldn't have changed a thing? She wanted to ask again, she couldn't believe that was her final answer. Had she asked the question clearly enough? Did Grandma understand it? She couldn't possibly feel like that. Nancy was certain that almost everything she'd done wrong in her life, she would happily retract or change paths if she'd been given the opportunity. She made constant mistakes but recognised and reconciled them as quickly as possible as she got older. She saw both sides after a moment of blind rage. With age, grudges faded. She didn't sulk like she used to, and she forgave quickly. She couldn't believe that this 80 year old woman had just said that given her time again, she would have still chosen a life with that sordid pervert, even though she was now fully aware, if she hadn't been before, that her Granddaughter's life had been ruined because of his actions.

"I'd like to go now please" Nancy said, facing her father.

"Yep" Dad said, standing quickly and pulling Nancy up to standing.

They walked out of the lounge door and along the hall, passed the frames hanging on the wall. There were none of her, as her parents requested, but a few of Dad and his brother as young boys, and her cousins. There was a young, handsome man in a graduation hat, and another of a small boy, dressed smartly in his school uniform. She wondered if his parents knew that his photo was being displayed in this house.

She opened the front door and Dad was right behind her, stepping out onto the drive way. Grandma had followed them down the hall and stood at the door.

"Do you still love me?" she asked, eyebrow raised, hopeful.

Nancy stopped for a moment, the question bouncing from ear to ear. She did. Why, she didn't know, but she did. But she couldn't answer and continued towards the car.

"Do you still love me?" Grandma asked again, this time more concerned, as they got into the car and closed the doors without answering.

CHAPTER 43

Then

Age 29

Dear Nancy,

How are you? It's been so long. I don't really know what I plan to say, I don't even know if I'm going to send this, but I just had to write down what's playing over in my mind.

How's Tilly? I bet she's growing up fast. I don't really need to bet, I see beautiful pictures of her on your Facebook (yes I occasionally check your Facebook…) and she is turning into a beautiful young lady. She looks just like you.

How's Alex? How's work? What have you been up to?

New York is so different to home. I loved it at first, it was like being in a film, the yellow cabs, Grand Central, Fifth Avenue, the steaming grates and the pretzel and hotdog venders on every corner (although no self-respecting New Yorker actually eats the hotdogs. There's but a scrap of pork present, I'm pretty sure they're made mostly out of cereal and eyelashes). Work is tough. Everybody is shouting all the time, and I've been called a 'British Cunt' more times than Alex has opened bottles of wine. I can take it, I knew what I was getting into, but day after day, you wonder if it is really how you want to be living. My Dad insists that it won't be long before I've worked my way up and I'll be doing the name calling, but I wouldn't really say that was me either. I suppose I just have to give it a chance and thicken my skin.

I have made a few friends, mostly American, who spend more time laughing at the way I pronounce things, than asking me how I actually am. Shit listen to me, could I sound more precious? I know you will probably be laughing at this, taking the piss out of me for being a spoilt brat in the big city. I wish you were here. I keep trying to enjoy things, throwing myself into nights out, experiences, tourist attractions, but I keep looking left, waiting for a sarcastic comment, or an outburst of excitement, an idea of what we should do next, but you're not there.

I know we made the right decision, or more to the point you did. If I'd have stayed I could have ended up resenting you, and you've got a different life to live with Tilly, it made sense. But now I'm here, without you, it doesn't make sense. It doesn't feel right at all Nancy. I know I shouldn't say this, but I still love you. I should be with you and Tilly, and Alex of course. You are my family. I know that seems a ridiculous thing to say when we were only together a few months, but you are. I don't know what I intend to get from this email, or whether I'll even send it to you. But I just had to say it. I have thought it for a long time, but knew you would just say that I'm homesick and need to give it a chance. I don't know if you feel the same, but I needed to tell you, so that if you don't, I can pull up my big boy pants and move on (I know you -and probably Alex- will be rolling your eyes at 'big boy pants', so I just had to leave it in. Hi Alex btw!). But if you do, and you think that there is any way I could come home to see you, or if you all want to come out to see me, on me of course, I would absolutely love it. It doesn't have to mean anything, I don't expect anything from you, but if you want to come to New York and to spend a bit of time together and see the sights, then it would make me so happy Nancy.

I think I will just stop being a pussy and send this now. This could all be a complete waste of time, you will have probably have met someone else over the last 6 months and will simply ignore this. But let me know what you think, even if it's just a polite Fuck Off and Have A Nice Life kind of email.

Yours,
Rupert

Nancy read the email on her laptop, she'd logged on to tidy up the last of her inbox, before putting her Out of Office on for the next year, redirecting her emails to the new girl who was standing in for her whilst she was on Maternity Leave. Her heart stung. The longing tugged like a fishhook in a guppy's cheek. She was a big fat fucking liar. He loved her. And he wanted to be with her. And she was about to have his baby and he didn't even know about it. What a piece of shit she was. She read the email again, feeling worse. The baby pushed it's elbow or knee into her rib, and she winced, pressing gently on her skin until the baby moved into a more comfortable position for her. She felt bad for it, like it was inside a water balloon, desperate to get out. She felt breathless just thinking about it. She wondered if it would be a boy or a girl, and whether it would it look like her or Rupert, or a mix of both. She hoped it looked like her, and not him, so she wouldn't need to look into its eyes and be reminded every day of what she'd done.

She wanted to press reply, to tell him everything, that the baby was due in 2 weeks, and if he came home now he would make it in time for the birth, he could move in with her and they would raise the baby together and be a happy little family. She loved that he'd mentioned Alex in his email too. Some would think he only mentioned her because he knew Nancy well enough to know that Alex would be the first and only person she'd show his email to. But she knew that wasn't why. It was because he knew the bones of Nancy, and that Alex was the bones of her. They were family, and if he was to stand half a chance in their life, he would need a life with Alex too, not to mention Tilly, of course. But she couldn't. She couldn't tell him. Yes, he'd told her he loved and missed her, but he was clearly lost and homesick. He wasn't saying he would give it all up for her, and she wasn't sure she'd want him to, even if he had. There were still too many 'ifs' and 'buts'. It was all too risky. She'd lied. She'd made unforgiveable mistakes. His father had lied and manipulated to get what he wanted for himself, to secure a future for his progeny and his family name in America. It wasn't as easy as confessing, it wouldn't end well. Rupert's relationships would be shattered, he wouldn't want her and the baby, and the life-changing money she'd been promised would be gone. She hated that she'd become this person, but she had children to care for, and the money Nate gave every month didn't give them any luxuries, just the basic contribution to housing and bills. And there would be three of them now. This money would be the difference between getting by and really living. And any good mother knew that she put the needs and wants of her child above anything else. If she allowed herself to dream, Rupert would come back, he wouldn't be angry and they'd live happily ever after. But it wasn't a dream, and it was much more likely that he would hit the roof, quite rightly, his father would cancel their deal and she would be raising both girls on her own. She couldn't believe this was how her thought process was now, that her moral compass was so far off. But she'd followed her heart before and look where it had got her. Broken hearted, alone and broke. She swore she'd never make the same mistake again, and she wouldn't. She would feel guilty for the rest of her life, but she tried to convince herself that in time the feeling would fade. It wasn't about her and her feelings anyway, it was about her baby and what was going to give them the best start in life.

The baby kicked again, right on her bladder. She pulled up her pelvic floor before she wet herself. She hovered over the delete button. She needed to end this once and for all. To have this baby and forget Rupert ever existed. She had to accept the situation for what it was and move on, or she was going to drown. This was about survival, not how she really felt. She'd got them into this position and she wasn't going to drag everyone down with her. She had to pretend. She had to forget. She wasn't worthy of happiness and peace. She had made mistakes and had a duty to protect as many people from her as possible. She pressed delete and then slammed the laptop shut. She dashed to the toilet, and sat with her head in her soaking wet hands.

CHAPTER 44

Present

The murky sky strained, bowing like a market stall roof on a rainy Saturday, threatening to overflow and soak the shoppers below. It was one of those days where it seemed the sun refused to rise. It was stubbornly sulking behind the grey ceiling, fighting against getting out of its pit, and everybody felt it. Snooze buttons were pressed, duvets pulled over heads, bodies rolled over to ignore the world outside. But Nancy couldn't ignore today. She'd been waiting for this day spanning three decades. But now that it was here, she didn't know why she'd wished her life away waiting for it.

She'd reluctantly risen and shuffled to the bathroom, wearing a backpack of dread and doom. She refused to catch her reflection. Her under eyes tight from crying, her head thick from dehydration. Her eyes scratched with every blink, and her neck sore from falling asleep sitting up, too afraid to lay down and accept she couldn't nod off.

After being engulfed in a hot, steamy shower, Nancy sat on the edge of her bed in a damp towel, head bowed. her breathing anxiously intermittent. She tapped her phone screen to check the time, which loyally sat next to her thigh on top of the duvet. An hour until she had to leave.

She reached for her moisturiser, deposited a dollop in her cupped hand, and smeared it on her freshly shaven shins, and massaged it into her tender calves. She squeezed another blob and smoothed the coconut-scented lotion from wrist to shoulder, circulating in gentle movements until her skin was shiny and damp. She smeared what was left on her hands onto her face, pressing and massaging her aching eye sockets and brow bones, looking down into her lap.

This was a day she had pictured in her mind over many years, but the reality felt quite different from the fantasy she had created for herself. She'd hoped she'd feel strong and satisfied, focused and validated, but the heaviness she felt in her heart, made her so tired, that she wanted to crawl back into bed and sleep until it was over.

With a resigned sigh, she lifted her heavy head until she was staring straight in the mirror at a woman, she barely recognised. This woman had a pale grey complexion smattered with dull freckles. Under her eyes a pressing of purple and green thinning skin, showcasing how many nights she'd lain awake with tattered insides. Her lips were dry, a thin white line of cracked skin ran along the centre of her plump bottom lip, and the rosebud on her top lip was cut, where she'd nervously sucked and chewed the callas off, during her restless night. Her reflection was so depressing. A woman so lost, so confused, so unbelievably sad. Nancy couldn't remember what it felt like to be happy and she knew she never would be again. She didn't even recognise the person sitting on the edge of her bed. She knew she had to cover herself in make-up, mask her sadness with products that promised joy, health, sex, beauty, success. She'd bought so many, lured in by the guarantee that she would get her life together like the women in the adverts; so confident, attractive, self-assured. It hadn't worked, but it didn't stop her buying into it.

She worked quickly to mask her face in foundation and concealer, and swept bronzer across her cheeks to brighten her skin, which had been the same colour as the clouds outside, but a few moments ago. She artificially flushed her cheeks with a smearing of liquid blush and used the same product to dab her eyelids and combed two layers of black mascara over her mousy lashes. Her wet blonde hair fell, framing her lost milk-chocolate, brown eyes. The thought of styling her hair right now seemed like hiking up a hill, whilst suffering from the flu, so she roughly dried it with the hairdryer and opted for a simple bun and pulled a few pieces out, which framed her ashen face.

Once she was ready and had tidied the products away, she stood up, brushed some fallen face powder off her smart black dress onto the floor and straightened herself out. But this time when she looked in the mirror, she did not look away. Somehow, by some miracle, she looked different. She felt different. Something had shifted. She stared at herself, she hardly blinked. She looked right into her own pupils in the mirror, and remembered that the eyes she was looking into, were the eyes of a child. A sweet, innocent, kind little girl. One that was excited for everything, that was gentle and pure. One that laughed; a loud and joyful laugh that made others chuckle, when they didn't even know what was funny. A child that had been hurt, beyond full repair, but one that was not going to allow what had happened to her define her forever. It was ridiculous to think that one horrible thing had managed to wash away everything good in her soul, like a tsunami enveloping a village.

She looked at her freckles, the bump in her nose, her rosebud upper lip. She was still there. But wiser, somehow. *Hello you* she thought. She suddenly felt love, compassion and empathy for her inner child. She'd loved life and found enjoyment in the smallest of things, and shared it with others, infecting them with her enthusiasm and passion. But Nancy's fuel and fight had run out, and she'd been running on fumes, believing she wasn't even worth refilling. Nancy didn't know what had caused the shift in her thought pattern, what had changed, and how. Was it the work of God, fate, stars aligning, or her own strength rising up from the depths of despair? She didn't know, but she did know in that moment, her soul had had enough. She said two words to herself. *No more.* She wasn't going to drag this around with her for a second longer. It was over. Well, as over as it could be. She had to make the choice to stop the pain. She couldn't prevent or change what had happened to her. But she could change how she stepped forward in the next part of her life. She didn't recognise the person looking back at her, but she liked her. She loved her. She was scared of her. She wanted to hug her. She wanted to be her friend. And she knew then, she would do everything she could to keep that person alive and present and never lose her again, no matter what, for the rest of her life. And if she couldn't do it for herself, she would do it for her girls. Did she think her daughters were blind? Wouldn't they end up like her, if she was treating herself like that? She thought she hid it so well, but the looks of concern when she regularly emerged from the bathroom with red eyes, were increasing. *Everything will be alright, won't it, Mummy? You'll never leave us will you Mama? What if I'm unhappy when I'm older Mum?* The questions that cropped up at bedtime were becoming darker, and something had to change. And she knew it had to start with her.

The black car slowly followed the curve of the pavement outside the Crematorium, where friends and family stood. They gathered like penguins in their black suits and white shirts, their heads hiding in their coat collars, huddled together to protect themselves from the storm, which wouldn't wait a moment longer to start its show. The guests held large black umbrellas above their heads, creating a shield from the chaos above. The wind roared, forcing them to clutch their jackets to their chests, squeezing their bodies tight together to try and resist its power. Rain, that was unable to reach them through the umbrellas, found its way in by blasting from the side, spitefully stinging their cheeks and bitterly bouncing into puddles and soaking tights, socks and shoes.

Nancy unbuckled her seatbelt and looked across to her father, whose clear grey eyes were glossed with moisture, framed by his bristly, peppered brows, which drooped down just above his temples. She reached over and gently placed her cool, clammy hand on his, and with her touch, he blinked out of his trance, and quickly smiled at her and placed his other hand on hers, like a sandwich, gently squeezing it with reassurance. She decided, at that point she'd never loved her father more and she felt a deep sadness inside, that his life had known so much pain, loss, betrayal and disappointment. He'd tried to think only of others and had sacrificed his joy and peace for hers, her brother's, his wife's and his mother's. Nancy treasured his loyalty, never doubting for a second that his children were his priority, even though he'd remained a dutiful son to his widowed mother since he was 18 years old. Nancy understood entirely that being left as the man of the house, as a young lad bore a huge weight of responsibility, and as a good man, he'd loyally upheld his father's final wishes to take care of the family and not shirk his responsibilities.

Inside the crematorium, the soothing notes of Mozart floated out of the speakers.

Those with umbrellas shook them and propped them against the wall in the entrance and brushed the silver droplets of rain that sat on their jacket shoulders onto the welcome mat. Women checked the state of their mascara in their phone screens, fussing over their children's appearance and quietly repeating the rules of behavior once more that had been delivered in the car only moments before. Then they helped their windswept mothers and aunties backcomb life into their thin, damp bobs and guided their families into the pews.

Dad, Nancy, Robert and his wife took their seats front left, her mother sitting just behind them, with her new husband. Her mother placed a comforting hand on Nancy's shoulder and she automatically reached up and firmly squeezed it. They held hands for a moment, a private exchange of communication between mother and daughter, that silently spoke a thousand words of comfort. Nancy let go and placed both hands back in her lap, face down. She couldn't look up, so just let the quiet hum of respectful chatter wash over her.

Nancy looked at her feet. Her tights were damp, even though the driver had parked as close as he could to the entrance, and sheltered her with a company umbrella, as he opened the car door. She thought that by hopping quickly out of the car and elegantly leaping in strides to the door, she would avoid the rain, but instead hopped straight into a puddle and got soaked. She couldn't wait to go home and slip into the bath.

She looked towards her Dad's knee, which was bouncing up and down at quick speed as he tapped his foot nervously. She reached across for his hand, held it tightly and pressed their clasp onto his knee to soothe it to a stop. Her father's body language betrayed him. He cleared his throat, straightened up and gave her a reassuring nod. She mimicked him, and sat up straight too, with a light shake of the head to reset her thoughts.

Nancy could see him out of her peripheral vision and her heart smashed against her rib cage with every beat. It could have been any man over the age of 80 at the funeral, same white hair combed over a blotchy, mole-covered scalp, and a slightly curved spine, shoulders slumped forward with age. But it was him. He stared straight forward, hands clasped in his lap, his daughter Deborah fussing around him, turning back to speak to the people behind, to thank them for coming. His sister Mavis was in the pew behind him, and shuffled to the edge of her seat, using the back of the pew in front to pull herself up, being steadied by a younger female relative next to her, maybe her daughter or daughter-in-law, Nancy thought. Mavis tapped her brother on his shoulder and shakily held out her hand. He turned and took it and gracefully received the pity she had to offer. He patted her hand to tell her he accepted her condolences and that he was done with her offering and turned back to face the front and quickly resumed his position of staring forward. His disgruntled sister remained standing on her shaky legs, clearly put out that she'd wasted the effort of standing for that pitiful exchange, but her daughter took her elbow, and gently lowered her back into her seat. There was some twittering on his sister's row at the coolness, and like clockwork, he turned around with a flash of annoyance, hidden rapidly by his hand raised to his face pressing one eye and then the other followed by a sharp exhale, which earned instant forgiveness and sympathy from the row behind and beyond. A competition began between the women, as to who could provide a tissue first, and three were thrust forward, guests desperate to be of some practical use. He dabbed his eyes and nose with one of the tissues and popped the other two in his jacket pocket with a brave, wobbly smile and returned to face the front.

Bless his heart

It must be so hard for him

Love him echoed amongst the guests between sniffs and nose blows. His tears did not continue, not that they'd even started, and Nancy numbly shook her head. Dad stood, kissed Nancy on the head and walked to the back of the room with Robert.

The funeral celebrant walked out onto the small stage and spoke into the microphone.

"Welcome everyone. Today marks a sad day, but also a day of celebration. Please may I ask you to stand."

The congregation rose to its feet, and Nancy turned. Her father, her uncle, Robert and their cousins walked down the aisle to Eva Cassidy's *Songbird*, the coffin balanced on their shoulders, their mouths in a matching thin solemn line, their eyes straight ahead, as if everyone in the room was invisible. Nancy's knees felt like they would buckle. She could focus only on her father, and she'd never felt such sadness from simply looking at someone else. All the heartache and pain she'd ever felt in her life, did not compare to seeing her Dad so vulnerable and lost, in his smartest suit, ready to say his final goodbye to his mother. Nancy burst into tears, quickly placing her head in her hands and sitting down, trying to gather herself before her father saw her. Her Mum passed tissues forward and put her hand on her shoulder from the pew behind, comforting her, saying 'it's alright poppet' as Nancy blew her nose. She stared forward at the coffin now resting on the stand on the stage, flowers in the shape of MUM on top. Her father and the pallbearers took their seats.

"Today we are here to celebrate the life of Mary who passed away at the age of 82, in the peace of her own home, with her husband Granville, by her side. Although today is a painful one, we want to take the chance to remember all of the wonderful times we shared with Mary, how she impacted our lives, and the memories that remain. Although she may no longer be with us in body, may she live on in spirit through us, the memories we keep and the stories we tell".

Nancy held onto her father's hand. They both stared forward, numb.

The celebrant continued with the service, reading an account of Grandma's life, telling stories of her younger years and beyond. The words looked like they were being said but Nancy's head was underwater. She couldn't help but think she couldn't believe she'd been waiting for this day, and it was hateful, sad, empty, pointless. It didn't feel good. She wasn't the kind of person to dance on anyone's grave in any aspect of life; she certainly wasn't going to start now, when there was an actual grave involved. She thought she'd be glad, that she could move on somehow, that she would then be able to finally punish Granville without hurting Grandma. Or that Dad would be free from the obligation of duty to her, and they'd both be relieved that they could cut those ties. But all she thought about was how much she had loved her. How much she loved to play games with her, go out on day trips, to go for picnics, and listen to her voice, when she read her a story. She thought about when they'd go swimming, and Grandma would desperately try at all costs to keep her freshly blowdried hair out of the water, and her and Rob would splash her anyway. She remembered her nifty little hatchback injection, that she'd zizzed them around in and when she'd take them to McDonalds, and they could have whatever they wanted. She'd started every sentence with 'as I say...' and loved Malteasers, which Nancy bought for her every birthday and Christmas, even though she didn't deserve them. Nancy loved her, even though she didn't deserve it. And the last time she saw her, Grandma had asked Nancy twice if she still loved her. She hadn't replied and just walked away, and now Grandma was dead. And if that wasn't bad enough, Nancy had wished for it. And now it had come true.

Dad interrupted her dark thoughts with a squeeze of her hand, and stood to walk towards the front, and took the two steps up onto the small stage and stood behind the microphone. He cleared his throat, and straightened his black jacket and looked out over the sea of smartly dressed mourners.

"I'll keep this reasonably brief as we are pushed for time but I just wanted to say that I hope Mum finds peace, wherever she is now, and knows that she was loved and will be missed by me and all of us here. I hope you will join us for a drink and a sandwich at the village hall after this. Thank you' he said, and stepped away from the microphone and walked back to his seat.

The congregation shuffled awkwardly at the brevity of the eulogy. Nancy smiled at Dad and he folded his speech up and put it in his pocket.

"You didn't really need to write that down, Dad. I think even you could have remembered that" Nancy smirked.

Dad smiled back.

"Oh there was more. But I just got up there and thought, you know what, she had enough out of me. I gave her everything I had, and that was all that I had left" he said, raising his eyebrows and pressing his lips together.

"I can understand that. Dad" said Nancy, quickly rubbing his forearm.

Out of the corner of her eye, Nancy saw Granville rise to standing, the celebrant stepping down to cup his elbow and support him up the steps to the stage. Nancy's stomach sank. She was going to hear his voice rasping over the speakers, waffling bullshit about Grandma and their life together, fooling every old dear and gimmer there, extracting their sympathy and sadness to keep as his own, so that he could take it home and have his own little well deserved pity party.

"She was the love of my life" he said, his voice cracking. This got a reaction, and over half of the congregation yelped in empathy and reached for a tissue.

He went on, talking about their life, which mostly consisted of going down to the caravan they owned. Come to think of it, they couldn't do much else, seeing as they were segregated from most of their family.

Nancy stared at him. She hated him. She felt sorry for him. She was scared of him. She was disgusted, furious, repulsed, frightened, sad. She felt as though she wasn't really in the moment, she felt both

35 and 5, she felt like a teenager and a confused young woman all at once. She wished she could change out of this uncomfortable outfit and hop into some her jammies. Her knickers were bothering her, and she wished she could have a lovely long shower, and slip into something comfy with slipper socks, light some candles and watch something sweet and light on the television.

"To lose her so suddenly was such a shock, but I will always be grateful that she wouldn't have known what was happening. Just nodded off on our sofa and slipped away in peace".

The audience hummed in comfort, holding their hands to their hearts, some gently applauded, silent prayers filling the room with hope that they would go the same way. He returned to his seat with assistance.

The celebrant resumed his position at the microphone, thanking Granville for his eulogy, to which he nodded humbly. Nancy hated him, but returned her gaze to her Grandma's coffin.

The service was clearly running to an end, and the celebrant was rounding up with words of comfort for Grandma's family and friends. He asked them to bow their heads, and take a moments silence to reflect. The congregation obeyed, and lowered their heads, some clasping their hands in prayer on laps. Nancy went inward, praying for forgiveness for wishing ill on her Grandma, for not telling her how she felt sooner, for not reminding her she loved her before she died. She hoped Grandma would be in Heaven and receive her prayer. Though she thought if she wasn't willing to repent the day before her death, then she probably wouldn't have made it to the pearly gates, and had most likely had to set up camp next to a pit of lava, just below the earth's core.

"Mary's family would like to invite you to join them at the village hall for refreshments, for those who would like to" the celebrant said into the mic, and nodded to Dad.

Dad gestured to Granville to walk out first. Debbie supported him, as they stood up and walked back down the aisle towards the door, eyes on them, silently sending their well wishes to his broken heart. Dad stood and pulled Nancy up quickly by her elbow.

"Jeez" she said, stumbling to her feet.

"Sshh" he said, and Nancy frowned in confusion.

He kept a hold of her elbow, and they walked behind Granville. Nancy looked at Dad, confused at why they had to be so close to that monster. Dad was standing tall, his chest out, his mouth grimaced. He did not let go of Nancy. She wanted to resist and wriggle out of his grip, away from being so close to Granville, but there was something about the look in Dad's eyes that made her submit. The rest of the congregation were on their feet and following, most likely eager to get to the buffet Dad was providing.

Debbie opened the doors for her father, and he walked through to the lobby. Dad caught the door from Debbie as she let it go, and held the door open, wafting Nancy through, asking her to hold the other side of the door for the congregation as they left.

"Come on, come on, everyone outside, let's go" he said, as he wafted them rudely through the door, herding them like cattle.

Nancy wondered why Dad was acting like this, his eyes urgent and his jaw, hard and set. She smiled apologetically at the insulted ladies as Dad beckoned them forward, ushering them outside. They twittered about being rushed, but Dad just ignored them.

When everyone had walked through the lobby and outside, Dad let go of his door, which slammed against the frame. He stepped towards and grabbed her by the elbow again, her door slamming as she let go too, and marched her outside with everyone else.

"Ow, Dad! What the actual fuuuuuuu" she stopped talking as she stepped outside.

Blue lights. Lots of blue lights. Police. She weaved through the crowd to see what was happening, Dad right behind her.

Then she saw him.

Granville was pressed against the wall of the crematorium, hands cuffed behind his back.

"What the fuck's going on!?" he yelled, his cheek smushed against the brickwork, a police officer's hand on the back of his head.

"Stop! He's just had his wife's funeral! What are you doing!?" Debbie screamed at the police officer, being restrained by another.

The crowd surged forward to get a better view, pushing Nancy closer to the arrest.

She turned to her father.

"Dad, what the fuck happened?" she asked him.

By the look on his face, he knew. He put his arm around her shoulder and squeezed, and told her to keep watching.

He was read his Miranda rights but Granville was shouting and swearing so loudly over the statement, Nancy could barely hear the copper's voices. She'd watched enough crime thrillers know them off by heart, so it didn't really matter.

The officers were obviously having trouble with him, swaying back and forth as they tried to keep him steady, as he tried to thrash out of their grip. It was when he spat in the arresting officers face, that things really got lively, several other's bundling in to rough him up. When they finally got him in a firm hold, he was marched over to the police car and had his head firmly pressed down at the open car door until he crumpled onto the back seat, the door slammed in his face. He looked out the window at her, beetroot-red and snarling. She resisted the urge to wave. The sirens sounded, which made everybody jump, before driving him away, blue lights twirling on top of the car rooves.

Nancy stood there, staring at the space where the police had just been. The crowd gobbled like a rafter of turkeys behind her, and she didn't want to be asked any questions, as she did not know the answers. She was struggling to comprehend what she'd just witnessed. She'd dreamt of him being arrested since she was a little girl, of course, but why now? What had they found out about him, and how?

"Thank you for coming. Buffet's cancelled, I'm afraid!" Dad announced to the sea of baffled faces.

"Come on" he said to her, placing a hand on her back and hurriedly walking her towards the limo.

"Go please mate, go" he directed the driver, as they clambered in.

The chauffeur put the car in gear, and proceeded to do a gentle three-point-turn at his own leisurely rate. Nancy went straight in with the questions, whilst Dad told the driver to hurry up in a less than polite way.

"Why was he arrested Dad? Was it because of me? How do the police know?" she asked, panicking, hands clasped in front of her mouth.

Dad went to answer but didn't know where to begin. He held his finger up to signify he needed a minute, and took a deep breath. Nancy looked at him, waiting for an answer.

Then Nancy saw her. Over Dad's shoulder, through the tinted glass of his door window, there she was. Standing just away from the crowd, around the side of the crematorium, looking right back at Nancy.

She wore black trousers, a smart black coat and black heels on her feet. She had almost white blonde, curly hair. Pale skin and a button nose, and large, glassy blue eyes with thin shadowy skin underneath. The girl she saw by the shops. It was the girl that had knocked on her door. The girl who knew her name. The girl she kept seeing. Was she the one who texted her? What the hell was she doing here? Nancy's face flushed red with annoyance, and panic. The panic rose further when she saw who the girl was standing next to. She couldn't believe it. It was Stephen.

CHAPTER 45

13 Days Earlier

Dad walked out of the police station into the dark, looking around nervously, jumping as someone shut their car door in the carpark. He was cold; he'd left his fleece in the boot. He picked up the pace and ran towards his car, unlocking it and sliding in. He pulled out quickly onto the main road in front of another car, which almost went into the back of him.

"Wanker!" yelled the driver.

He's got a fair point Dad thought and sped off quickly.

He had handed his recording pen into the police station, a detective had placed the item in a bag, and it had been carried off 'into the back', whatever that meant. Dad had agreed to be interviewed, and explained that he had laid the recording device under the sofa, to capture a confession from his step-father, admitting to the years of abuse he'd inflicted on a small child. His small child. Dad was asked the same questions over and over, and Dad had responded in the same way. He hadn't added new information, just kept it as simple as he could.

He didn't divulge that he had taken sugar cubes over to their house that day, one of which had been laced with arsenic. He hadn't decided for certain whether he was going to use it, but he wanted the option. He knew which one it was, it was the slightest bit darker than the others, until he'd dropped the bowl on the floor and mixed the cubes up.

When he'd agreed to organise the meeting with them for Nancy, he'd hoped he'd be able to record it, and give Nancy the evidence afterwards, so she could report Granville to the authorities afterwards, should she want to. But he wasn't convinced she'd ever really have the strength to send Granville to prison. She'd never enjoyed revenge. So, Dad decided he'd have to take matters into his own hands to make sure they didn't waste the opportunity to get the bastard out of their lives, once and for all.

The night that followed their visit, Dad had received the phone call to say that his mother had passed away. He'd sunk to his knees, devastated, and sat still, on the cold floor, until the sun had come up. He felt numb. Had he killed her? How could he ever forgive himself? Later that morning, the morgue had phoned following the postmortem, and Dad couldn't hardly breathe. He was waiting to be told she'd been poisoned. But she hadn't. She'd suffered a fatal heart attack and died quickly, but the 'p' word wasn't mentioned. He breathed a sigh of relief, and then felt horrendously guilty for being so self-centred. He'd sat still for a while, staring at nothing, thinking. Thinking about his mother no longer alive. The sadness, the loss, the relief. The guilt for feeling relief. But then his eyes caught on a photo on the fireplace. It was a picture of Nancy and Robert, aged three and five, squealing by the English sea, as the foamy waves rushed over the pebbles to chill their tiny little feet. They had rolled up their jeans to paddle, and Nancy's nose was pink and her eyes and mouth wide, as the cold water swallowed her toes. Robert was laughing, trying to pull her away, farther up the stones, before the next wave got them. Dad remembered what had happened after he'd taken the photograph. He'd put his camera away in its case and hung the strap over his body, then grabbed a towel and scooped her up in it. He'd kissed her nose and her pink cheeks, and held her close to him, and told her how much he loved her. Grandma and Granville had been on that holiday too. Grandma had wrapped Robert in a towel and Mum had unrolled their socks and unstrapped their shoes, ready to put back on after their paddle. Granville had watched. Dad dreaded to think what had happened to Nancy whilst they were all obliviously trying to make happy memories.

The day after she'd died, Dad had to go back to their house. It was under the proviso to speak to Granville about funeral arrangements, and to collect something for his mother to be buried in. He knocked on the door and waited for an answer. After a minute, it opened, and he silently stepped through the doorway, onto the welcome mat. He hung his coat on the hook opposite, brushed his boots like he always did, and walked down the hallway into the lounge. He knew she wasn't going to be there, but it still felt strange. He hadn't even had the chance to say goodbye. He swallowed the lump in his throat.

"Tea?" Granville said gruffly.

"No, no" Dad replied, holding his hand up, refusing to make eye contact like always.

"I mean yes, actually yes, thanks" Dad said, remembering what he had to do.

Granville turned and walked into the kitchen, and Dad perched on the sofa he was sitting on the day before. He reached down and touched the carpet with his fingers, keeping his eye firmly on the door and slid his hand under the couch. Nothing. His heart thundered. He slid it back and forth, still nothing. Shit, shit, shit. He shuffled to the edge of the sofa so that his hand could reach further under.

"Biscuit?" Granville asked, poking his head round the door.

"Yes!" Dad almost shouted, smiling widely.

Granville returned to the kitchen, the click of the kettle announcing the water had boiled. Dad franticly swished his hand back and forth like a windscreen wiper and hit something. He grabbed, and shoved whatever he had in his fist into his fleece pocket.

"There we are" said Granville, pleased that his step-son finally accepted a drink from him for the first time since he'd molested his daughter.

"Sorry, got to go. Loads to do to sort everything out for Mum. Thanks for the tea" he said, and was out the door before Granville could even set the drink down on the coaster.

As Dad drove away from the police station, he felt an invisible weight lift from his shoulders.

"Just one more thing to do", he said to himself.

CHAPTER 46

Present

"Pull over" Nancy said.

The chauffeur looked over his shoulder at her.

"But Miss, I thought…"

"Pull over now!" she barked.

"Nance, wait" Dad said, but her door was already open, and she was sprinting towards them. Dad climbed out of the car too and ran after her.

"Someone needs to tell me what the fuck is going on, right fucking now" she breathed, as she approached Stephen and the girl.

They stood closely together, looking at her, and then at each other.

"Seriously, tell me right fucking now, what is going on?" she said, furious and impatient.

Dad had caught up with her, and stood next to her, in front of Stephen. They exchanged a curt smile. Dad smiled softly at the girl.

Nancy noticed and was red with rage.

"Am I invisible?! Did anyone hear what I just said?" she squeaked, almost hopping.

"I'm sorry, I'm just scared, that's all. I don't really know where to start" the girl said.

"You could start by telling me who the fuck you are" Nancy advised sarcastically.

"Don't you remember me Nancy?" she said.

"I'm Chloe. Grandville's granddaughter".

Nancy stared at her, all of a sudden seeing a small child that she'd been introduced to when she was about twelve. Chloe. She knew her. Grandma had brought her to meet Nancy and Robert. She was small and wobbly, a mass of curls falling around her face, her blue eyes dancing. Nancy had felt such fondness for her, followed by great fear that the small child was staying with such a monster. Nancy didn't feel equipped to do anything about it at the time being only twelve, but had worried herself sick about Chloe and her safety. She only hoped because she was a blood relative of Granville's, that he'd have left her alone. It seemed that she was wrong.

"He did it to me too, Nancy" Chloe said, looking down at the ground.

Nancy gasped, clamping her hand over her mouth. She lunged forward and held Chloe, whilst she cried on her shoulder. Nancy put her hand on the back of her curls, pulling her in closely.

"I'm sorry, I'm so sorry" Nancy whispered in her ear, over and over again.

Nancy stroked Chloe's hair, shushing her until she stilled. *He did this to his own flesh and blood.* She felt sick. *Who else had he hurt?* The sound of a throat clearing next to her, made Nancy turn her head. She let go of Chloe gently, and wiped the tears from her face with her thumbs. She smiled bravely at her, with a nod of reassurance. *You are going to be alright, my darling.*

"Chloe came and told me last week Nancy, and she told Pete too, sorry, your Dad" he gestured towards her father.

"She'd been trying to talk to you but wasn't getting anywhere. Her mother didn't believe her, so she came to me. And obviously I believed her, because I already knew about what he did to you, I've known for a long time" Stephen said.

"Hold on? Stephen, what are you talking about? Why would Chloe tell you? And how did you know about me?" Nancy questioned, her head spinning.

"Because, well, Nancy" he said.

"I'm Chloe's uncle"

"And Granville's my Dad."

CHAPTER 47

Two Weeks Earlier

"I'll stick the kettle on then" Granville said, the sound of him shuffling to the edge of his arm chair, heaving and groaning until he pulled himself up, huffing and puffing to the kitchen to make a brew.

Dad was parked in a layby next to the woods, after rushing out of the house, leaving Granville standing there with a cup of tea, bemused. There was another car parked in front, empty. It was a place where families with dogs parked, to go for a stroll. He was anxious, he felt like he'd been followed. He kept looking round but no one was there. A few cars had passed on the main road, the noise causing Dad to click on the pen to pause the recording, and shove it under his thigh and gaze out of the car window casually. He was making himself look way more suspicious and probably more like a dogger waiting for someone, than anything else. He reminded himself that he only had 'a pen', but he'd never really done anything wrong in his life. Until now. His guilt of what he'd done, what information he may possess in the recording device was making him sweaty, jumpy and suspicious. When he saw that the coast was clear, he clicked the pen to play again.

"There we are" Granville said, the sound of the cup being placed on the coaster. A pause.

"What?" he asked.

"Nothing" Grandma replied.

"No, come on, out with it" he said gruffly.

"I just…it's just upsetting that's all"

Dad held the pen up to his ear, straining to hear what his mother was about to say.

"What?" he barked, indignantly.

"Just to see Nancy like that, after all these years."

"Yeah and I said sorry, didn't I?" he near shouted.

"That's what she wanted, an apology, and that's what she got! What more do you want?"

"Nothing. It's fine" she said.

"I'm not actually feeling that well, I think I might take myself off to bed".

"I see. I agree to this ridiculous meeting, and now you're turning on me? Is that what's happening here?" he growled, the speaker crackling against Dad's ear. He was frozen solid, listening with bated breath.

"No, not at all Granville. I'm just tired" she reassured.

"What are you going to do if the others want to confront me eh? Are you going to be like this then too?"

Others. Dad couldn't breathe.

"No. I'm sure Nancy is the only one that will come forward, and even she's not going to do anything, Granville, she just wanted to talk. I told the others you weren't well back then and they moved on. I know Chloe can be difficult, but she is too scared to say anything, I'm sure of it. You wouldn't have had a relationship with your daughter if she knew the truth about what you'd done to Chloe. As for the other girls, they wouldn't have told their parents, or we would know about it. It's fine darling" she coaxed.

"Don't talk about the others! We said we would never talk about them again" he said, rage radiating from his voice.

"I'm sorry, I didn't… listen, I'm going to go to bed, I'm really not feeling well all of a sudd-"

Smack. Silence. Dad's eyes shot from side to side, the pen pressed against his ear, his heartbeat echoing inside the car.

Another smack. A cry.

"Granville, please, you're hurting me"

"Granvil–" his name was muffled.

There was the sound of material being swished, his grunting, her muffled cries. A struggle. Dad sat up in the driver's seat, wanting to intervene, and remembering it was in the past. It had already happened and there was nothing he could do. Then the sounds of thrashing slowed until they stopped altogether. Silence.

Dad unclicked the pen. His breath was erratic. Murder. He rewound the recording and played it again. She was silenced.

CHAPTER 48

Present

"I'm Granville's son Nancy" Stephen said, when she didn't reply.

Nancy felt like her knees were going to give way. Dad cupped her elbow.

"Wh…what?" Nancy near whispered.

"I'm his son. Estranged son, might I add"

Nancy head felt like it might explode. She couldn't even process what he was saying. Questions that didn't even make sense flew around her mind.

"I wanted to tell you. But how do you tell someone something like that. I had a strange relationship with my father anyway, he was a cruel man. When he did…what he did… to you…your father called me to tell me. He wanted to warn us, in case we had children in the future" he nodded towards Dad.

"Debbie didn't believe him, but I did. I tried to warn Debbie when she had Chloe, but she wouldn't listen. She told me to 'fuck off to America and leave them alone', like I had before. I kept trying but eventually, our relationship became too strained, and she stopped me from seeing Chloe. I wish I'd gone to the police, but without any evidence that anything was even happening, I knew I wouldn't get anywhere. I was haunted by what I knew had happened to you Nancy. I'd seen him behave inappropriately when I was younger; walking

220

in on Debbie's friends when they were changing into their pyjamas at a sleepover, or telling them they weren't allowed to lock the door when they went to the toilet. One time I'd walked into the bathroom and he was washing his hands right next to one of Debbie's friends, who was having a wee. She'd looked upset and he was furious with me. I didn't say anything to my mother or anyone else. I just decided when your Dad told me what my father had done to you, to believe him. It was completely plausible, and I just felt dreadful that I'd seen him behave like that and never did anything to stop him. I told Audrey and we decided to cut ties. We were moving to New York permanently for my job and we didn't want to bear a child to ever know such a disgusting human being, and he didn't deserve to have family round him for what he'd done".

Chloe sniffed, and Stephen handed her a tissue, and rubbed the top of her back.

"I'm sorry Chloe, this must be really hard for you to hear all this" he sympathised.

"No, no, it's okay. Carry on" she said, giving them a watery smile.

"Debbie, your mum" he said to Chloe.

"Well, she was livid that I'd believed Pete over our own father, and said I was using it as an excuse to leave them all behind to go to the Big Apple and get rich.

I've haven't talked about my father since. Rupert thinks he's dead" he said.

Rupert. The mention of his name. Rupert. Rupert. No. No. No. No. Please. No. Shit. No. Oh God no.

"I'd seen your photos up in Dad's house before they were obviously made to take them down. And when Facebook took over our lives, I looked you up. I wanted to see that you were alright. You looked happy, in your pictures" he said.

"And then when you were sitting at my dining room table that night, I couldn't believe it. I didn't recognise you at first, but when you mentioned your brother and where you were from, it clicked and I dropped my glass. Even though I had gotten in the habit of checking on you online. Not in a weird way, just every time I saw your smiling picture, I convinced myself, in that moment, that my Dad hadn't ruined your life".

Nancy turned away from them and threw up on the floor. It splashed up onto her tights. Dad, Stephen and Chloe did their best not to grimace. Dad stroked her back and handed her his hanky. She wiped her mouth and stood up. She apologised and encouraged them to step a few steps right, away from her sick.

"Listen…I've told Rupert. About the baby" sighed Stephen.

"The baby? What does he mean Nancy? Are you pregnant? How do you know Stephen, Nance?"

"No, no Dad I'm not pregnant. He means Lottie" Nancy explained flatly, folding the hanky to hide the vomit on it.

"Lottie? What's Lottie got to do with it. And who the fuck's Rupert?" he asked, becoming furious.

Nancy turned to her father. Unsure of where to even begin.

Maybe start with the fact that Lottie's father was the grandson of the man who abused had her, all those years ago.

CHAPTER 49

Three Weeks Later

Nancy had heard from Rupert, of course she had. Mostly via email, or he left voicemails, as she couldn't quite pluck up the courage to pick up and explain. She listened to the messages afterwards, hands shaking as she pressed play. He was all over the place; sometimes furious, sometimes apologetic. Always emotional. Everything was fucked. Her daughter's bloodline was that of a molester. She'd ended the deal with Stephen. He'd insisted, as he'd broken their agreement by telling Rupert about Lottie, that she would be entitled a payout, to even more money. But she didn't even want what he had given her, let alone any more. She had believed the payout was so that Rupert could go and make a successful name for himself and follow in Stephen's Wall Street footsteps, which Nancy's pregnancy was threatening, which was bad enough. Now, she knew it went deeper and darker than that, and the truth was, that Stephen never wanted Nancy to find out that he was Granville's son, and that Rupert his grandson. He had refused to stop the payments, and she didn't know how to send it back. She'd written him cheques, but he'd never cashed them. The money sat there like a goblin in her account, reminding her how foolish she was to think she could escape her past. Not only could she not run from it, but now she was intrinsically linked to Granville via her sweet little daughter. Rupert had no idea of course and had taken the news badly about his Grandfather. He'd thought he was dead, and now knew that he was alive but in custody for manslaughter and ever-increasing charges of sexual assault against minors. He didn't know what Granville had done to Nancy. He didn't know he had a cousin, or that the same thing had happened to her, either. Stephen agreed he wouldn't tell Rupert about Chloe, as Nancy was worried if he started pulling at that thread, he might find his way to the truth about Nancy too. Debbie was knee deep in trying to prove her father's innocence, and Chloe hadn't wanted to stick around to see it play out, so packed her bags and bought a one-way ticket to South America to go travelling. Nancy had given her a chunk of Stephen's money to do it. It was the least she could do and felt that the money should have been for her anyway.

When she finally plucked up the courage to answer the phone to Rupert, she paced around the lounge, staying silent, whilst he begged to meet his daughter.

He wanted to fly back, to come and see her and meet Lottie, but Nancy needed a bit of time to process what she now knew. She wasn't being difficult, but a few weeks ago she'd found out a lot of new information, which changed almost everything in her life as she knew it. It had changed her feelings; it had changed her longing. What she'd longed for was Grandma and Granville to be punished, jailed or killed. She'd got that. And as one hand gave, the other took away. Her love for Rupert had diminished, through no one's fault but a pure disgust that flooded through her veins that she'd made a baby with a relation of Granville's. She was furious for Lottie, and vowed that she must never know, another secret that would burden Nancy for the rest of her life. Would Rupert want to be part of Lottie's life? Would he move back here and be present or be a father that flew over sporadically and leave Lottie feeling abandoned and unwanted. It was all fucked. And she blamed Stephen for telling him. No, she blamed herself. For being careless and reckless, for lying and manipulating, for hurting others. But she'd done it all for the girls. That's what she had to keep telling herself, anyway. She wrapped her hand around the back of her neck and squeezed, her muscles tight and tender with stress.

"Please Nancy. I want to meet my daughter. I know this is all a lot to process, it is for me too. But I am going to come home. And I want to meet her. Please" he said, desperately,

"Yes" Nancy whispered, a silent tear dropped onto the carpet, knowing if she wanted to be the best mother she could, she had no choice.

"Of course, you can".

CHAPTER 50

Three Weeks Earlier

"Nance? Nancy? Are you okay?" Dad asked.

She sat on the wet, crematorium bench, feeling weak, limp and numb. She stared at nothing, her thoughts sounded like someone was holding a car horn down in her mind.

"I'm…I'm…I'm so tired, Dad" she said slowly, looking forward with drooping eyelids.

"I know Poppet, I know" he said, clasping her hand.

She couldn't cry anymore. She had nothing left.

Dad had just told her about the recording pen he'd handed into the police. About how they now had evidence of what he'd done to her, and to Chloe, and with a statement from both of them, Granville would be locked up for the rest of his life. Dad had told her was going to work on a line of enquiries to help the police. He was to make a list of anyone he could think of that Granville might have had access to and could have done the same, as he had to Nancy and Chloe. Dad wanted it to be over, to move on and forget, but it haunted him that there could other people out there, like Nancy, living in the pain that Granville had inflicted. He was determined to help in any way he could, to ensure that every victim received the retribution they deserved.

Then he'd told Nancy about how the recording device had picked up on how Grandma had actually died. Dad had kept it brief, sparing Nancy the details. Her eyes twitched, blotchy and blood shot, and she blinked slowly, dryly, the new information settling like dust on a shelf.

Everyone had left hours ago, she had no idea what time it was, or how long they'd been sitting there. She couldn't think, she couldn't move. She felt like when she'd just finished meditating but without the peace, just a state of nothingness before her brain started working again and she remembered she had problems.

"It's going to be alright, you know" Dad said, quietly.

Nancy blinked.

"It is. You can't even begin to believe me right now, but it's the truth. It's over Nance. It's going to take time, but in the end, it is going to be better than alright. I know it" he said, placing his large, warm hand over hers.

The heat of his hand made her fingers twitch, like she was waking up from a general anesthetic.

She lifted her chin up to the clouds and breathed in through her nose. She closed her eyes, listened to the distant traffic, the birds chatting, the woosh of the wind, making the leaves swish on the branches of the trees. She could smell the damp grass and a hint of a burning bonfire in the breeze. She felt the wet wood against the back of her legs, and the hard ground under her feet. The clouds parted slightly, enough to allow a small streak of sunshine through, warming Nancy's face, like when she held her hot morning coffee up to her nose to smell it. She could see light through her closed lids, and the feeling of hope cascaded over her, tingling her skin. She breathed out through her mouth and a single, salty tear escaped from the corner of her right eye. She squeezed Dad's hand back. It was over. He was right. She didn't know how, or when it would be, but it was going to be alright. It was going to be better than alright. It was going to be bloody brilliant. She was free.

Epilogue

Dad pulled into the driveway. He walked up to the front door, and opened the door with a single key. He wiped his boots on the mat, but didn't take his jacket off and put it on the coat hook this time. He shut the door behind him, and walked down the hallway past his mother's bedroom. He saw her hairbrush on the side, the teeth interlaced with her white hair. He took a deep breath in and walked into the lounge. The pot of tea was still sitting there. He picked up the tray and took it into the kitchen and tipped the cold, scummy tea into the sink, discarding the sodden dumplings of teabags that remained, into the bin. He filled the kettle and clicked it to boil. He washed the cups and saucers, the milk jug, the sugar bowl and the biscuit plate, and put them on the drying rack on the draining board. He pulled a pair of latex gloves out from under the sink and placed them on his hands, before reaching into his fleece pocket, and pulled out a fistful of sugar cubes and tossed them into the sink. He could tell which one it was, it was slightly greyer than the others. He tapped his foot whilst the kettle boiled and when it whistled, he poured the bubbling water over the cubes, watching them dissolve and disperse down the plug hole. He sprayed the sink with disinfectant and wiped it round, removed his gloves and put them in his pocket to dispose of later.

He filled the milk jug with water, and walked around the house, watering the wilting plants that had been dotted about by his mother. He sprinkled a generous amount of food into the gold fish bowl, the pungent flakes skating around on the surface of the water, the single fish gratefully swimming up to eat them. He walked to the front door, and pulled the wadge of post from the letterbox, it slamming shut and making him jump. He fanned through the post and seeing nothing of importance, tossed it onto the side table for his brother to sort through another day.

He looked down the hallway to remind himself that the evidence was well and truly gone, along with the two people who had tried to destroy his family. He opened the front door, stepped out of it and slammed it behind him, for the very last time.

Acknowledgements

My family and friends were so supportive when I told them I'd started writing a book in the middle of the night. I have no doubt they thought I was crazy to believe I could produce a novel at nighttime when I should have been sleeping. A lightning bolt moment hit me when I was making coffee for someone else, that I should turn, what started off as journaling, into a book. It felt like a huge project, to turn my feelings into a story but I am so glad I have done it, and I hope it will inspire my children to set their mind to something and achieve it. The people that inspired that characters are essential in my life. I know you will find yourselves in there, you arrogant bunch. But it's true, you are all in there, and I couldn't have written this and been able to inject so much humour into what is a dark subject, without you. If you can't find yourself in there, you aren't looking hard enough! Buy it and read it again eh?

My children– you are the reason I now have ambition. I work hard because of you and hope that you will too. I want you to know that you can do absolutely anything you set your mind to, and I cannot wait to witness your journey's through life. You are both so funny, kind and thoughtful to everyone and you will forever be the loves of my life, my greatest achievement, the best thing I've ever done. If you read this when you are older, I hope you feel in the text how I would lay down and die for you. Because that's how I felt when I wrote it, and still do. I won't, because you need me, but if I had to, I would.

To my nephews, nieces, Godchildren, and all the poppets born of the people I love – I could explode with the love I feel for you all.

Parents- please can you pass on to them that their Auntie loves them more than words can say, because they can't read this yet - it ain't no bedtime story.

Something I wish I could have told my little self now I am older and going a little bit grey... Be yourselves, little people. Don't change or mould yourselves for anyone but you. Be honest with yourself and others about what you want and need. Remember to be kind to others, and be kind to yourself too.

Remember that whatever challenges you face, we will all be here for you, supporting, guiding, consoling and celebrating.

And thank you to all of my lovely couples for getting it on, and making the cutest babies of all time.

The women who make up Alex – I couldn't create enough characters to honour you all individually. You are complex, powerful, ferocious, loyal, kind, funny, strong, determined, soft, and loving soulmates. I've made sure you are all represented, one hilarious, supportive and honest comment at a time. When I have lost touch with reality, you have the ability to ground me, and I would be truly lost without each and every one of you. If I list you, there will be a kick-off of what order your names appear, so just shut your gorgeous faces and know you're in there. I wouldn't have my favourite character in the book without you all. I feel very blessed every day to know you and share my life with you. In the words of Alex... "I fucking love you".

To my parents – Thank you for always being there no matter what. For always talking to me and helping me understand everything. For making me and my brother feel loved and important. For showing us how to be open and honest, how to be kind and thoughtful, polite and silly. You've taught us how to be grateful and how to celebrate. I love you both so much and have always felt very loved, and still do. I am very thankful every day for the life you have given me.

To my brother – for always being hilarious, annoying and the other half of the weirdest brother sister band in the UK. I hope this book shows you how much I look up to you, and how valued you are. There's no one quite like you. Celebrate and treasure it. You are truly loved by us all. The rest doesn't matter.

To the Kerns Castle – You are my people, always have been, always will be. Thank you for all your love and support and not laughing (in my face) when I told you I was going to write a book. I'm so thankful for all of the good times been, and all the good times to come. I feel beyond blessed to share my life with you, which essentially consists of eating, drinking, playing games, dancing, hugging, singing, crying at the sad songs on the iPod, watching films and discussing them in detail and taking the piss out of each other when we mispronounce something. Is there any better way to spend your time? Not to me. Ilymtwcs.

To the Hole Traggambyllerns – To my huge, wonderful family. Your characters are laced through the book, I hope you can find yourselves, a bit like Where's Wally. Not that you're wallies, but you know what I mean! Standing around singing 'how old are you now' on one of the many birthdays in our family is one of the happiest moments in my life and each time we do, I feel blessed beyond belief. The children in our family are an utter gift, and the fact that they just keep on coming brings me utter joy and excitement for our ever-growing crew. I love every single person that makes up our massive, bonkers, joyful, weird and loving family. Thank you for making me feel so loved and accepted.

If I can help one person by reading this book, I will be so happy. If something in this book has happened to you, or to someone you love, you are not alone. Or maybe you can relate to how Nancy feels for another reason. It's okay. Seek help. You can recover. You can be happy. Tell someone how you feel. You may think there is no hope, but there is. Never, ever give up. Because there have been times I have wanted to, that there was no light, just darkness. But just hold on and believe that things will get better. Even if you can't feel it, just keep telling yourself to have faith that it will be okay soon and hold onto that faith in whatever form. Believe me, you will be glad you did.

Printed in Great Britain
by Amazon